Luminous

The Story of a Radium Girl

Samantha Wilcoxson

Other books by Samantha Wilcoxson

The Plantagenet Embers Series

Plantagenet Princess, Tudor Queen: The Story of Elizabeth of York
Faithful Traitor: The Story of Margaret Pole
Queen of Martyrs: The Story of Mary I
The Last Lancastrian: A Story of Margaret Beaufort (novella)
Once of Queen: A Story of Elizabeth Woodville (novella)
Prince of York: A Story of Reginald Pole (novella)

Children's Fiction

Over the Deep: A Titanic Adventure
No Such Thing as Perfect

Luminous

The Story of a Radium Girl

Samantha Wilcoxson

Copyright © 2020 Samantha Wilcoxson

All Rights Reserved. This book may not be reproduced or distributed in any printed or electronic form without the prior express written permission of the author. Do not participate in or encourage piracy of copyrighted material in violation of the author's rights.

ISBN: 9798637237388

Printed in the United States of America

Cover Art by Tyler Wilcoxson.

It's too late for me, but maybe it will help some of the others.
— *Catherine Wolfe Donohue*

Chapter 1

The scientific history of radium is beautiful.
Marie Curie, 1921

Another mosquito buzzed in Catherine's ear as she brushed dirt from the freshly pulled carrots in her hand. With her hands full and covered with the rich, loamy soil of her aunt's garden, her only remedy was to shake her head and try to shrug her shoulder against her ear. After finally dropping her share of the harvest into her aunt's basket, Catherine swatted at the pest with a vengeance and was rewarded immediately with a satisfying end to the noise.

"I am so thankful for your help," her Aunt Mary sighed, waving her hands at more of the swarm that had been attracted by the sweat of their hard work. Aunt Mary groaned as she dropped more produce into the basket and put a hand to the small of her back as she straightened. "The whole neighborhood will benefit from this final harvest. I think we have enough put up, so why don't you take some of this bunch to Shirley?"

"Yes, Auntie," Catherine demurred, immediately beginning to separate the vegetables into those that their own household would use in the next few days and those that their neighbor, Shirley, would turn into delicious soup.

"She'll want some of those carrots . . . and some onion," Aunt Mary called from the next garden row, as if Catherine didn't already know.

"Yes, Auntie," she simply replied again, knowing that no insult was intended. "Should I take some potatoes?"

Aunt Mary straightened again and squinted into the sun. Catherine squinted that way too, in subconscious imitation. Finally, Aunt Mary made up her mind.

"Just a few. I'd like a few more bushels in the cellar as well." Aunt Mary looked down at the ground and rubbed her back. "I think that's enough for now. I just don't know what I would do without you, my dear."

"Then it is good that you don't have to worry about such a thing," Catherine reassured her with a kiss on the cheek. "I'll run this bundle to Shirley and be back before you can miss me."

"That's a good girl." Aunt Mary was already carrying the remainder of their vegetables into her cozy kitchen as Catherine cut through backyards toward a little, grey house that stood with all the doors and windows open to the crisp breeze.

Shirley hastily closed a brown glass bottle into a cabinet as Catherine strolled into the kitchen, shouting, "Hello," to announce her presence.

"Look at you loaded down with veggies, child!" Shirley exclaimed happily. "You know I love nothing better than a rich, vegetable soup."

Catherine tipped her head in agreement as she dumped Shirley's share of the produce onto the table.

"Very nice. Very nice," Shirley murmured as she inspected the haul. "I'll bring you and your auntie a fine pot of soup tomorrow."

"Thank you, Shirley." Catherine scooted out before the older woman could strike up more conversation. It was easy to find oneself trapped in the little house all afternoon if the friendly woman got talking.

Reentering her own home, Catherine picked up the *Ottawa Daily Times* that her Uncle Winchester had left on the kitchen table.

Girls Wanted

Catherine gazed at the advertisement, absentmindedly gnawing at the inside of her cheek. She had heard of Radium Dial. The factory was across the road from St Columba, where her family worshipped each Sunday morning. Running her tongue over the tender spot her teeth had created, Catherine weighed her options. A job as a watch dial painter would take her away from home during hours that her auntie might need help, but it would provide income to cover medical bills that had been increasingly occurring as her aunt and uncle aged.

The thought of those wages was more than Catherine could deny. It took her only a moment to firmly scoop up the paper and charge out of the house. Indecision was not one of Catherine Wolfe's weaknesses. Her course determined, she forged ahead confidently.

Superior Street was quiet. Soon children would fill the yards as they were released from school, allowing them to run off the energy that they were forced to hold in throughout the day. For now though, scurrying squirrels and dry leaves blowing across the cobbles were the only sounds. It was out of Catherine's way to walk along the river, but the autumn splendor made it worth it. The trees did not maintain their colors for long. Soon snow would fall, and shades of grey would blanket the fallen leaves.

The Fox River flowed a few blocks from Catherine's house, and the vibrant views refreshed her soul, giving her the boldness she needed to request a job that she knew many other Ottawa girls would apply for. Radium Dial had been in town since the Great War, and all the girls knew that it was the best paying work they could hope for in this part of Illinois.

At that thought, Catherine accelerated her stride, suddenly

irritated that she had frivolously chosen the scenic route. What if the positions were filled before she arrived?

Where the river met the end of Washington Street, Catherine turned west and forced herself to remain calm. The few blocks extra that she had walked couldn't possibly make a difference. Could it?

An old saloon stood with its windows boarded shut, looking dark and desolate. Catherine knew that to be the furthest thing from the truth. Once the sun dipped below the horizon, a secret door in the back would welcome in more people than the front entrance had before Prohibition had begun. She tried not to examine the saloon too closely. You never knew who was watching, and Catherine would not want to be responsible for giving away her neighbors' secrets, even if she did not imbibe herself.

Catherine paused in front of the old high school that was now the home of Radium Dial, gazing up at the brick façade. A faint smile curved her lips as she admired the craftsmanship and variation in color in the arched window frames. The new high school might be more practical, but it lacked the Victorian beauty of this building. Her smile broadening, Catherine marched inside, her dark, bobbed hair bouncing as she ascended the steps.

She was directed to a smartly dressed lady who appeared to be about her Aunt Maggie's age. However, Lottie Murray had an air of sophistication that the middle-aged housewife could never attain and didn't desire. Miss Murray was one of those progressive women, who pursued a career instead of marriage. Catherine couldn't imagine making such a choice for herself but was somewhat awestruck at Lottie's evident success.

Trying not to compare her off-the-rack dress to Miss Murray's tailored suit, Catherine carefully answered questions about herself. She was a dedicated parishioner at Ottawa's St

Columba Church and had recently turned nineteen. Since there were no marriage proposals apparent in her future, she wished to contribute to the household she shared with her Uncle Winchester and Aunt Mary. They had raised her since the death of her father almost ten years ago.

Miss Murray, who was kind but seemed to hold her head up just enough to look down her nose at Catherine, seemed satisfied with her answers.

"Please, report to Mrs Mercedes Reed promptly at seven tomorrow morning," Miss Murray ordered to indicate that Catherine was hired. She stood and gestured toward her office door. "She will see to your training. If you complete that satisfactorily, she will direct you as to the next step."

"Thank you!" Catherine gushed, quickly rising from her seat to follow Miss Murray's instructions. She tried to temper her excitement, for she felt it gave away her youth and naivety, but a grin lit up her face as she repeated, "Thank you, Miss Murray," and left the small office.

Miss Murray rewarded her with a perfunctory nod before closing the door the moment Catherine was through it. Crossing her arms to give herself an enthusiastic squeeze, Catherine stood outside Miss Murray's office basking in her good fortune. Dial painting was a lucrative job in an exciting new industry. Girls were dying to get into Radium Dial's studio.

Catherine repressed a squeal as she made a show of slowing her footsteps and strolling out of the building as though she obtained exciting new jobs as a part of her daily routine. Once outside, she allowed herself to quicken her pace. Safely away from view of the old school windows, she cheered and leapt into the air, finally able to channel her joy.

She was halfway home before she realized that she should

have crossed the road to give thanks within the familiar walls of St Columba. It could wait until Sunday. She was too anxious to tell Aunt Mary and Uncle Winchester about her great news.

Superior Street was filled with playing children upon her return, and Catherine felt that it had been a lifetime since she had been a part of that group, though it had been just a few short years ago.

In the middle of a block, half hidden behind a tall maple tree, stood the white house with black shutters that Catherine called home. She jumped over the porch steps and called for her aunt as she opened the door.

Catherine did not remember much about her mother. It was her Aunt Mary who had nursed her when she was sick, comforted her when her heart was broken, and guided her along her path to becoming a respectable young woman. Much of the time, Mary could be found in her small galley style kitchen preparing the day's meals or putting up canned goods for the future. That is where Catherine found her.

"Auntie, I have the best news!" She kissed a softly wrinkled cheek and leaned against the counter.

"What is it that has you so excited?" Mary asked as she slid a roasting pan into the oven.

"I got myself a job at the dial studio." Catherine grinned openly, any doubts she had about leaving the home for outside work buried deep beneath her sense of victory.

"Why, that's just wonderful. It will be a good thing for you to be able to set a little money aside."

"And help you and uncle."

Shaking her head, Aunt Mary protested, "Now, we don't need your money. It would be wrong for us to take it from you."

Catherine just smiled and kissed her aunt again. She would

find ways of contributing without having to put cash into Aunt Mary's hand. "Where is uncle?"

Aunt Mary gestured vaguely toward the back yard. "I believe he is working in the vegetable garden. Go tell him your news."

Catherine skipped out the door, eager to do just that. Her Uncle Winchester was indeed pulling weeds with an eye out for anything Catherine and Mary might have missed. He took longer breaks to stand and stretch between rows these days and couldn't seem to completely straighten any longer.

He did not notice Catherine until her arms wrapped around him.

"Well, where did you come from?" he laughed, squeezing her to his side.

"You won't believe it. I've just come from Radium Dial. They've given me a job!"

"Good for you, little Cat!" He patted her shoulder and eyed the next row of plants.

"Let me finish that for you," Catherine insisted, knowing how his back must be aching. "I'm sure Aunt Mary could use your help inside."

She was actually certain that Aunt Mary would provide him with a glass of lemonade and send him out to the front porch swing. He likely knew that as well, but he nodded and shuffled toward the house.

"Thank you. I will see what she needs."

Catherine quickly completed the work in the garden, energized by her new adventure. By the time she had finished ridding the garden of weeds, Catherine, too, was ready for a tall glass of lemonade and a couple of her aunt's famous oatmeal cookies.

†

The next morning, Catherine found her way to Radium Dial's training room. Her heels click-clacked on the oak floors in an animated rhythm until she reached the door Miss Murray had indicated. With a deep breath, Catherine grasped the handle of the heavy, wood door and went inside.

The room was clearly an old classroom, large and high ceilinged. Sun shone in, but a dusty haze hung in the air. Upon further inspection, Catherine realized the girls being trained were even sitting at old school desks. She sighed. At nineteen, she thought she was done sitting at school desks. However, her smile was quickly back in place. What did it matter where she sat when she was one of the lucky few chosen to paint using the wondrous new material that made watch faces glow in the dark?

"Name?" A brusque voice tore Catherine from her reflections, and her eyes pivoted to its source. The instructress was somewhere between Catherine's age and Miss Murray's with no memorable features. Catherine thought she was the kind of woman one could pass on the street and not realize you had done so.

"Name?" she repeated.

"I'm sorry, ma'am," Catherine said, moving forward with her hand extended. "I am Catherine Wolfe, and Miss Murray instructed me to present myself to you today. That is, she did if you are indeed Mrs Reed."

"Of course, I am," the thereby introduced Mercedes Reed huffed. "Take an empty seat," she ordered without taking Catherine's hand.

Feeling awkward, Catherine quickly dropped her arm and lowered herself into the closest seat. Before she could wonder if

Radium Dial would be as fantastic as she hoped under the tutelage of women like Mrs Reed, the girl next to her smiled her welcome, and Catherine was certain she saw her wink. Catherine recognized her from around town but wasn't sure of her name.

Two more girls came in after Catherine and received the same treatment from Mrs Reed, but the instructress seemed to brighten once they had all taken their seats. Her face relaxed as she took up the tools of the trade that she would train them to use. With the items lined up on a low table in front of her, Mercedes Reed addressed the ten girls who leaned eagerly forward to hear.

Catherine glimpsed at the desktop in front of her to confirm that her own brushes and dials were within easy reach.

"Painting dials is important and delicate work," Mrs Reed began as she held up a brush with bristles too small to be seen from where Catherine sat. In her other hand, she held a paper watch face. "You will affix the dial like so," Mrs Reed continued as she demonstrated, "and then apply the paint – very carefully – to the numbers."

She paused as the girls got their dials in place and picked up a brush.

"The best way to be certain of a fine point on your brush is to dip it into the radium paint."

She did so.

"And then sharpen the tip of the brush with your lips."

Mrs Reed pursed her lips and gently inserted the bristles. Then she held it up and walked around the classroom, allowing each new employee to see her perfect point. The girls picked up their brushes, and she nodded to encourage them to try.

"Those of you able to perfectly lip-point and trace the numbers on your dials will be selected to become permanent employees of Radium Dial."

Catherine's brow furrowed, even as she slipped the brush between her lips and examined the resulting point. She was glad when a more outspoken girl asked, "Are we not all employees, Mrs Reed?"

Mrs Reed laughed in a not entirely unfriendly manner. "For now, yes, but this is skilled work, and not all of you will take to it. Have you got the point?" she asked, looking at the girl's brush. "Good. Now let's try with some paint."

The girls looked at each other questioningly. None were certain about the radium paint, which appeared a dull greenish-white but they knew to possess special characteristics that made it glow.

"Go ahead then!" Mrs Reed encouraged while demonstrating the technique once again. "Dip. Point. Paint."

Catherine sat up straighter in her seat, took a deep breath and clutched her brush tighter. She dipped the thin camel-hair bristles into the mixture and peered at it for a few seconds before touching it to her lips. Then she grinned happily at her perfect point.

"Very good!" said Mrs Reed as she walked by Catherine's desk. "Now try to trace the numbers on your dial."

Catherine's grin transitioned to a look of determination as she accepted this new challenge. Ever so slowly, she slid her brush along the straight lines of the number one. Finishing, she realized that she was holding her breath, so she released it and looked around the room to observe her co-workers.

Some shared her look of determination. Others took to the work lightly, and Catherine guessed those would be the girls who had a difficult time succeeding at Radium Dial. The girl next to her looked up at the same time and said, "I'm Charlotte. How did you do?" as she leaned over to peer at Catherine's dial. "Nicely done!" she said, leaning back.

"Thank you. And yours?"

Charlotte nodded, her lips pressed together. "I think I've done alright."

"I'm Catherine. It's very nice to meet you."

They smiled at each other and took up their brushes to dip in the paint for the number two. As the girls worked their way around their first watch face, a few questions were asked and frustrations vented. Catherine ignored most but perked up when she heard Charlotte speak.

"Can whatever makes this stuff glow hurt us? I mean, is it safe to put in our mouths?"

Catherine raised an eyebrow. She hadn't thought about that, but it was a good question.

Mrs Reed's laughter was thick with condescension. "Of course, it cannot harm you! In fact," she elaborated as she returned to her table, "the radium that gives our paint its special properties is beneficial to your health and will give your cheeks a rosy glow."

To convince them, she took her mixing spatula and used it like a spoon to scoop up the paint and eat it. The girls gasped as Mrs Reed swallowed and took a sip of water.

"As I said, our paint is perfectly safe. If anything, you will feel better after working with it."

Tension fled from the room and the girls laughed together, taking up their brushes and dipping them in the paint. By the end of the day, Catherine not only felt that she had mastered pointing the brush and tracing the fine numbers, she had made a new friend. When she and Charlotte Nevins parted ways upon reaching Superior Street, Catherine was already looking forward to work the following day.

Continuing down her street, Catherine was surprised to

realize that less than forty-eight hours had passed since she had seen the advertisement for dial painters. She was so glad that she had followed her instincts and applied. It was a decision that would change her life.

Chapter 2

*It is such a fascinating element,
such a magical element.*
Dr Ellis Fischel

Low conversation and laughter ebbed and flowed throughout the large, well-lit room. It had been a gymnasium back when Catherine's parents had attended school in the building that now housed Radium Dial. It made the perfect dial painting studio with its tall windows and vast space. The girls were lined up at school desks with pots of paint and water on one corner of their workspace and a stack of paper dials on the opposite corner.

Catherine tried to suppress giggles when Mary Vicini started painting her fingernails while Mrs Reed's back was turned. Mary held her hand under the desk to see the faint glow in the darkened space. As much as Catherine enjoyed the camaraderie of the other girls, she also took her work seriously. Since they were paid based on how many pieces they completed, it literally paid to be diligent.

"Mary is so young. It's a shame that she is here rather than in school," Catherine whispered to Charlotte, who sat at the desk to her right.

Without missing a beat in her routine, Charlotte nodded. "She is five years short of the eighteen that Radium Dial claims to require," she agreed before pointing her brush with her lips and continuing, "but I heard that Elizabeth is only eleven."

Catherine gasped, but before she could protest one so young spending her days at work, Charlotte continued.

"For those who have to help their family, this work is a blessing, regardless of age."

Bowing her head lower over her work, Catherine did not respond. She was adequately admonished, but she still thought it was wrong for the company to break their own rules and hire girls who weren't yet eighteen. Then again, she thought, glancing over at Charlotte, even her best friend had been only sixteen when they were hired.

They had just recently celebrated her seventeenth birthday with a gathering of young people crowded into Charlotte's home. Catherine allowed her mind to drift back to that day as her fingers automatically applied the paint to number after number.

Gramophone music and strawberry cake had been enjoyed by all, and Charlotte had glowed as the center of attention. Preferring to observe the more boisterous party-goers and listen quietly to the music, Catherine had remained at the perimeter of the room and taken advantage of moments of escape when Charlotte's mother requested help in the kitchen.

At the end of the evening, the other guests had left, and Catherine felt special that she was the one Charlotte asked to stay. Catherine had listened as Charlotte gave a brief review of each boy who had been in attendance. She noticed a soft smile touched Charlotte's lips when mentioning Albert Purcell. Catherine hadn't been brave enough to speak much to any boys and wondered at Charlotte's boldness with them.

"Well, Catherine, they aren't that intimidating," Charlotte had insisted. "You won't find a husband by hiding in the kitchen with my mother."

Blushing, Catherine realized she hadn't been as discreet as she had believed. "I wasn't hiding," she protested.

But Charlotte had been adamant. "The next time we go out,

you are speaking to a boy. A cute one!"

Her mind returning to the present, Catherine smiled at the memory. Charlotte was just the sort of friend she needed, and she hoped there was something that she brought to the relationship that enriched Charlotte in return.

With a sigh, Catherine decided that it wasn't up to her to worry about the younger girls in the studio, so she said no more and dipped her brush into the paint.

From Catherine's left, a new girl piped up. "I don't like the taste of this paint, not one bit." The redhead dropped her brush and scrunched up her freckled nose at it.

Catherine offered a reassuring smile. "Once you get used to it, it's not so bad. It doesn't have a flavor really, it's the sandy texture that is off-putting."

Pursing her lips, the girl considered this. "I don't know....but the wages sure are good." With a sigh, she retrieved her brush and pointed it with her mouth as quickly as possible.

"There you are," Catherine encouraged. "Soon, you won't even think about it."

The redhead looked like she didn't want to grow accustomed to the work, but she begrudgingly carried on. Catherine turned to Charlotte, who knew what she was going to ask before she could so much as raise an eyebrow.

"Peg," she whispered under her breath.

The new girl was Peg Looney. Now Catherine remembered. She was a girl with more siblings than she knew what to do with, though they all seemed close and happy enough with their lot in life.

The thought made Catherine look toward another young woman who worked at Radium Dial. Marie Becker also was here to help alleviate the stress on her mother and step-father who struggled to feed their children. Catherine decided she would have to stop judging the other girls who worked in the studio, even if they were young. They certainly all had their reasons.

She dipped her brush into the radium paint, pointed it with her lips, and determined to get ten more dials done before it was time to go home.

However, Catherine did not go home after work. Charlotte and Peg convinced her to join them on the trolley to Utica. Starved Rock was a popular place for young people to hang out, and the trolley ride along the river was a fun time too. Catherine didn't typically run with any crowd, but she loved the natural beauty of Starved Rock standing tall with the river coursing past and trees covering its surface.

During the trolley ride, Catherine learned that Peg had nine siblings. She couldn't imagine being a part of a family that large. How loving and cozy it must be, and oh so different than being an orphaned only child. It made Catherine wonder how many children she might have one day.

But she didn't think of it for long, because the girls' conversation grew animated. That thirty minute ride made Catherine feel closer to each of them. She knew which of them had marched with their mothers for Prohibition and which could escort you to a speakeasy. Most surprisingly, Peg announced her affinity for reading the dictionary.

"I would love to be a teacher," she murmured as if it were a confession. Peg's blush made her freckles almost disappear.

"Well, that's nothing to be ashamed of," Catherine said, speaking up for the first time. "You will make a wonderful teacher someday. Why, you almost take care of an entire classroom of children already!"

The laughter of the other girls embarrassed Catherine, but

Charlotte gave her a nudge. "It is a good thing," she whispered in Catherine's ear. "People are supposed to laugh when you make a joke."

Catherine smiled shyly. Charlotte was correct, but Catherine still kept quiet for the remainder of the trolley ride. Once they arrived in Utica, the girls trekked toward Starved Rock, splitting into pairs and smaller groups to gossip along the way.

Charlotte and Catherine strolled slowly, appreciating the wild scenery and the scent of dried leaves in the air. When they came to a large stump, they sat close together to rest upon it.

"Look at that!" Charlotte cried. She pointed at a small yellow and black bird that perched so close one of the girls could have reached out and touched it.

"It looks like a canary," Catherine whispered. She didn't want to scare it away.

Charlotte lowered her arm and pressed her lips together to follow Catherine's lead. "Where do you think he lives?" Charlotte asked, looking around as though the bird's nest would be obvious.

Shrugging, Catherine laughed quietly and watched the canary bop about. He gazed at the girls from time to time but didn't seem to think they were a threat. After a few moments, he flew away, and the girls waved to him like an old friend.

"What do you want to do, Catherine, besides paint clock dials?"

Catherine frowned. "I don't really know, I guess. Since I started working at Radium Dial, I haven't thought beyond that."

"Really?" Charlotte stood and stretched. Holding a hand out to Catherine, she said, "I want to design dresses." She twirled and her skirt fanned out around her.

They began walking down a narrow path, and Catherine said, "That sounds mighty fine. I suppose, I've always thought I would be a mother and spend the day in the kitchen the way my auntie does."

"So, you have a beau?" Charlotte's eyes lit up in hope of a romantic story.

"No," Catherine shook her head and felt just as disappointed that she had nothing more interesting to share.

"Well, that's alright," Charlotte encouraged her by taking her arm and pulling her faster through the woods. "Maybe we will find a few handsome boys at the Rock."

Giggling, they continued toward the sound of those who had already arrived at their destination. It didn't take long for them to break through the trees into a clearing where several of the other dial painters had already gathered. Charlotte winked at Catherine when she noticed that a few young men were also in attendance.

Catherine was glad the sun was beginning to go down. It would make her blush less obvious. Charlotte pulled her forward, and she was caught up in a swirl of conversation and joviality.

One boy was enthusiastically announcing his plans to join the local police force.

"Why would you want to do that?" his friend asked. "You looking to get shot?"

"No, of course not," the first boy protested. "Don't you see how good them policemen are doing these days? You know why?"

He was smug when no one had a response.

"Why, it's the bribes! Don't you know?" He put his hands in the air and shook his head at their ignorance. "All the speakeasies and moonshiners - they're paying the police to look the other way. You know they make more from bribes than they do from their paycheck!"

"And just how do you know all this?" a skeptical friend

inquired.

Either protecting his source or afraid to admit who it was, the boy simply said, "You don't need to take my word for it. I'll be strutting down the street in my uniform with cash stuffing my pockets, and you'll be busting your butt down at the factory for twelve hours a day."

He walked away to emphasize his point and end the argument. New discussions and debates filled the space he left, and groups formed and reformed as interest waned and grew. It was an experience that Catherine had never really had before. Even in high school, she had been one of the quiet kids, not one invited out to the Rock. Working at Radium Dial was proving to be a blessing in every way.

The next day, Catherine was relieved when Peg took the seat next to her.

"I was afraid you might not come back," Catherine admitted softly.

Peg's grin revealed straight, white teeth. "I couldn't stay away."

The girls laughed, but Marie interjected more seriously.

"My step-father would be furious if I quit. He is already counting on my $15-a-week. It's twice what I made at my last job."

Although Catherine's lips pressed into a thin line, she successfully kept herself from saying anything derogatory about Marie's step-father. He did have ten children to feed and not all of them were his own, she reminded herself.

"It is good of you to help out. You'll find the work gets better."

Charlotte chose this moment to break in. "Especially as you get to know your fantastic co-workers!"

The girls laughed again and settled into their work. Once

they had found a steady pace, Catherine spoke again.

"She's right though, you know. We're like a jolly family here. We look out for one another and have a good time."

As the days passed, Catherine stopped worrying that Peg would leave Radium Dial. Her family needed the wages too badly, and the girls grew attached to one another. Days in the studio and evenings at the Rock or cozied up at one of their homes deepened their friendships, and they forgot about the taste of the paint.

During this time, Catherine also discovered that Mr Reed was a friendlier boss than his wife. He seemed to like to think of the girls as his own daughters, teasing them and spoiling them as a father would. When Peg needed to leave early to help care for her siblings, he practically pushed her out the door, and when Daisy got married the girls joked that he should be the one to give her away.

Catherine kept her head down when they talked of marriage this way. She longed for a family but had no prospects, nor did she have a father to walk her down the aisle should her day ever come. It made it a difficult subject to joke about for her.

Mr Reed somehow noticed Catherine removing herself from the conversation. "Don't you worry, sweetling. Some fine fella is going to find you, and I'll be losing another of my gals!"

Catherine smiled at his thoughtfulness but said nothing. Throughout high school, she hadn't worried too much as many of her classmates paired up and planned to get married after graduation, but now that she was twenty she wondered if she should have tried harder to attract a boy when she was surrounded by classrooms of them. One didn't realize how much harder it was to spend time around boys once those school days were over, and then it was too late.

Mr Reed had already moved back to teasing Daisy along

with the rest of the girls. So many girls. How was Catherine supposed to meet a man?

†

Held up by her aunt needing help in the kitchen, Catherine was a few minutes late to work, so she quietly slipped into her seat, hoping that Mrs Reed would not notice.

"You look quite nice today," she murmured, indicating Marie's dress.

"Thank you, dear," Marie replied with a flip of her dark, curly locks. "I decided that my mother's husband could do without my earnings this week. I do the work and deserve some of the rewards."

Catherine eyes widened. "You bought the dress?"

"And the shoes."

Ruby red high heels peeked out from under Marie's desk.

"You didn't!"

"I did," Marie proclaimed, her eyes bright with victory. "And after wearing it to work today, I'll go out tonight, glowing like a starlet!"

Catherine shook her head, not sure if she was impressed by her friend's boldness or disappointed by her impetuosity. There was no turning back now, so she smiled and said, "Well done, Marie."

She turned to see Charlotte's reaction to Marie's news and was surprised to find her quietly at work, not paying the least bit attention to them.

"Did you see . . . ."

"I did," Charlotte interjected before Catherine could say more.

"Are you alright?"

Charlotte sighed and put down her brush. "Now is as good a time as any, I suppose."

"I don't think I like the sound of that."

Charlotte leaned closer to her friend and gently moved a dark lock of hair from Catherine's pale forehead.

"You're mothering me," Catherine objected, brushing Charlotte's hand away. "What is it?"

"Alright. You're right." Charlotte searched the room, as though looking for an easier answer. When her eyes returned to Catherine, she sighed again. "There's no easy way to say this, so I'll just say it."

"I wish you would," Catherine encouraged when the pause grew uncomfortably long.

"I've found a new job."

"What? Why?"

Charlotte took up Catherine's hands. "I've found work as a seamstress. You know how I will miss you all, but a person can only find so much fulfillment in painting tiny numbers day after day."

"But...."

"We will still go to the Rock and dazzle the boys." Charlotte dimpled as she said it, "but I have to follow my passion while I can, before I get married and have a family."

Catherine breathed in deeply and released it slowly. "If this is what you feel is the right decision for you, who am I to argue?"

"Oh, thank you, Catherine!" Charlotte caught her up in an embrace, causing the other girls to stare and wonder. "I was so afraid to tell you, but no matter what we will always be the best of friends!"

With the girls all quietly watching, Catherine heard a

familiar tune at one of the windows.

"Why, look! It is our little friend," she exclaimed pointing to the black and yellow canary perched on the sill.

Chapter 3

*It is possible to conceive that in criminal hands
radium might prove very dangerous.*
Pierre Curie, 1905

Catherine tried to be strong in order to support her friend, but she was heartbroken the first time she slipped behind her desk at Radium Dial and Charlotte was not next to her. She would have been lying if she claimed that it was any easier for some days after that first. The other girls still had their fun, painting luminescent rings on their fingers and buttons on their dresses, but Catherine became more reserved and focused solely on her work.

Peg and Marie tried to draw her out of her gloom, but they quickly gave up in order to pursue their own fun. Even Mr Reed stopped trying to pull Catherine into the group conversations. Catherine didn't blame them. They were young and impatient with her dark moods. She wouldn't have said it aloud, but Catherine found a perverse comfort in her depression and isolation, or if not comfort, contentment of a sort.

After work, Catherine did not feel her typical eagerness to get home. Guilt tickled her conscious, but only slightly. Instead of striding toward Superior Street, she turned south and strolled to the park instead.

Washington Square, in the center of Ottawa, was a point of pride for those who lived there. Not only did the park boast memorials to townspeople who had fought in Illinois regiments in the Great War, but it was the home of Ottawa's life-size statue of

Abraham Lincoln and Stephen Douglas.

Following one of the square's paths that all eventually led to the Lincoln-Douglas monument, Catherine wondered what it would have been like to be here on that day sixty-five years earlier when two of the country's most impressive orators fought for votes to become the next US senator from Illinois.

Catherine tipped her head and looked up at Lincoln's bronze face. Curious that had he won that senatorial race, he would not have begun his presidential campaign the following year. Funny how things seem to work out for the best.

Then she looked down at Lincoln's large, bronze shoes, her mind wandering. Did things always go the way they were supposed to? Was Charlotte supposed to leave her here all alone?

Catherine heard her name called from the edge of the square, and she looked up to see Peg and Marie waving at her.

"Come with us to the Rock!" Peg yelled while Marie gestured for her to join them.

An unenthusiastic smile briefly touched Catherine's lips. It was so kind of them, but she just wasn't in the mood.

"Maybe next time," she said, not really loud enough for them to hear her, so she also shook her head and turned away. A smidgen of hope flickered in her heart that they would understand and forgive her. She would want invitations again someday, she was sure.

When she looked back toward the street, the girls were gone, and Catherine decided to go home. Helping Aunt Mary would take her mind off her loneliness.

†

It was in the midst of this that Pearl Payne joined Radium

Dial. She was exceptional in that she was married and, at twenty-three, old compared to many of her dial painting coworkers. Pearl had a joyful round face and short, blonde hair in perfect fat curls. The youngest of the girls tittered when Pearl walked in, but Catherine felt instantly drawn to her. Here, she could tell, was someone who would appreciate Catherine's more serious demeanor.

The first day Pearl was with Radium Dial, Catherine simply observed her bowed low over her brush and taking no breaks. At lunchtime, Pearl stayed at her desk and ate swiftly without putting away her paint, as did many of the girls. Pearl seemed to be a quick study, for Catherine did not see her ask a single question of Mrs Reed.

The next day, Catherine arrived early to ensure that she would have a desk next to Pearl Payne. She couldn't say exactly why the need to do this was so overwhelming, but she trusted her instincts. After just a few moments, she was rewarded with a brief word of greeting from Radium Dial's newest employee.

"Hi there."

"Hello, I'm Catherine." She held out her hand.

Pearl, hiding a momentary surprise, took Catherine's hand and replied in kind. "How long have you worked here?"

"Just over a year."

They both took up their brushes and commenced working before Catherine asked, "You are married?"

"I am."

Catherine cleared her throat. She had not thought of what else she might say. Thankfully, Pearl continued.

"His name is Hobart, and he is a mighty fine husband."

Catherine glanced up at Pearl long enough to see a slight blush cross her face.

"He is an electrician, a real knowledgeable guy." Pearl paused to point her brush before continuing, "We thought I could make some money to sock away until we start our family."

By the way Pearl's words had faded to nothing by the end of this explanation, Catherine assumed that Pearl had been trying unsuccessfully to get pregnant. She felt that encouragement was called for.

"That's a wonderful idea," Catherine said, enthusiastically nodding. "Radium Dial is just the place to earn some good wages in a short period of time."

Pearl smiled tightly but gratefully at Catherine's words before they settled silently into their work.

Later, Catherine passed Peg's desk on her way out. Peg was surreptitiously stuffing clock dials into a bag alongside a pot of paint and several brushes. She paused only for a second when she noticed Catherine gazing at her.

"Whatever are you doing?"

"Taking these home so that I can get more done," Peg whispered as she cinched the sack closed and stood quickly to walk out next to Catherine.

Unsure what to say, Catherine chose to say nothing. Peg must need the money, and they were paid by the dial. When they reached the street, Catherine placed a hand on Peg's arm before they went their separate ways.

"You would tell me if you needed help?"

"Of course," Peg lightly assured her with a toss of her hair, which gleamed copper in the sunlight. Before Catherine could say more, Peg was marching toward her tiny two room home and all those brothers and sisters.

†

Catherine was glad that the next day was Sunday. Just the thought of being inside that big, old church soothed her nerves and calmed her fears about Peg Looney. She just wanted to make a little extra, and who could blame her?

Carefully smoothing her best dress, Catherine went into the kitchen for breakfast. Her auntie and uncle were already chatting animatedly and did not stop when Catherine entered. As a greeting, Aunt Mary slid platters of pancakes and sausages onto the table. Catherine nodded her thanks and tuned her ear to their conversation.

"It's nonsense. That's what it is!" Uncle Winchester was fired up, and Catherine was willing to wager that she could guess the topic.

"Oh, Win," Aunt Mary sighed, and Catherine felt certain that he must be ranting about Prohibition. Again.

"Good morning, Uncle," she cheerily greeted him with a kiss on the cheek before repeating the routine with her aunt.

He cleared his throat and lowered his voice to say good morning, his fiery temper quickly cooled.

"I am hoping to see Charlotte today," Catherine introduced a new topic as though she was unaware that she was interrupting, and her aunt smiled gratefully as she set her breakfast before her.

"Well, I for one love her dresses. That girl has skill with a needle, and - I know you miss her - but I think it was the right thing for her to follow her dreams and become a seamstress," Aunt Mary said.

"It was," Catherine had to admit that Charlotte was happy in her new job, and she used her time off to sew lovely items for herself. She had even given Catherine a few small items for her hope chest.

"And how are her parents?"

"Well, I think," Catherine shrugged.

Uncle Winchester only grunted and nodded as he dug into his breakfast. He was content to leave matters such as these to his wife.

Taking some pity on him, Catherine asked about his plans for after church.

"Oh, I suppose I'll see to the garden and fixing that section of fence." He nodded at Mary as he said it, and she smiled in return.

"Thank you, love. That will help keep those rabbits out of my vegetables."

"More soup for me come winter," he said, rubbing his stomach at the thought as though he had not just filled it with Mary's delicious pancakes.

As they cleaned up and prepared to leave, they chatted about the daily chores that needed to be completed before Catherine could have the balance of the afternoon for leisure. By silent agreement, the conversation ended when the front door of the house closed behind them.

The family of three strolled down Superior Street with ample time to arrive at St Columba and enjoy small talk with their neighbors before mass began. Catherine savored this time and squeezed her uncle's arm as they walked. When she was young, he had held her hand to keep her safe as they walked to church. Now, she gave him support, though neither of them admitted that this was Catherine's reason for taking his elbow.

They continued the charade as he leaned on her more heavily to ascend the concrete steps that led to the church's front doors. As she absorbed his weight, Catherine tried to remember when the transition had occurred, but it had been so gradual that she wasn't certain. It made her wonder how many more times they would make this trip together. She would be sure to pray for her dear uncle this morning.

It was easy to tell when a visitor attended church. The seating arrangement would be casually set aside by the guest who was not aware of its existence, and regular parishioners would eye each other suspiciously, silently accusing each other of taking the wrong seats.

On this particular morning, someone unfamiliar was sitting where the Catherine's guardians had prayed for more than half a century. Before Winchester could begin to grumble about it, Catherine cheerfully pointed out that there was plenty of space near one of his good friends from the Masonic Lodge. He gave her a look that acknowledged her ploy and ceased his complaining.

They slid into the pew and knelt to pray as their friends and neighbors continued filing in. Once seated, Catherine relaxed and let herself be calmed by the comfortable surroundings. The pillars that soared up to St Columba's arched ceiling were poorly coated with peeling paint, and a few of the lights were out, but Catherine didn't mind. This church was home, even more than her house was.

She felt connected to her parents here. It was something she had never admitted to Aunt Mary, for Catherine didn't wish her to feel an inadequate guardian, but, of course, a girl misses her mother. Sometimes, Catherine wondered how her life would be different if her parents had not both died young. Returning a smile from her auntie, she decided that it would probably be much the same.

Catherine's worries and burdens that she carried throughout the week dissipated as the sweet voice of the cantor soared through the air. When the congregation responded,

Catherine confidently contributed her imperfect but faithful alto to the harmony alongside Aunt Mary's airy soprano and Uncle Winchester's rumbling bass. It made her heart feel full and happy, as though all was right with the world.

She thought she couldn't be happier until Charlotte found her after the service and enveloped her in a breathtaking embrace.

"How I have missed you!" Charlotte cried, and Catherine felt the heat of tears threaten.

Somehow, Catherine always found herself questioning whether her friends truly loved her the way she did them. She wondered if Charlotte knew how much her words meant to her and hoped so, for it was impossible for Catherine to express.

"How shall we spend our afternoon?" Charlotte asked, holding Catherine's hand as they left the church.

Catherine explained that she had a few tasks to complete at home. "But maybe then we could go down to the river."

"That sounds perfect. We can catch up, and someone will probably start up a game of baseball." Seeing Catherine's face, Charlotte laughed. "We will watch."

Catherine's laughter joined Charlotte's, and she squeezed her hand. "I'll meet you there as soon as I can."

It wasn't long before they were strolling along the edge of the river on a path that had been worn down through decades of children playing and couples courting underneath the canopy of trees. They spoke of inane things, content to simply be in one another's company.

"Do you think you will ever return to Radium Dial?"

Charlotte pressed her lips into a thin line. "I don't want to disappoint you, Catherine."

"No, it's alright," Catherine said, and she hoped her smile was convincing. "I am happy for you."

Charlotte's face lit up. "I'm so glad. It really is wonderful, even though I miss you and the other gals." She winked, and they both laughed at the reference to Mr Reed. "How is the old man?"

"Same as always. Miss Murray hasn't been well, but the Reeds seem content to take on more work."

"That's a shame," Charlotte murmured, but they did not dwell on Miss Murray's problems. No one was particularly close to the stern spinster.

Catherine indicated a tree that must have blown over in the last storm. It had grown there for many decades before its demise, and thick roots splayed from one end while the limbs twisted in the branches of another tree. The result was a makeshift bench where the girls climbed up to sit.

As Charlotte was excitedly describing some new dress designs she was eager to try, a black and yellow canary fluttered into view and came to rest upon the upward reaching roots of the girls' tree.

"Would you look at that!" Charlotte cried, pointing at the curious bird.

It tipped its head as if examining these strange creatures, and the girls laughed.

"That is our little bird," Charlotte stated with certainty. "The same one we saw before."

"How could it be? How can you tell?"

Charlotte crossed her arms over her chest and shrugged. "It is. I just know."

"Alright," Catherine acquiesced. "He must be fond of you then."

"Of course, he is." Charlotte put out a hand as if she might try reach the canary but thought better of it. "He is happy that we are friends, as we were meant to be."

Catherine smiled and rested her head on Charlotte's shoulder. They watched the bird scamper and listened to him sing until he flew away to find his dinner.

Catherine sighed as though the bird had given her instructions by leaving. "I should go too. Auntie will want me home for supper." She was climbing from their perch but looked up at Charlotte. "Would you like to come?"

"Oh, I couldn't just show up like that."

"You know she will have made enough. She is probably planning on having you."

"Are you sure?"

"Of course!"

Charlotte smiled, revealing a dimple that Catherine was sure the boys found charming. "Alright then, but I'll have to get home to mother directly after. She will worry if I am too late."

"She is a sweet woman." Catherine wasn't sure why she felt the need to defend Mrs Nevins's strict curfew. It was an impulse she blamed on her deep longing to have known her own mother better. Charlotte was unoffended.

As they strolled toward the little white house on Superior Street, she grasped Catherine's hand once again. "She is. I am blessed to have a mother that cares for me so, the way your Aunt Mary cares for you."

Catherine nodded thoughtfully. "She does, and she adores your dresses," she added to lighten the mood.

"Thank you, Catherine. You are a good friend."

†

The dial painters were working diligently on Monday morning, but that didn't mean they couldn't have a bit of fun.

They chatted and teased Mr Reed when he misheard their conversations. He took it good-naturedly and responded in kind.

"You gals would make fun of an old man's hearing!" he bellowed unconvincingly. "I'll have your job for this!"

Peg just patted his cheek and went back to gossiping with Marie. Mr Reed walked away with a faint handprint on his face that he wouldn't notice until he was getting ready for bed that evening and the glow caught his eye.

Across the room, Catherine and Pearl murmured quietly as they worked, feeling less inclined to share their conversation with the entire room.

"I didn't realize you had a nursing degree," Catherine said. "I knew you cared for your mother, but I just thought..."

"I must not be trained if I'm working here?" Pearl finished for her.

"Well, yes."

Pearl set aside one complete dial and took up another before answering. She dipped her brush in the radium paint, pointed the bristled perfectly between her lips, and said, "I love caring for others and was so proud to earn my certificate, but painting dials pays better."

"Does it now?"

"Don't be so surprised," Pearl admonished with a grin. "You know that Peg has long dreamed of being a teacher, but she will stay here because it means more money for her family."

"Yes," Catherine agreed, frowning. "That is true."

As she dipped her brush and pointed it for the next number, Catherine thought about these women giving up their dreams for the repetitive work they did here. It made her realize that she was truly happy for Charlotte, who was doing what she loved instead of tracing numbers all day.

"It's not so bad," Pearl said, as if reading her friend's thoughts. "Hobart and I are able to set plenty aside for when we start our family."

Catherine forced herself to smile, knowing how Pearl longed for that day. During her free time, Pearl spent hours sewing tiny clothes and knitting warm, cozy blankets that would one day swaddle her little ones. Catherine would have to set aside her concerns. It was not up to her to make these decisions for her friends, even if she did think they could put their intellect to greater use in other employment. Maybe she was just jealous of their lofty dreams, not having one of her own.

"I am sure your house will be blessed soon," she said, reaching over to pat Pearl's arm. "You will be a wonderful mother."

Pearl smiled radiantly and returned to work, pursing her lips to point her brush.

Leaving work that afternoon, the girls decided to congregate at Peg's house. Though it was small and filled with children, it was a friendly place where the young people were always welcome. On the way, Marie decided to manufacture a minor scene.

"This is one, I tell ya," she murmured to the group as they approached Lutz's Drug Store. "Just watch."

Without giving them time to respond, Marie strutted toward the door. Her hand was inches from the door when she came to a sudden halt. Instead of grabbing the handle, Marie's fingers flew to her forehead. She closed her eyes and swooned convincingly, just as a handsome young man was passing.

He caught her awkwardly, and Catherine was certain she saw a repressed smile on Marie's pale face. The man held Marie as though he was trying to do so without touching her more than necessary. The rest of the girls quickly took pity on him and went to his rescue. As they clumsily lowered Marie to the sidewalk, the pharmacist opened the door a few inches to peer at them.

Peg looked up at him with begging eyes, but Catherine kept her head bowed over Marie. She did not wish to be a part of this ruse.

"Oh, Mr Lutz! Could you please help us?" Peg whined in a childish voice.

Taking a few seconds to make up his mind, Mr Lutz nodded once, turned, and disappeared. The door swung fully open just moments later to reveal the pharmacist with a medicine vial in hand. He handed it furtively to Peg with a gesture toward Marie, who moaned in melodramatic fashion.

"Give her this," Mr Lutz grunted, and then he was gone.

Peg giggled as soon as the door slammed shut behind him.

"Here, darling. I do hope it restores you," she sang in false concern.

Marie laughed aloud, swiping the medicine from Peg's hand and swallowing it in one swig.

"Mmmm...the good stuff," she whispered with her eyes closed in appreciation. Marie grinned up at her friends and jumped to her feet. "Why, I believe I am entirely cured!"

"What do you mean?" Catherine demanded. She was growing cross with the tasteless display.

"What do I mean?" Marie gently mocked with sideways glances at the other girls. "Catherine, honey, it is moonshine. The best in Illinois, too."

Marie was licking her lips, and Catherine's jaw dropped open. She stared at the apothecary door as if she was seeing it in an entirely new light.

"Oh, relax, Catherine," Marie said patting her too firmly on the back. "Everyone knows. If the Eighteenth Amendment has done anything, it has ensured that everyone wants to drink more than before!"

The girls laughed as one and resumed their trek to Peg's house. Only Catherine hung back, feeling naïve and foolish as she stared after them. Finally, clamping her mouth shut, she hurried to catch up.

Peg's home had a weary but well-loved look about it. The roof drooped, but flowers lined the path to the front door. The paint peeled, but cheery curtains fluttered in the windows. For reasons Catherine couldn't quite explain, the place gave her a feeling of calm contentedness.

Then Peg's younger siblings began spilling out.

The air was filled with giggling and a variety of shades of red hair from copper to deep russet. Peg lifted up the smallest of the bunch and placed a loud kiss on her cheek.

"Have you been helping mother today?" Peg asked sternly. The toddler nodded gravely, and Catherine grinned as Peg praised her profusely.

One of the children – Catherine could never remember all their names – pulled at her skirt, so she squatted down to be eye-to-eye with the quiet girl.

"Do you paint numbers like my sister?"

"I do."

"Will you paint my fingernails so that they glow in the dark?"

Powerless to deny the blue-eyed gaze, Catherine promised that she would. Inside though, Catherine wondered if it was prudent to share the luminescent paint with the children.

"Well, I suppose if it is safe enough to be in our mouths, it's safe enough for children's fingernails," she muttered to herself as they filed into the small house.

Once they were settled in the tiny bedroom that the children shared, Catherine realized that all of them were waiting to play with the radium paint. One begged for buttons to be covered, another for some in her hair. A girl who couldn't be more than a couple of years younger than Peg asked for glowing makeup on her face.

Peg laughed as she pulled supplies from her bag and filled the requests one by one. Then the children crawled under their blankets to see each other glow.

"Isn't she just everything you could wish a big sister to be?" exclaimed one joyous little sibling.

Catherine smiled and nodded her agreement, silently watching Peg with her family. A small part of her was envious of the chaotic but loving atmosphere that filled the Looney home. The household Catherine kept with her uncle and aunt was calm and quiet, their love less demonstrative. An insistent request for glowing cheeks distracted Catherine from her thoughts as she turned her attention to dotting radium paint onto sweet, tiny freckles.

Then she painted the frame of her round-lensed glasses at one of the children's urging, sending them into hysterics when she popped her head under the blankets with her eyes aglow.

The time passed too quickly in this happy home, and it was soon time for Catherine to return to her aunt and uncle. She hoped they had managed to get themselves some supper without her help.

Catherine swatted at mosquitoes as she hurried down the street. She didn't like to be out on her own after dusk, so her heels drummed a quick, staccato rhythm on the sidewalk. The scent of illegal home brew overwhelmed her as she walked past some homes, but she had never noticed a patrolling policeman stop to investigate.

She shrugged and quickened her pace. Prohibition was not a great concern of hers. Getting home before the last pink ribbons of sun disappeared was.

When she reached for the handle of her front door, Catherine noticed her fingertips were beginning to glow in the deepening dusk.

†

The next morning was crisp as Catherine made her way to Radium Dial. She filled her lungs with as much of the refreshing coolness as she could before slowly releasing it. A bright sun hung low in the sky and promised a warmer afternoon. A smile on her face, Catherine practically skipped the rest of the way to the old high school.

Pearl looked as though she had already been at work for some time, her paint mixed and a few dials already completed in front of her.

"Good morning, Pearl. Is everything alright?"

Without pausing in her routine, Pearl admitted, "No, not everything. I need to take dinner to my mother after work. Sometimes, it is so difficult to take care of her needs and my own house, too."

"I'm sorry," Catherine murmured. "Is there anything I can do?"

Pearl smiled. "No, dear. You have your own aunt and uncle to worry about. I know they need you more and more."

Catherine raised her eyebrows. She did not talk about helping Winchester from his chair or cutting the vegetables for Mary. Slowly, she had taken on more around the house as they had aged, but it only seemed right. Other girls her age were married and caring for children. But how had Pearl known?

"It is easier to recognize a caregiver when you are one," Pearl explained, answering Catherine's unasked question.

"Does Hobart mind that you have to split your time between your house and your mother's?"

Pearl took a deep breath. "No, he doesn't mind that."

Catherine could tell Pearl was leaving something unspoken, but she did not press. She would be ready to listen when Pearl needed to talk.

Chapter 4

*I would suggest that every operator be warned of the
dangers of getting this material on the skin or into the
system, especially into the mouth.*
Dr M Szamatolski, 1923

As the weeks passed and the weather cooled, the young women fell into a routine of work and leisure that gave Radium Dial a familial atmosphere. The threat of ice and snow temporarily ended the trips to Starved Rock, but they found other places to gather and have a good time.

One of those places wasn't much more than a large shack. Back in the far corner of a property, a boy named Chuck had turned an abandoned structure into a hang-out, complete with gramophone and root beer still. He was the kind of boy all the girls swooned over, a football player with hair that begged to have fingers run through it. Chuck, however, had set his eyes on only one girl: Peg Looney. Because Catherine was Peg's friend, she frequently found herself attending impromptu shack parties.

It was not the kind of thing Catherine would have done of her own volition, but she found that her horizons were often broadened at the urging of her Radium Dial cohorts. Without them, she knew that her evenings would be spent quietly at home with her aunt and uncle. She felt brave and impetuous when she joined the girls strolling out to the shack.

Some of the girls would wear their going-out dresses to work when a party at the shack was planned. That way, they could show up faintly glowing in the low light. The dust that was omnipresent in the painting studio would settle throughout the day, giving a magical quality to the girls' clothes and hair. Catherine could never bring herself to do this. She blushed at the idea of putting herself in the center of attention that way.

Catherine had to admit to herself that she didn't only attend the parties to please her friends. She was single and lonely. When she watched Chuck hold Peg close as they danced, Catherine wondered what it would be like to be embraced that way. Pearl didn't attend the parties, but she told stories about Hobart all day long as they painted their dials. Catherine wanted someone to make her own memories with. Maybe, she would find him at the shack.

On this particular evening, Catherine had herself tucked into a corner. She watched the couples dancing and groups of girls laughing uproariously, but she was content to observe. Her dark hair fell around her pale face, helping to guard her expression from anyone who might glance her way. She was surprised to notice that there was another quiet guest on the opposite side of the room.

Making her way through the crowd, Catherine attempted to match the girl's face to a name she was sure she should know. She bit her lip to jog her memory. Inez. How could she forget? They had both grown up in Ottawa and been casual friends early on at Radium Dial. Catherine said a quiet greeting and waited, something telling her that the girl was ready to talk if she was supplied with a willing listener.

After a few moments of mundane small talk, Catherine's hunch proved correct. "Did you hear about poor Della?"

Catherine furrowed her brow in thought. "Della Harveston?" She tried not to allow her face to give anything away, but Catherine did know Della. They had begun work at Radium

Dial at approximately the same time. She had hoped that Della had left the company for marriage or to help at home.

Nodding, Inez continued. "She's in a bad way. They say it's tuberculosis."

"I'm so sorry," Catherine said as she avoided looking directly at the tears in Inez's eyes. "She was at Radium Dial."

Another nod, and Catherine could tell Inez was trying to keep her face from crumpling into sobs.

"You are close to her?"

After a deep breath, she was able to say, "Yes, and I don't believe for one moment it is tuberculosis. I had a cousin who suffered from tuberculosis, and this just isn't the same." A floodgate seemed to have been opened. "I don't know what it is, but it's just not that. The weakness might be the same, but poor Della just aches all over. It's more than wasting away. She is in constant pain."

Catherine didn't think she could add anything useful to this, so she simply put her arm around the young woman and gazed at her with what she hoped was obvious compassion. When Inez didn't continue, Catherine spoke, "It is terrible to watch our loved ones suffer, but it is also a privilege to serve each other at our times of greatest need. Della will be comforted by your great love for her."

Inez gave herself over to sobbing, and Catherine wondered if she had said the wrong thing. Silenced, she rubbed the girl's back and murmured as she would to a hurt child. Just when Catherine was thinking that she should have stayed home, Inez looked up.

"Thank you, Catherine," she said in a voice heavy with sorrow. "Everyone tries to tip-toe around the issue or pretend everything is fine." She shook her head in disbelief. "You are the first to name it for what it is. Suffering. Suffering that will only end with sweet Della's death."

"With her heavenly homecoming," Catherine quickly corrected as she embraced Inez.

She was rewarded with the shadow of a smile. "Yes. I will remember that. Thank you," Inez said, wiping her nose and looking around the room. "I should go, but I am glad now that I came. Please, pray for me . . . and for Della." She gave Catherine's hand a final squeeze and walked away without waiting for a response.

Catherine decided to leave as well. She did not resent that others would continue to have fun, but, with her mind on Della Harveston and the dear friends who had already begun grieving for her, Catherine felt that her place was at home.

†

Pearl seemed unusually quiet as they painted their dials. Catherine could almost hear the bristles of her brush as they slid along the digits leaving a faintly green residue behind. Catherine did not wish to break the silence. Her mind was again on Della, and she wished that she had thought to visit Inez since that day at the shack.

So caught up was she in her own thoughts that it was midmorning before Catherine wondered what made Pearl so quiet. She took a deep breath and cast a sidelong glance at her friend. Only then did she notice the red rims of her eyes and the blotchiness of her normally perfect skin.

"Dear Pearl, whatever is wrong?" Catherine asked, carelessly discarding her brush and dial as she moved to her knees at Pearl's side.

Pearl only shook her head with a vehemence that pushed

Catherine back into her seat. Whatever it was, Pearl had no desire to discuss it here.

"I'm sorry," Catherine whispered as she took up her work and tried to pretend nothing had happened while curious girls peered their way.

Pearl sniffed and gulped. When Catherine had given up any hope that her friend would be able to speak, she finally did. "It is my mother."

"Oh no!"

Her lips pressed tightly together, Pearl struggled for self-control.

"We can speak about this later," Catherine assured her with a gentle hand on Pearl's arm. "Whatever it is, I am by your side."

A flat smile was gone almost before it formed on Pearl's face, but she whispered, "Thank you."

Catherine had to pretend that not knowing wasn't driving her insane for the rest of the day. When they could finally retrieve their coats and hats, she breathed a sigh of relief and then felt guilty. Surely, whatever Pearl was coping with was much worse than having to wait to hear news.

Pearl did not want to wait any more than Catherine. As soon as they were away from the crowd of women pouring through the doors of Radium Dial, she blurted, "My mother's illness has returned. I must go to Utica to serve as her nurse."

"No!" Catherine hoped that Pearl believed her outburst was in sympathy for Pearl's mother, though it was truly the thought of Pearl leaving that caused it.

"I know, Catherine. I do not wish to leave Radium Dial either, but I trust no one else to care for mama."

"Of course. I am being selfish."

Pearl smiled. "No, you are being a friend. Is it wrong for me to say that I am glad you do not wish for me to leave?"

"Of course, I do not!"

"I know," Pearl grasped Catherine's hand and held it as they moved slowly down the sidewalk. "I am being vain, taking some pleasure in your pain."

"Oh, Pearl. Utica isn't so far. Maybe we won't see each other at work, but . . . ." her words trailed off as she considered the reality of Pearl having a sick mother and a husband at home. Little time would remain for frivolous friendships.

"You're right," Pearl insisted, squeezing her hand. "We will still make time for each other. I will need your support more than ever."

Catherine smiled, despite her sorrow. Pearl had known that empty platitudes would not have comforted her, but that knowing she was needed would.

"You know I am here for you. Always."

†

Work wasn't the same without Pearl. In addition to that loss, Charlotte was hopelessly distracted by love. She spent all her free time with her new beau, leaving Catherine feeling quite alone. In an effort to keep her spirits up, Catherine focused entirely upon her work and was making more money than ever. It was the one favorable consequence of her friends' resignations.

Pearl and Catherine made a point of seeing each other on Sunday afternoons. It was the only time they could carve out between work and home responsibilities, so it was all the more treasured. They also started writing each other letters. At first, Catherine had thought this silly, Utica and Ottawa only being separated by a few miles, but once the first letter arrived Catherine realized it was wonderful to have words from a dear one that could be read over and over again.

She was thrust back into the present by Mr Reed's raised voice.

"Come on, gals! No dilly-dallying! The quicker everyone gets outside, the quicker we can get back to work."

Catherine realized that the girls were filing out the door, but she hadn't the faintest idea why. With a shrug, she stood up and followed them.

When she saw they were being directed to line up on the wide steps in rows according to height, she remembered. Today was the day for Radium Dial's company photograph. Well, maybe she shouldn't have worn her black dress today, but it couldn't be helped now. It would not have been so bad if they hadn't placed her in front. She sighed, crossed her ankles, and folded her hands in her lap to keep her from fidgeting.

The portrait was taken before she knew it, and dozens of young women hurried back to work. Mr Reed and the men who worked in the lab strolled more casually to their tasks. They, of course, were not paid according to how much they accomplished.

That night, Catherine was still feeling depressed, so she sat at the small desk in her room and penned a note to Pearl. She had nothing new to say, besides that Pearl had left before picture day, but it was still nice to feel a connection to her friend.

Realizing the lateness of the hour, Catherine turned off the light and put her hand out to feel her way to bed. She gasped as light emanated from her body, dimly revealing her surroundings. Catherine held her hand in front of her face to examine it.

"The dust," she whispered to herself, thinking of the hazy air in the painting studio. "It must be the dust."

With a low chuckle, she climbed beneath the covers. If lip-pointing her brush gave her rosy cheeks, the dust of Radium Dial would ensure her perfect health!

Catherine did not think of the glowing again until several weeks later when she received the news that Della Harveston had died of tuberculosis.

Then she remembered the ghostly glow of her own body and a chill coursed through her veins.

†

"I couldn't be more proud of you gals," Mr Reed announced as the dial painters smiled and blushed. "You will be happy to hear that Radium Dial is now the largest studio of its kind in the entire United States!"

The women whooped and cheered until Mr Reed held up his hands to continue.

"As every year does, 1925 will bring us some challenges, but I know that you gals are a match for anything that comes our way!" After more enthusiastic cheering, he added, "Your successes will not go unrewarded. Starting next month – free of charge – the company will begin providing health check-ups, just as though you were family."

His satisfied grin filled his face so that his cheeks pushed up the frame of his round-rimmed glasses. After adjusting them and nodding to a few girls who looked eager to ask questions, he said, "I will contact you when it is your turn for a physical. Can't fit in all you gals at once, of course."

Catherine frowned. All around her was excitement for the future, but she had awoken feeling poorly. She would not press right now, as some of the less patient girls did, but she hoped that Mr Reed would agree to let her be one of the first to visit the doctor.

It wasn't until the end of the day that an opportunity arose. Catherine dawdled over cleaning up her desk and scrubbing her hands in the tepid water. Finally, the last girl left the studio, and Catherine shoved her things aside and rushed to Mr Reeds office.

She knocked softly as she opened the door.

"Mr Reed?"

He cleared his throat and furrowed his brow at her. "Yes, what is it?"

"Sir, I was hoping, if you don't mind..."

He tilted his head as if to say, "I'm waiting."

Catherine decided she must simply spit it out. "I was hoping I could be included in the first medical tests." There. Why would he say no?

But he did.

"I'm sorry, Catherine." Mr Reed was already shaking his head remorsefully and rearranging papers on his desk. "Those appointments have already been taken." He opened and closed a few desk drawers without apparent purpose. "Is there a reason you ask?"

"Well," Catherine began timidly. "I've been a bit poorly, but I'm sure it's just a seasonal cold."

The relief that washed over Mr Reed's features seemed excessive to Catherine.

"I'm sure you're right. I'm sure you're right," he repeated while his attention was on keeping his hands busy. "You get home and get some rest now, gal. You'll feel better tomorrow, I'm sure."

"Yes, Mr Reed."

Catherine quietly retreated and closed the door, angry with herself for not going to Mr Reed immediately. She felt foolish and hot tears burned in her eyes as she rushed through the hall with her head down. She wouldn't think of it. What else could she do?

Catherine was successful in setting aside her concerns. She felt better after a few days and assumed she had been concerned over nothing. Then she received a thick letter from Pearl.

She always carefully opened the notes so that she could tuck them back into their envelopes and keep them that way in a violet box under her bed. When Catherine gently tugged the papers from this envelope, she saw that it was more than Pearl's letter. A news clipping was included. She read the note first, but the only reference to the enclosed clipping was a vague question.

"*Have you read about this?*"

Bemused, Catherine unfolded the news sheet, going pale as she read the headline.

Dial Painter Sues Claiming Injury to Health

It was what she had been afraid of since Della's death, since her own ineffectiveness in ridding herself of fatigue, and since Radium Dial started offering medical testing. Was radium paint making them sick?

The article was frustratingly short on details and left Catherine with more questions than answers. She started furiously writing them in a letter to Pearl, thankful as she did so that her friend, at least, was no longer exposed to the substance that Catherine became increasingly concerned might not be as beneficial to the dial painters' health as they were led to believe.

How she wished she could speak to this woman in the article who worked at US Radium Corporation! But she was in New Jersey. She may as well have been on the moon. Catherine added a postscript to her letter, begging Pearl to send her any other news articles she saw.

The very next day, water pots appeared on each desk at Radium Dial. Catherine's stomach felt twisted and heavy when she saw them. The feeling was not alleviated when Mr Reed made his announcement.

"Good morning, gals!" he began with false cheer. "You will have noticed that you have been provided with water for dipping your brushes in. Some of you have requested it, and I always try to do what I can for you gals."

Catherine peered discreetly around the room and noticed that the others appeared to be doing the same, all wondering who had requested water and why. She thought of Peg complaining about the taste of the paint when she started working there. Maybe a new girl had insisted upon water. Catherine shrugged and picked up her first dial of the day.

Later, she noticed a man she had never seen before slowly walking through the studio. He appeared to be inspecting every detail of their work. Catherine observed him as he watched Peg dip her brush in paint and point it with her lips, ignoring the water pot. He wrote something in his notebook and kept moving through the room, peering into water pots and watching women paint. When he met Catherine's gaze, she quickly lowered her eyes and picked up her brush, but she could not bring it to her lips.

She bit her lip and set the brush down, careful not to look up. Instead of painting her dial, she set it aside and began to mix more paint. Catherine's hands shook and she spilled some of the powder, so she brushed it away in frustration.

Then, she accidentally looked up and realized the stranger was watching. And he looked even more horrified by Catherine covered in the radium paint powder than he had by Peg lip-pointing her brush.

Catherine's face felt hot with the blush that she was sure made her cheeks glow like fire. Tears in her eyes, she left her desk and ran to the restroom. The door closed securely behind her, she sobbed, though she wasn't sure why.

"I must be going crazy," she muttered to herself as she splashed cold water on her warm skin. Catherine forced herself to breathe slowly and be rational. She loved her job and had no reason to be worried. Why was she letting one news article invade her mind and impede her happiness?

She took one more deep breath and released it as slowly as she could before returning to the studio. At the door, the sound of voices caused her to pause.

"Several girls have derived benefit from their exposure to our products."

That was the voice of Miss Murray. Catherine had scarcely interacted with her since her interview almost four years ago. The answering voice had to be the stranger.

"They do seem healthy and vigorous. Do they all point the brushes with their lips?"

Miss Murray had her response ready before he had finished asking the question. "All of the girls have been admonished not to tip the brushes with their mouths."

Catherine heard Miss Murray sigh in exasperation, but she could only wonder when those instructions had been given.

"You know how difficult it can be. They insist on doing things their own way."

Catherine could hear the stiff fabric of Miss Murray's tailored suit shift as she shrugged in despair of getting poor working girls to follow simple instructions. She realized she was leaning forward in anticipation of the inspector's response, but she was disappointed.

"I see," was all he said, and Catherine did not see him again.

Chapter 5

*We are a long way from speaking of the
ill-effects of radium therapy.*
Dr James Ewing, 1925

Nothing filled Catherine's heart with joy quite like a wedding at St Columba. The fact that two of her friends were being joined together before God and congregation only made it better. Albert Purcell had swept Charlotte off her feet. It meant less visits between the two friends, but Catherine couldn't be upset. In fact, she squeezed herself to contain her delight. They would make each other so happy.

Only occasionally did Catherine feel sorry for herself as her friends married and started families. As she witnessed Albert and Charlotte make their vows, Catherine felt certain that her turn would come, and she was content to wait for the just the right man.

She would not be one of these overly eager women who got herself into trouble and ended up married to a womanizing drunk – not that anyone was supposed to be a drunk anymore with alcohol illegal.

Catherine returned her attention to Albert placing a delicate ring upon Charlotte's slender finger. She was glowing with happiness.

Catherine frowned. Was Charlotte faintly glowing in the dim light of the church? She shook her head. It was the effect of the candlelight and an overactive imagination.

It had to be.

Then the church bells were ringing, and Catherine thought of it no more. There were happy greetings, hugs, and kisses for all who congratulated the bride and groom.

Catherine was content to wait while others pressed to see the couple first. She stood and looked up at the stunning stained-glass windows that encircled the chapel until she was startled by a deep voice close to her ear.

"Did you know that my grandfather donated the money for that window?"

Catherine automatically stepped away from the voice while looking to see who it was.

"Oh, Tom Donohue, you made me jump!"

He grinned at her and was instantly forgiven.

"Now, just which window is your grandfather's?"

"Well, I don't think he still has claim to it, but it is that one," he said, leaning close to her again and gesturing toward a colorful Biblical scene.

"It's beautiful," she murmured.

Catherine did not move away as quickly as she should have this time. Tom wasn't the type of man that girls swooned over, but Catherine wasn't the swooning type of girl. She preferred his serious, studious ways to flashy charm that deceived and quickly faded.

"Are you going down for the reception?" Tom asked, holding his arm out to her to escort her to the potluck dinner in the church basement.

Praying that her face wasn't aflame with a blend of nervousness and pleasure, Catherine placed her hand in the crook of his elbow and smiled.

Albert led Charlotte in their first dance as a newlywed couple. Copious amounts of food were eaten, and illegal booze was smuggled around the room. In this joyful atmosphere of love and laughter, Tom remained at Catherine's side.

For once, she was more than an observer, and she wondered what had changed. Where had Tom Donohue come from and how had she captured his interest? Even more importantly, would that interest last beyond this one enchanted evening?

Catherine was still swaying with bliss as she arrived home and noticed a letter from Pearl on the hall table. She squealed as she hadn't since her elementary days and scampered up the stairs with it clutched close to her heart.

She hadn't even removed her hat, when her smile faded and a sudden chill overtook her. Pearl had enclosed another news article.

Suits Are Settled in Radium Deaths
"Deaths?" Catherine whispered to the empty room.
Were women dying – did Della die – because of radium?

†

"I heard you spent quite a bit of time with Tom Donohue last night," Aunt Mary announced as Catherine settled at the breakfast table. She didn't even have time to wonder where Aunt Mary had gotten the news so quickly before she was speaking again. "Do you know that he studied to be a priest? A girl cannot marry a priest!"

"Tom has not become a priest, Auntie."

Aunt Mary narrowed her cloudy eyes at Catherine. "Is he yet preparing for the priesthood? What is that boy up to?"

Catherine laughed. "I assure you that he is entirely honorable, not that a priest isn't," she quickly amended. "But Tom decided that was not his calling."

"And what is?"

"He works as an engineer, Auntie."

"Well, I suppose that's alright," she huffed, slapping scrambled eggs onto Catherine's plate. That was as long as it took to recall another objection. "He's a rather short man."

Trying not to grin, Catherine countered, "He is not tall, but, thankfully, neither am I."

Aunt Mary harrumphed, and Catherine wondered if there was anyone in Ottawa that she would approve of her niece courting. She didn't have much time to consider it. Scarfing down her eggs, Catherine stood to kiss her aunt before the elderly woman had taken her own seat.

"I'm sorry, Auntie. I must get to work. I slept too late."

Catherine could not make out her aunt's response, so she simply called, "I love you," as she dashed out the door.

At Radium Dial, the girls were at their desks but not working when Catherine slipped in. Mrs Reed was standing before them, holding up a small item that Catherine couldn't identify.

"You will find on your desk," Mrs Reed started as though she had been waiting specifically for Catherine, "a glass pen." She paused as each girl located and took up a strange clear cylinder of mysterious purpose.

"You will use this for dial painting in place of your brushes."

"Eliminating the need to lip-point," Catherine said before she could stop herself.

"Yes," Mrs Reed surprised her by agreeing. "Too much of the material is wasted by the practice of lip-pointing. Therefore, you are to use the glass pens instead."

With that, Mrs Reed strode from the room without allowing for questions.

Catherine was thankful to have a different method to paint

the dials, and she was relieved that Radium Dial was taking seriously the concerns regarding radium safety. Now Catherine wouldn't have to worry.

Except that the pens were impossible to use. Even before lunchtime, some of the girls had begged for their brushes and shoved the useless glass pens to the back of their cubbies. Catherine soldiered on. She would make less money this week because of the difficulties using the pen, but she would be safe.

When Peg noticed Catherine still struggling with her glass pen the next day, she slid into the desk next to her and asked, "Why are you still messing with that thing? You know our old brushes are just in Mrs Reed's desk. She'll give you one. You've only got to ask."

"Oh, I know," Catherine muttered as she ruined another dial with clumsy paint drops. She tossed it aside and took up another, but Peg's hand stopped her.

"What are you doing?" Peg asked again, this time with genuine curiosity.

Catherine dropped her work in frustration and covered her face with her hands. "Oh, I just don't know!"

Peg shushed her comfortingly as she would one of her younger siblings and gently pulled Catherine's hands into her own. "What do you mean?"

Catherine gestured hopelessly at her discarded dial and dripping glass pen. "I am trying to do this the way they say we should. The way that is safe. But it just doesn't work, does it?"

Peg's face scrunched up in confusion. "What do you mean, the way that is safe?"

Shaking her head, Catherine scraped the paint from the pen and back into her dish. "It's silly, I suppose, but I thought that the paint must be unsafe if they were giving us another way to apply it."

"Oh dear, Catherine!" Peg exclaimed in relief. "You have yourself in a *tizzy* over nothing. You know how penny-pinching they can be. They just don't want us to use too much paint. As you can see," she gestured to the ruined dials, "it is more efficient to use the brushes after all."

"I guess you're right," Catherine gave in.

"Oh, sweet Catherine. You would know better than anyone if the luminous paint made us sick. Haven't you worked here for four years?"

"More or less."

"See," Peg enthusiastically encouraged, ignoring Catherine's morose tone, "and you are a picture of health. No more worries. Party at the shack tonight. Chuck and I will pick you up."

Peg stood and kissed her on the head as Catherine imagined a mother would do, without giving her an opportunity to respond. Catherine retrieved her brushes and hurried to catch up on her work.

"Tom will be there!" Peg had called out when she walked away, and there he was.

Good to her word, Peg had sweet-talked Chuck into picking up Catherine, sacrificing the opportunity to drive around alone with Peg. The shack was already filling up with people, but Tom looked out of place. He looked too much like someone's older brother, there to make sure things didn't get out of hand.

Catherine smiled and approached him. She blushed as his face lit up when he saw her.

"I'm so glad you're here, Catherine."

"I didn't have much of a choice," she joked with a meaningful look in Peg's direction.

"She's a real pal, ain't she?" Tom shoved his hands deep into his pants pockets to keep from fidgeting. Catherine found it hopelessly endearing.

"She is." After a moment of awkward silence, she asked, "So, how did they get you here?"

Tom pushed his hands so deep into his pockets, Catherine was afraid he might rip them. His eyes were on the floor when he admitted, "Chuck told me you would be here."

Catherine couldn't help grinning like a crazy person. She wished she could say something flirty, like she knew other girls would, but she just stood there. Grinning.

Tom cleared his throat, forced himself to meet her eye, and said, "Can I get you a root beer?"

"That sounds wonderful." Catherine had only previously tried small sips of Chuck's homebrew, but she would have accepted a glass of creek water from Tom's hand. She watched as he pushed his way through the crowd as though on his way to an emergency. She laughed and covered her mouth with her hand.

He was here to see her!

She tried to calm herself and think of topics of conversation before he returned with the root beer. Her heart fluttered in her chest, despite her commands for it to calm itself. When Tom strode toward her with mugs in hand and a boyish grin on his face, Catherine knew that she would be powerless to control her animated heart.

"It's quite good," Tom assured her, handing off one of the mugs and taking a sip from his own.

Catherine followed his lead and smiled as the sweet brew cooled its way down to her stomach. Tom must have also been thinking of what to say as he retrieved their drinks, because he had returned more confident, asking about Charlotte and Albert, her work at Radium Dial, and the health of her guardians.

"You're just so thoughtful," Catherine gushed, feeling a bit like she had just completed an interview. "Now you must tell me what is going on in your life." She almost asked what had made him chose engineering over the ministry but decided that she didn't want to mention the possibility that Tom Donohue might have taken the path of celibate bachelorhood.

Tom talked of his family, especially his twin sister Margaret, to whom he was particularly close. However, he didn't seem to have much to say. Instead, they watched as some of the partygoers danced. They laughed together and shared innocent bits of gossip.

When Tom asked if he could take her home, Catherine happily said, "Yes."

Chapter 6

Why didn't you tell us?
Grace Fryer, 1925

"Aren't you having lunch?"

Peg only shook her head without looking up from her work.

"Why, what do you mean? You must be hungry?" Catherine wanted to squat down by Peg's desk to force her to look her in the eye, but her leg was too sore.

"I'm not," Peg muttered.

"Well, if you're sure," Catherine gave in reluctantly. She wondered if Peg's family was short on money again. It could be such a struggle just to get by sometimes. Not wishing to embarrass her friend if that was the case, she patted her shoulder and left her alone.

Finding a quiet corner, she wrote a short letter to Pearl. Catherine still missed her so, and she wanted to tell her all about Tom. She felt a pleasant tingle at the thought of him, so she took up her pencil to share her secret feelings with Pearl.

As she walked back to her desk when the lunch break was over, Catherine slipped a fresh baked cookie onto Peg's desk.

"Auntie made them," she whispered. It was something at least. Tomorrow she would bring more to share with Peg. Now that she thought about it, she realized her friend was looking startlingly thin. Catherine admonished herself for not noticing sooner but was quickly distracted by her work.

The next morning, Catherine stuffed an extra sandwich

into her lunch sack before rushing to sit at her desk before the church bells tolled the hour. It was not until they broke for lunch that Catherine had the opportunity to tell Peg that she had brought enough to share.

"That's too kind of you, Catherine, but I couldn't take advantage."

"You wouldn't be," Catherine insisted, thrusting the sandwich into Peg's hands.

"You don't understand."

Peg's voice was quiet, her words oddly slurred. Catherine realized that she hadn't heard Peg speak much lately.

"Then help me understand." Catherine placed her hands on Peg's shoulders, gently but firmly. "Tell me what is wrong. Let me help you."

Peg sighed and gave in, gesturing for Catherine to follow her into the tiny bathroom shared by all the dial painters. Once they were snugly closed inside, Catherine examined Peg's face and saw her own concern mirrored there.

Peg surprised her by not speaking. Instead, she opened her mouth wide and pulled at the side of her mouth for Catherine to see inside.

"Oh, Peg! How in the world?"

"They just fell out," Peg whispered.

Having seen the inside of Peg's mouth, understanding flowed over Catherine. Her friend wasn't avoiding food and conversation because of money problems. She must be in constant pain from the throbbing, angry abscesses that flared irritably where two of Peg's teeth should have been.

"You poor thing!" Catherine wrapped her arms around Peg, which was easy to do in their close quarters. Peg's shoulder blades and ribs felt sharp. "How long have you been suffering?"

Peg only shook her head as her tears began to fall.

"Oh, shush, love," Catherine murmured, swaying slightly on her feet. "We will talk about it when you're ready, and we will find you help."

"That's just it," Peg suddenly cried out. "I've been to the dentist. He doesn't know what could be wrong, and four more of my teeth are loose."

"Four?" Catherine's voice was scarcely more than a whisper, and she felt a sliver of fear pierce her heart. What could be wrong?

Someone knocked on the bathroom door, making them both jump and then laugh half-heartedly at themselves. Peg swiped at the tears on her cheeks and took a deep breath.

"Thank you," she whispered as she nodded for the door to be opened.

They both ignored the shocked look on their coworker's face when they left the small bathroom together.

"Can you come home with me for dinner?" Catherine asked before they separated to go to their seats.

Peg just nodded. Poor girl, Catherine thought as she took up her paint and brush.

They didn't speak as they walked the few blocks to Catherine's house that evening. Peg seemed content that she had shared her troubles with someone who cared about her. Catherine was distracted by a pain in her hip. She must have sat too long in the same position, she thought, trying to ease the pain by lengthening her stride and stretching a bit to each side.

They could smell Aunt Mary's bangers and mash almost before they could see the house, and the hungry girls shared a grin. It was Catherine's favorite, and the smashed potatoes should be tolerable for Peg to eat with her sore, inflamed jaw. They weren't giggling and gossiping as they often did after work, but, at least, they were content.

"Hello, dears," Mary greeted them as they stepped into the aromatic kitchen.

"Hello, Auntie," Catherine said before placing a kiss on her velvety cheek.

"You two look famished," she said, eyeing Peg's thin form, and Catherine felt once again admonished that she hadn't noticed Peg's misery sooner.

Peg reached out and squeezed Catherine's hand as though she had read her mind. Catherine flashed her a grateful smile, and they took seats at the small kitchen table.

"Have you heard from Pearl?" Aunt Mary asked after they had said the blessing over their meal and inquired about Peg's family. Auntie quickly picked up on the fact that Peg was not comfortable speaking. Without needing to know why, she had changed her line of questioning.

"She sounds well and praises Hobart in every letter." Catherine and Peg shared knowing looks of young girls in love as she said it. "She sends me news clippings after she has read the paper to her mother."

"That sounds lovely," Aunt Mary said. "How is her mother?"

"I've heard nothing new. I know Pearl does not begrudge caring for her, but I do so miss her at work. I suppose it is selfish that I hope Pearl might be able to return soon."

"Now, now, don't you be silly. Of course, you may think of those besides the dear lady herself," Aunt Mary encouraged.

"How was your day, Auntie?" Catherine asked to take the focus off herself.

"Well, that there's something I need to tell you."

Catherine could tell by the way her aunt shifted and kept

her eyes on her food that she had news to impart that Catherine wouldn't want to hear. Normally, she may have urged her on, but today Catherine was content to wait. Her mind was already full of Peg's problems. Her aunt could not hold back for more than a few bites.

"I'm so sorry to tell you girls this, but that sweet thing, Ella Cruse, passed away this morning."

Catherine gasped and she saw raw fear in Peg's pale features. Ella was the same age as Catherine. They had gone to St Columba together their entire lives. They had worked at Radium Dial together until Ella had left work a month ago not feeling well.

"God have mercy."

"Yes, God rest her poor little soul," Aunt Mary agreed. She hadn't realized that Catherine had been talking about herself and the terrified friend across the table.

"What happened?"

Auntie shrugged. "It was like nothing I've ever seen. Nothing but a pimple when it started out, but it turned into an infection that just . . . . well, it's not appropriate for the dinner table is it? But God has ended her suffering in His mercy, and Ella is healed in the presence of her Savior."

"Amen," the girls whispered together as they both crossed themselves reverently.

They ate without speaking for a few moments. Catherine watched Peg cut her sausage into pieces tiny enough to swallow whole as memories of Ella flashed through her mind. Their first communion, youth group outings, and high school graduation. They hadn't been close friends, but they shared a common history.

And now she was gone.

"What do they think it was?" Catherine asked, breaking the silence awkwardly, but she had to know. "The pimple?"

Aunt Mary slowly shook her head. "I'm not sure those doctors have any better idea than her poor mama. I just cannot imagine having to watch that girl as the evil spread through her face."

Aunt Mary abruptly stopped speaking, realizing that she was saying too much while caught up in her own grief. She shoveled a huge bite of potatoes and sausage into her mouth to avoid the temptation to say more.

Catherine set down her fork. An infection in her face killed Ella. She couldn't look at Peg, whose teeth were falling out with nasty looking infection taking their place.

What was happening to them?

†

More Deaths Raise Radium Paint Toll to 17

Catherine stared down at the headline of the *Ottawa Daily News* with her heart sinking.

She could no longer deny it. None of them could. The radium paint was poisoning them. Killing them. And they weren't alone. Complaints about radium had started in New Jersey, where girls had filed a lawsuit against US Radium Company in 1923.

"Why that was five years ago," Catherine uttered in amazement, though no one was present to hear her.

The newspaper fluttered from her hands. They've known for years that the radium is harmful, Catherine thought as she dropped heavily into a kitchen chair. The impact sent pain pulsing through her sore hip, but she scarcely noticed.

She picked up the paper again, mesmerized by the doom announced on the front page.

"It simply can't be," she whispered slowly as she read.

Then she thought of the clippings that Pearl had sent her, articles that she had ignored because she didn't think they could be true. She'd been warned and she'd ignored it. Catherine shook her head and read on.

It had not been quite a year since Ella's death, but Peg was still feeling poorly. And what about Della Harveston? Had she really died of tuberculosis, Catherine wondered.

What would it be like at work now that the local paper had picked up the story?

Catherine tossed the newspaper into her room. She didn't want her Aunt Mary to read it until she had a chance to learn more. Surely, Mr Reed would address this horrifying news, and Catherine would be equipped to calm her auntie's fears. And her own.

She wasn't sure what she had expected, but the eerie silence that greeted her when she walked into the studio wasn't it. Girls at work did not look up as she passed, and the laughter and conversation that normally accompanied their tasks was entirely absent. Catherine took her seat, careful not to make a sound.

Someone would ask. Someone had to. If only Charlotte was here. Maybe Marie, she wasn't afraid to be bold. Catherine wished she wasn't. Catherine looked to where Marie Rossiter sat, but Marie was peering toward the door. When Catherine followed her gaze, she saw Mr Reed entering with two unknown men closely behind.

He was pointing out different women but whispering so they couldn't hear why. Finally, Mr Reed addressed the dial painters.

"Good morning, gals. I have two medical experts here with me today, and they are going to put your minds at ease regarding news you may have heard or read about. Radium Dial is like a family," he nodded his head enthusiastically to emphasize this point in case anyone might disagree. They didn't. The women just stared back at him in silence, so he continued.

"They will be splitting you into groups to make the medical testing go more efficiently." He looked around again, but the girls did the same, all wondering if anyone else would speak up.

Nobody did, so the medical experts began calling women up by name. When Catherine was called, she wasn't sure if she felt relief or fear, but she followed the man from the room, trying to keep her stride steady despite the pain in her hip.

"Miss Wolfe, I just need you to breathe into this tube."

It seemed innocuous, so Catherine shrugged and complied. As he pulled the tube away, she tilted her head to watch, as though something from her breath might be visible inside. He caught her gaze and smiled slightly.

"I will also be taking a blood sample," he explained, gesturing for her to stretch out her arm.

"Alright."

Her slender arm was exposed for a long, fat needle. Catherine looked away as he inserted it into her pulsing vein. It hurt, and she willed nausea away. It was quickly over, and she breathed deeply in relief.

"Only one more thing," the doctor said. He stood, so Catherine did as well. "We have an x-ray machine set up in one of the offices. We will take a few pictures of your skeleton."

"But why?" Catherine asked, rubbing her hip as she followed him. He didn't hear or didn't wish to answer.

Once the x-rays were taken, Catherine was sent back to the studio. She felt let down. Somehow, she thought she would feel reassured if she was tested, but the process had only left her with more questions. What on earth were they looking for that might be in her blood, her bones, and in the very air she breathed?

Later, she mentioned her concerns to Marie. She wasn't sure why it was Marie that she chose to confide in, unless it was because she hoped that some of the young woman's boldness would rub off on her.

If that was her subconscious goal, it was fulfilled. Marie was just as upset as Catherine, and all it took was knowing that at least one other person felt the same way to march into Mr Reed's office and demand more information.

When he saw them, he appeared taken aback. "What can I do for you gals? Shouldn't you be headed home?"

"Yes, we should be, Mr Reed," Marie stated confidently, "but we have concerns that have not been addressed."

"What do you mean?" Mr Reed asked without seeming concerned. He took off his glasses and started polishing the lenses on the edge of his shirt.

"When will we receive the results of our medical testing? Just what were they looking for?"

"If I were to give the medical reports to you gals, there would be a riot in this place."

Marie and Catherine's eyes widened at his words, and Marie stomped her foot and cried, "Are we in danger?"

"There is no such thing as radium poisoning. There is nothing to these stories." Mr Reed grumbled and turned away as he said it, waving them out of his office.

They reluctantly shuffled out, but his words had given Catherine a chill. Marie's voice seemed to come from the end of a long tunnel.

"What do you think is in those reports?"

Catherine shook her drooping head. "I don't know. I just don't know."

The New Jersey girls and their own unknown fate were all the Ottawa dial painters could think or talk about for the next two days. They knew no more than they had the day the supposed medical experts had come and gone without providing any encouragement. Then a full page article in the *Ottawa Daily News* got them all excitedly murmuring again.

Statement by the Radium Dial Company

Catherine eagerly read on.

All the distressing cases of so-called 'radium' poisoning reported from the east have occurred in establishments that have used luminous paint made from an altogether different material, mesothorium.

"Oh, thank God!" Catherine cried, releasing the breath she hadn't realized she'd been holding. Tears of joy sprang to her eyes, making it impossible to read the remainder of Radium Dial's statement for a few moments. "Oh, we are safe!" she announced as she ran through the house looking for Aunt Mary.

They hadn't spoken about their fears, but Catherine knew there was no way she had been successful at hiding all from her auntie.

"What is that, child?" Aunt Mary demanded from the back yard where she worked in her small vegetable garden.

"It's not radium poisoning! Look! It says so in the newspaper."

Catherine could focus again now, and she read to her aunt.

Radium is being blamed for conditions which better knowledge of the facts indicates radium has not caused. We have at frequent intervals had extensive physical examinations made of our employees by well-known physicians, and nothing even approaching the symptoms of 'radium poisoning' has been discovered.

Catherine looked up from the newspaper to find her aunt sobbing into her garden gloves.

"I've been so worried about you girls!"

"Oh, Auntie. You needn't be upset. We were all worried over nothing."

"Thank God almighty," she sighed, rubbing away tears and leaving streaks of dirt on her face.

Catherine embraced her, careless of the grime that would be transferred to her work clothes. Her relief was greater than she could have imagined. Only now that the fear was gone did she realize how terrified she had been.

A few moments passed before Catherine and her aunt released each other. Tension was relieved and joy had taken its place. Catherine read on at a more leisurely pace.

"It says here that those poor New Jersey girls were using mesothorium, not radium like we use. That's why they're getting sick. I should have known that Mr Reed would look out for us. Oh, I just feel so relieved!"

"Indeed, I will be singing praises all day long!" Aunt Mary crooned, her worship thus commenced.

Catherine grinned and carried the newspaper back inside to study it more carefully while Auntie serenaded her roses.

At work, the newspaper announcement was pinned to the wall where everyone could see it, but Mr Reed was taking no chances. As the women settled into their desks, he raised his voice to address them.

"I want to make sure that all you gals pay particular attention to this notice," he said, pointing to the page and waiting for them to nod their agreement. "It was in the paper yesterday and will be included a few more times, just to make sure that everyone in this town understands the truth about radium." He smiled at them in what he seemed to think was a fatherly manner, and continued, "It makes all you gals good looking!"

After the obligatory chuckling quickly faded, Mr Reed added, "Radium Dial has been ever watchful of your health. That is why we ran tests as soon as there was any concern. We would have shut down this studio if there was any truth to this 'radium poisoning' business, but that would have been a shame since Radium Dial has been such a good employer to all of us."

The women all nodded and turned their attention to their work. Except Marie. She spoke up.

"Mr Reed, when will we receive the results of our examinations?"

"What do you mean?" he snapped. He paused to state in a kindlier tone, "I have already told you. Each of you gals is perfectly healthy. There is nothing more to know."

Catherine was so relieved; she hardly noticed the dull throb of pain in her hip as she dipped her brush in the paint and pointed the bristles perfectly with her lips.

Chapter 7

*One cannot doubt for a moment that we have here a
case of death caused by mesothorium.*
Notes of a German Physician, 1912

Young women were squealing and crowding around Peg Looney. She proudly held out her slender hand to give everyone a glimpse of the engagement ring that Chuck had placed on her finger.

"It's beautiful, and I pray that you two will give each other so much joy," Catherine said softly, so quietly that she was sure Peg wouldn't notice her low voice amid the cacophony of excitement, but she did.

"Thank you, Catherine." Her smile was wide, but Peg kept her mouth closed. She didn't want her friends to see where her once winning smile was missing teeth. Catherine understood.

"You have been feeling . . . ."

"Fine," Peg was quick to reassure her. "Just fine." Then Peg allowed herself to be swept into the giggling and joking of the less serious girls, and Catherine eased herself away.

She prayed fervently that Peg really would enjoy a long, happy marriage with Chuck. But she was so very thin and ate less and less. Catherine hoped that Peg ate more at home, where she didn't have to worry about hiding her dental issues. Chuck would take good care of her.

Catherine was excited to have happy news to share with Aunt Mary and Uncle Winchester at dinner that evening. She told them about Peg, praising Chuck at length for his devotion to Peg and their rosy future.

"Why, he even pulls her around town in that little red wagon when she isn't feeling up to walking!"

"I have seen them," Aunt Mary said, nodding thoughtfully. "He is a good boy."

"And quite handsome, too."

Uncle Winchester only grunted, leaving the discussion of romance to the women.

Aunt Mary smiled. "Not more handsome than your Tom."

Her cheeks warm, Catherine shook her head. "He's not my Tom."

Aunt Mary's smile widened. "No, of course, he isn't."

After a few moments of companionable silence, Catherine saw her aunt's face fall.

"What is it?"

Aunt Mary fidgeted and grew flustered. "Oh, I've just remembered something. That's all."

She stood to clear away the dinner things, though a few bites remained on her plate. Food was never wasted. It was too dear. Winchester raised an eyebrow at her, but Catherine sprung into action before he could comment.

"Let me help you," Catherine insisted. She stood and indicated her aunt's plate. "You finish."

"Oh, silly me," Aunt Mary chuckled nervously and shoveled in the few bites before hurrying to her feet a second time.

Catherine struggled to hold her tongue. She didn't mean to be disrespectful. What could have upset her aunt, she wondered. Catherine couldn't think of anything in the newspaper or neighborhood gossip.

Winchester strolled out to the backyard while the women

stood side by side and cleaned the dishes. Catherine put them away while Aunt Mary straightened up the kitchen. When they were done, Catherine's patience ran out.

"Tell me, Auntie. What is upsetting you?"

She took a deep breath and smoothed the front of her skirt. Then, looking Catherine directly in the eye, she confessed, "Ella Cruse's family filed suit against Radium Dial."

Catherine floundered for a chair and heavily fell into the first one she found.

"They still believe the company is responsible for Ella's death? But the announcement . . . ."

"Was an advertisement paid for by Radium Dial," Aunt Mary interrupted. "They don't believe it."

"Do you? When did this happen?"

Aunt Mary only answered one of Catherine's questions.

"They filed suit on the day after the announcement appeared in the newspaper."

†

Green trees soared above and surrounded them, giving Tom and Catherine the sensation that they were the only two people on earth. It had been a treat to drive along the Fox River until they were on the shore opposite Starved Rock. In just a few weeks, all this green would turn to gold, red, and orange, but today everything was vibrant and full of life.

Tom had been telling her about his work, but now they strolled quietly down a sandy path. Squirrels dashed across in front of them, and birds sang in the trees. Sometimes, Catherine wished she could identify them, but she had never been taught and looking them up in a book just wasn't the same.

"This is one of my favorite places in the world," Tom said with a sigh of contentment.

Catherine took a deep breath of warm, forest-scented air. Anywhere with him was fine with her, but she wasn't quite ready to say so.

He didn't seem to mind. Tom just kept walking, holding back branches for her to follow and taking her hand to cross rough patches. She felt so safe and comfortable when he did and wished he didn't let go once the path was level.

"Did I tell you that Peg has asked me to stand for her in her wedding?" Catherine's face grew hot as soon as she said it. She had only wanted to make conversation, but now she worried that Tom would think she was being forward, dropping hints about weddings.

His mind did not go where she had predicted though. "Will the poor thing be healthy enough to get married?"

"Why, I should think so," Catherine quickly defended her friend, but the seed of doubt had been planted. Tom wasn't cruel or heartless. He would only ask in genuine concern.

"It just about breaks my heart when I see big, ole Chuck pulling little Peg around in that wagon," he said, shaking his head.

"I think it is sweet," Catherine protested.

"Oh, he's devoted, alright," Tom agreed. He stopped in the middle of the sun-dappled path and took Catherine's hands into his own. She could feel the callouses from the physical labor he performed every day. It made her feel soft and fragile. "Chuck and Peg are two of the nicest people I know," he continued, absent-mindedly rubbing her palms, "but her health must concern him."

"Do you think so?" Catherine asked. She tried to think about their friends, but she was electrified by Tom's touch.

"Are you not worried about her? It's uncommonly odd that

a young woman isn't strong enough to walk."

Catherine forced herself to concentrate. "I suppose it is. I've just gotten to used to it, and it's so endearing for Chuck to care for her so."

She pictured them as they were most Saturdays. Peg used to try walking about town, but lately Chuck drove or pulled Peg in her little sister's red wagon. It did seem strange, now that Tom had compelled her to think about it. A worm of worry wriggled in her chest.

"I'm sorry," Tom said. "We are supposed to be having fun." He squeezed her hands and gave her a lopsided smile. "Tell me what you'll wear."

"What?" Catherine giggled.

"To the wedding, of course," he clarified with raised eyebrows.

"Oh, Tom." She had to lower her face and hope that the brim of her hat hid her blush. "As if you've given a single thought in your life to a lady's dress."

"Only yours."

Her face burned hotter, and she couldn't respond.

"I would like for you to come for dinner and meet my parents," he said, releasing one of her hands so that he could tilt her chin upward. "You are very special to me, Catherine."

Her face was on fire, and she was sure that Tom must be able to hear her heart beating. Catherine's voice wasn't much more than a whisper. "You are special to me too, Tom."

He smiled and gently ran his fingers along her jawline, making her entire body tingle. "You will come? Tomorrow evening?"

"Of course."

She thought he might kiss her. She wanted him to, but Tom

was too much of a gentleman, and parochial school had taught him too well. He cupped her face for a moment with his strong, rough hand and then continued along the path. She was satisfied that he kept hold of her hand for the rest of their hike through the woods.

Catherine was more nervous than ever before as she prepared for dinner with Tom's family. She was desperate to make a good impression but distracted by increasing pain in her hip. A hot water bottle was pressed against it while she sat at her vanity examining her reflection.

She wasn't sure what Tom saw in her average features that attracted him to her. Her hair was dark and made a pleasant contrast with her pale skin, but her mouth tended to naturally downturn and her eyes were heavy-lidded. Catherine had never believed herself pretty, but, if Tom was content, she would be too.

She wore her best dress. It was olive green with white polka-dots and flattered her slender figure. Catherine hoped it was sufficient to impress a family well-off enough to have donated one of St Columba's stained-glass windows. A tan hat was placed on her head at a slight angle, and matching low heels buckled onto her feet.

Then she waited for Tom and tried to calm the beating of her heart. Catherine was ready to love Tom's family just as she loved him. Did he love her? She thought so, but he hadn't said it yet. That was alright. Catherine was a patient girl.

She sprung from her seat when he knocked on the door and would have run to fling it open, but pain flared in her hip and coursed down her leg, stopping her in her tracks. Catherine gasped and rubbed her sore hip to no avail. Nothing seemed to make a difference. Did arthritis run in her family? Her mother had died so young, Catherine wasn't sure.

Tom knocked again, and Catherine was determined to ignore her hip and enjoy the evening. She knew her face lit up as her eyes took him in. He was so handsome in his dark grey suit. It clung tightly to his chest and tapered down to his narrow waist. She could tell by the way he kept adjusting his cuffs that he was as nervous as she was.

"Why, Catherine, don't you look fine!"

Feeling emboldened, Catherine held his gaze instead of hiding her face. She smiled and offered a small curtsey. "Thank you, Tom. You are quite handsome tonight."

She was rewarded with a grin as wide as the Fox River.

"Shall we?"

Catherine happily placed her hand on his offered arm.

"We shall."

Her heart skipped with joy as she strolled down the street on Tom's arm. If only she didn't have to concentrate so hard on evening her stride. Pain throbbed in her side, but she didn't want Tom to know and couldn't allow herself to limp.

Thankfully, he was content to walk slowly, enjoying this time alone before they reached the bustling Donohue home, where his mother and sister were working in the kitchen as though a dozen extra people were coming to dinner rather than one slender young woman.

"You must be Catherine."

As soon as Tom opened the front door, his twin sister was there, looking as though she was filling out a mental scorecard to determine if this woman was good enough for her brother. Although they were the exact same age, she mothered Tom and was certain that she always knew what was best for him.

"Yes, and you must be Margaret," Catherine quietly replied and extended her hand.

"That's right." Then she turned to Tom. "Mama has made your favorite bread pudding."

"Sounds delicious. Catherine, you will love it. I'll have to have mama tell you her secret."

Margaret's eyebrows shot up at this, and Catherine took it as a sign that their relationship was more serious than she thought if Tom was ready to share the secret of bread pudding. It was silly, but it made her feel warm inside all the same.

She simply said, "I can't wait to try it."

In the dining room, Catherine was introduced to Tom's brother, Matthew, and his parents. Of course, they were nowhere near as intimidating as she had thought they might be. She was able to relax and enjoy the meal more than she had anticipated, and every time Tom looked at her like he was proud to have her at his side her heart fluttered in her chest.

Tom's father must have looked just like Tom when he was younger. Catherine felt certain that she was looking into the future when she looked at the sinewy, bespectacled older man. He spoke something like a preacher, and Catherine understood why Tom had considered the priesthood.

Mrs Donohue was timidly quiet, making it almost seem as though Margaret rather than her mother was the mistress of the house. Struggling with her own natural tendency to fade into the background, Catherine made a point of including Tom's mother in conversation.

"Your dress is just lovely, Mrs Donohue. I have a dear friend who works as a seamstress. She loves trying out new fashions, and I know she would adore your dress."

"Why, thank you, Catherine," she replied with an I-told-you-so look at her husband. "Maurice scarcely seems to notice when I get a new dress, but I do confess that it is one of my vanities to be among the first to try new designs."

From that point, Catherine found conversation flowed easily with Tom's mother. She had plenty to say about Charlotte, and Mrs Donohue had plenty to say about dresses.

"But you don't work as a seamstress, do you?" Margaret interrupted, silencing the table.

"Um, no," Catherine stammered. She had never felt ashamed of her work. In fact, many people thought Radium Dial was the best place in town for a girl like her, but she couldn't bring herself to say where she worked with Margaret glaring daggers at her.

Tom was her salvation. "Catherine is an artist. She paints those watch dials, and I don't know how she manages such fine work. The bristles on those brushes are barely visible they're so thin."

"Thank you, Tom," Catherine recovered. "I do enjoy my work and the friends that I have made there."

Mrs Donohue surprised Catherine by speaking before Margaret had a chance to comment. "I think it is exciting how young women are able to work and contribute to their household. If anything good came out of the Great War – and I have to believe that some good must come out of so much suffering – some of that good has to be the opportunities for you young ladies."

She smiled at Catherine, who hardly noticed the professorial opinion that Tom's father carried on in response. Maybe it would take a bit longer to win over his sister, but Catherine felt she had, at the very least, made an ally of his mother.

Peeking at Margaret, Catherine had to admit that she didn't blame her. It was a virtue to protect and defend those one loves. Catherine just had to make sure that Margaret decided that she loved her.

"Oh, she will," Tom assured Catherine when she had shared this strategy during the walk home.

"How can you be so sure?" Catherine asked without concern. The dinner had been so fine, and Tom was holding her hand.

"Well, I love you, so Margaret will, too."

Catherine gasped and halted mid-stride. He had said it. He looked a bit embarrassed, as if he were a gangly high school student, not the capable thirty-year-old standing before her. Catherine opened her mouth to respond, to reciprocate, but nothing came out.

Her heart wanted to shout, "I love you, too!" but her brain wasn't connecting to her mouth properly, so she clamped it shut.

"I'm sorry if it's too soon," Tom apologized, shaking his head, but then he had an injection of confidence. "But I do love you, Catherine Wolfe, and if you don't love me yet, that's alright. I will work on that."

That lopsided grin! Her heart was aching to be heard.

"No," she exclaimed, and then shook her head. "No, I don't mean that . . . . I mean, no, you don't have to wait." She took a deep breath, looked directly into his eyes, and her voice became firm. "I love you too, Tom Donohue."

He kissed her softly as they stood on the edge of the cobblestone street, the soft glow of a gas streetlight almost reaching them. When he pulled away, too soon, Catherine knew he was the one she would spend the rest of her life with. He seemed to come to this conclusion as well, because he leaned down to kiss her again.

†

Catherine felt like she was floating on the walk to work the next day. She wouldn't have known her feet were touching the cobblestones if it weren't for the persistent ache in her hip. Even that couldn't bother her today though. Everyone dealt with a few aches and pains, but she was in love and nothing could be more glorious.

Sleep had come reluctantly as her heart raced long after she had gone to bed, but she still felt perky this morning. Catherine imagined Tom next to her, the feel of his firm arm as he escorted her down the street and the scent of the rosemary sachets he must keep in his closet. She smiled to herself and skipped up the steps into Radium Dial.

A few girls were chatting amiably when Catherine walked in. She was early, so most of the desks were empty and the sun was only beginning to brighten the room, making dust particles almost sparkle in the air. Catherine collected her supplies for the day and took her seat.

She had just finished mixing her powder with water to create the sticky, glowing paint when Peg took the desk next to her.

"Are you alright, dear? You look tired."

"I suppose Chuck and I stayed out too late."

"Young love," Catherine said with a wink, but her heart felt torn in two.

Peg didn't just look tired. She was emaciated, and her once glorious auburn hair hung dully. But Catherine knew better than to comment any further. For weeks, Peg had been insisting that she was fine as her condition continued to deteriorate. With the truth hanging awkwardly between them, the girls picked up their brushes and dipped them in the paint.

Some of the girls gossiped all day, but that had never been Catherine's habit. She was not a naturally talkative girl, and she preferred to concentrate on her work. Peg was lately of a similar mind, so it was comfortable for them to quietly pass their morning, tracing numbers with their thin camelhair brushes. Therefore, Catherine was surprised when Peg spoke before the bell for lunch rang.

"Are you alright, Catherine?"

She glanced at Peg without pausing her routine, only raising an eyebrow as she pointed her brush with her lips.

"Of course, why do you ask?"

Peg set aside the dial she was painting and examined Catherine more closely. "You are shifting in your seat as if you cannot settle."

"Am I?"

Catherine was genuinely surprised. She hadn't realized that she was subconsciously adjusting to ease the pain in her hip. It had grown so constant that she hardly ever thought about it.

Peg was still looking at her.

"I suppose it's this pain in my hip. It feels better if I don't sit in one position too long."

"How long has it bothered you?"

Catherine quickened the pace of her work as Peg's attention increased her anxiety. "Oh, I don't know," she tried to blow it off. "It's nothing."

This only made Peg's eyes narrow more. "Nothing?"

"Just a touch of arthritis."

"You are twenty-six."

Catherine peeked sidelong at her friend. "Well, yes, but that's not so very odd."

"Have you seen a doctor?"

"The doctors here," Catherine said with a nod toward Mr Reed, who always organized the medical testing at Radium Dial.

Peg was already shaking her head. "You should see someone else – a real doctor."

Catherine was ready to give in, talk more about her issues, and ask Peg what she meant. But that was when Peg decided to turn away and return to her own work, leaving Catherine with an uncomfortable sensation in her gut that had nothing to do with arthritis.

That afternoon, Peg stood, and Catherine assumed she was going to retrieve more supplies. However, Peg grasped the back of her chair for support, and she was unable to take a single step. She was swaying on her feet when Catherine glanced up at her. Before Catherine could react, Peg collapsed onto the floor of the studio.

"Mr Reed!" Catherine screamed, and other girls' cries joined her own. "It's Peg! Send for a doctor!"

Catherine knelt at Peg's side, brushing hair from her face as she checked her head for injuries. Not finding any bumps or blood, Catherine felt a glimmer of relief. Of course, her friend was weak. It was so difficult for her to eat with that state of her teeth. She needed rest and nourishment.

Catherine's thoughts got no further, for she was shoved aside by Mr Reed and another man he had recruited to carry Peg from the studio. Knowing there was nothing else she could do, Catherine remained on her knees and prayed fervently for her friend.

Chapter 8

Well, mother, my time is nearly up.
Peg Looney, 1929

"I am so worried about Peg," Catherine groaned, thankful for Tom's strong arm around her shoulders.

"What have the doctors said?" he asked.

"That's the thing. They don't say anything. They won't let anyone see her. Her mother is just in shambles." Catherine's rant ended with her in tears, so Tom pulled her close and said nothing.

When she could speak again, Catherine was resigned to the truth, "Radium Dial doctors are examining her. They are paying the bills."

Unspoken between them were the reasons Radium Dial would do such a thing. Was it really a small town employer caring for its workers like family or a corporation covering up the fact that its employees were getting sick and they knew it?

"She must be so lonely," Catherine said with a laugh that was half sob. "Peg is used to being home with nine siblings. She must be out of her mind with no visitors."

"You have a caring heart, Catherine. No wonder I love you."

The words caused her heart to beat faster, just as they had a few days earlier. He was keeping her from despair. She hadn't yet confided in him that her aunt's condition was also poor. Though Catherine loved her Aunt Mary, the pain of knowing her passing approached gave her nowhere near the agony of Peg's situation. People were supposed to live full lives and then go to heaven. Aunt

Mary had done that. Peg hadn't had the chance.

"How is Chuck?" she asked instead.

Tom shrugged. "I don't really know. We aren't close. He was just one of Peg's matchmaking tools." He managed a weak smile and a wink.

Catherine chuckled softly. "Poor thing. He loves her so."

Tom's arm became like a vise around her, and Catherine knew what he was thinking. What if it were her?

Days went by and nobody was certain of Peg's condition. Catherine prayed that she was improving, and her heart melted anew when Tom offered to kneel next to her. At first, Catherine thought it was curious how tragedy fueled their budding romance. However, on further contemplation, she realized it was natural for her to love Tom even more when he supported her through tough times.

He was there, at her side, when the terrible news came. Peg had died, alone and in pain. Her family relegated to a waiting room while she suffered. Catherine couldn't speak. She just sobbed in Tom's arms and prayed he would never let her go.

It wasn't until the funeral that Catherine discovered the full horrifying truth. Not only had Radium Dial doctors kept Peg's siblings from her room, they had tried to trick the family after her passing. Catherine's jaw dropped when Peg's sister, Katie, told her that Radium Dial doctors had performed an autopsy without the family doctor present, breaking an agreement they had made.

Catherine wasn't sure which was greater, Katie's anger at Radium Dial or sorrow that her sister had died, but it must be heartbreaking to deal with both.

"What did the doctors say?" Catherine managed to whisper. "Do they know what was wrong with Peg?"

Katie's smirk was out of place in the midst of the grief and anger that filled the funeral parlor.

"Diphtheria. They say she died of diphtheria."

Catherine's insides went cold. It couldn't have been diphtheria. She had watched Peg's illness from the time her teeth had started falling out. It didn't make sense. Katie had already walked away, so Catherine was talking only to herself when she whispered, "But if it wasn't diphtheria, what was it?"

†

The town of Ottawa was in mourning, especially the dial painters who were quiet as they completed their work in the days and weeks that followed Peg Looney's death. Catherine thought about quitting, but her aunt's medical bills were much more than her uncle could afford and Radium Dial continued reassuring them that the work was perfectly safe.

Maybe Peg had died of diphtheria. And Della had died of tuberculosis. And Ella had died of a mundane but fatal infection. Catherine's head hurt if she thought about it, so she did not. She just carried on doing what needed to be done.

She made breakfast at home before going to work. Her lunch consisted of whatever she could grab on the way out the door. When the evening bell rang, she rushed home to make dinner, do chores, and make sure that her aunt and uncle were comfortable. Recently, she had to help her aunt take sponge baths because she wasn't able to wash herself properly.

Catherine might have to quit working at Radium Dial, and, for the first time, that thought didn't sadden her. It would be a relief, if only her family didn't need the money.

That evening, Catherine had a few quiet moments to glance at the newspaper. She had no idea what the headlines meant and didn't realize what the impact would be. The stock market crashing wouldn't affect people like her. How could it?

Catherine set the newspaper aside and went to check on her auntie. Tip-toeing into the room, she was grateful to see that the elderly lady was sleeping peacefully, her chest rising and falling with slow, steady breaths. Catherine stood still for a few moments watching the mesmerizing motion. In, out. Up, down. It was calming and reassuring.

She didn't leave the room until sleepiness began to overtake her. Shaking her head free of mental cobwebs, Catherine left Aunt Mary to her rest and went in search of her Uncle Winchester.

He was sitting at the kitchen table with papers scattered in front of him, but he wasn't looking at them. His large hands covered his face as he wearily rubbed at his eyes before moving on to his temples.

"Is everything alright?" Catherine asked, startling him enough that it took him a second to get his unconcerned mask in place.

"Of course it is, my little Cat." He smiled and asked about her plans for the day.

"I am of an age to ease your burden," she replied, gesturing to the papers. "What can I do?"

He sighed and attempted to gather them up before Catherine could discern what they were. "I already expect too much of you – working and caring for your aunt."

Catherine put a hand on his to still them. "Let me help you with the bills."

His protest began before she finished speaking. Her heart ached at his broken pride.

"Please, Uncle," she softly begged. "That is why I work. We have been blessed with my income for this purpose." Seeing that he remained unconvinced, Catherine changed her strategy. "You don't have to share anything with me. I will give you part of my wages, and you decide where it can best be put to use."

When he began to object again, she stated firmly that it was her money to do with what she wished, and this was what she wished. With another elaborate sigh, he nodded his reluctant agreement.

"Thank you, Uncle," Catherine said sweetly. She kissed him on the cheek and began gathering ingredients for their supper.

That very week, Catherine found a way to contribute to the family bills without embarrassing her uncle. She left money on the kitchen table when she left for work, and it was gone when she returned. They never spoke of it again, but Catherine was certain that Uncle Winchester looked at her with greater respect and asked her opinion about an increasing number of mature topics, like the friends that suddenly found themselves out of work and rising prices at the grocer.

The headlines were full of financial news that Catherine didn't entirely understand, but she could see that things were indeed changing, even in little Ottawa.

Each day when Catherine arrived home after work, the first thing she did was check on Aunt Mary. Although she knew that Uncle Winchester and a flock of neighbors spent time with her all day long, Catherine liked to see for herself that Auntie was comfortable and cared for.

These visits varied in length depending on Aunt Mary's strength on any given day until the day came that her aunt grasped Catherine's hand tightly when she moved to leave.

"Please, stay," she whispered.

There was no urgency or pain in her voice, but something stopped Catherine in her tracks. She examined Aunt Mary's face, not knowing what she searched for and said, "Of course."

Catherine perched on the edge of the bed shared by her aunt and uncle, softly stroking the hand that had quickly become frail once her household duties had been relinquished.

"You have been such a treasure to me," Aunt Mary whispered wistfully. "I could never have children of my own."

They had never talked about this, but Catherine had assumed this to be true. "I'm sorry, but I'm also grateful that you were able to be a mother to me."

Aunt Mary smiled, and her eyes crinkled in deeply set lines. "It was all part of God's plan. He has much more in store for you."

Catherine nodded. She knew and accepted this, much as she often wished that she knew more details of this plan.

"Just trust Him," Aunt Mary said, patting Catherine's hand. "For a while, it will be your burden to comfort and care for your uncle."

She said it so casually, but a lump formed in Catherine's throat, leaving her unable to respond. Her objection would have rung false anyhow. They all knew that Mary was dying.

"It's alright," her aunt insisted. "This is part of everyone's plan. I have fought my fight and run my race. I will recognize His voice when He welcomes me into Heaven."

Catherine gulped as tears burned her eyes and spilled down her cheeks. Finally, she was able to croak out a few words. "That is beautiful, Auntie."

Aunt Mary started singing in a weak, raspy voice as if she had forgotten that Catherine was there, though she kept hold of her hand. Catherine took the opportunity to sniff and get herself under control. She was so focused on composing herself that she almost didn't notice when the grip on her hand loosened and the room went silent.

Chapter 9

*Is it not reasonable to say that the use of radium,
which is much more powerful than the x-ray, will affect
the body quicker and do more harm?*
Thomas Edison, 1903

Catherine no longer tried to walk without limping. Caring for her aunt had been too much of a strain upon her thin frame, and the pain in her hip was too much to hide. It didn't even seem that important as she mourned both Peg and her auntie.

At least Aunt Mary had died peacefully at home in her own bed. Catherine would be forever haunted by visions of Peg thrashing in pain and crying out for friends and family in an isolated hospital room.

Catherine was so grateful to have Tom to help her through it all. As her permanently uneven stride took her to the front steps of Radium Dial, Catherine was comforted by the memory of Tom holding her tight and praying by her side. Then there were the memories of soft, stolen kisses.

She shook her head and opened the door. This was not the time to think about those moments, much as she may wish to dwell on them.

The day she applied to work at Radium Dial came back to Catherine when the uneven clatter of her heels echoed through the hallway. She had strode in so confidently and quickly the first day she met Miss Murray. Catherine frowned. Miss Murray had died of cancer two years ago.

Catherine had been so happy to be a part of the Radium Dial family. Now she was only here because jobs had become so dear. Without acknowledging what was happening aloud, Uncle Winchester had been forced to leave more of the household bills to Catherine since Mary's death. His own health was failing, but it meant Catherine was stuck. She needed her pay from Radium Dial more than ever.

Catherine sighed with relief when she finally took the seat behind her desk. She couldn't help laughing when she remembered that she used to double the length of her walk just to follow the course of the river for a few blocks. Now the shortest route left her breathless and aching.

Her paint was mixed, and a stack of dials stood ready when Mrs Reed's shadow fell upon Catherine's desk. She looked up in curiosity. "Yes, Mrs Reed. Can I help you?"

Mrs Reed seemed to consider for a moment before she said, "Actually, it is I who have decided to help you."

Catherine's brow was as furrowed as a freshly plowed field. "I'm not sure what you mean."

"What I mean," said Mrs Reed, tapping her foot nervously, "is that Mr Reed has decided to award you with a vacation."

"But I can't . . . ." Catherine started, but she was cut off.

"It will be a paid vacation. We cannot help but notice that your health has suffered, probably due to the stress you are under. We would like you to take six weeks to recover."

Catherine fought tears. She could not afford to lose this job. Seeing the terror on her face, Mrs Reed seemed to soften. She placed a hand on Catherine's shoulder and patted gently.

"You will have a job here when you return. You rest and get better, you hear?"

Catherine could only sniffle and nod. She put away the

paint and dials that she had just placed on her desk and began the painful journey home.

Home didn't feel quite the same without Aunt Mary. Left with few precious memories of her mother, Catherine mourned the aunt who had raised her as well. It just wasn't fair. And now Catherine wouldn't be seeing her friends at work either. Tears welled up, so she quickened her pace. She would allow herself a good cry once she was alone in her room.

At least that was the plan, but when Catherine entered the house her uncle called for her.

"Catherine, is that you?"

She hurried to the living room, where he spent most of his days on the couch. However, Winchester was not comfortably situated on the couch, tucked in with pillows and blankets as Catherine had left him. He was on the floor halfway to the bathroom, shivering and in pain.

Catherine rushed to his side. "Are you hurt?" She moved hands over his arms and legs, looking for injuries. "I don't want to move you if it will hurt you."

"You're here," he said. He sounded like a wounded child, and it made Catherine's heart break.

"I am here, my dear uncle. Have you hit your head? Are you in pain?"

He shook his head slightly. "I don't believe so. Just had a dizzy spell on my way to the toilet, and . . . ." he didn't finish, but Catherine could see in his downturned mouth and watery eyes that he was ashamed. How difficult it must be for a once strong and vigorous man to need help from his petite niece.

"I will do my best to get you back to the couch, but you must help me," she said, pulling him into a sitting position and wrapping a slender arm around him. This awkward squatting position caused the pain in her hip to be almost unbearable. She gritted her teeth and said, "Make sure you tell me if I'm hurting you."

Then she gathered all her strength and tried to stand. Her uncle groaned and struggled to get his feet under him. It was all Catherine could do to keep pressing upward and not scream.

"There we have it," Winchester cried, just as Catherine was about to collapse. His weight on her narrow shoulders lessened as he found his balance. Catherine released the air she was holding captive in her lungs.

"Hold on. Just stand here a moment." She wasn't ready to support him walking yet.

"I'm sorry, Catherine."

"Don't be silly," she gasped as she caught her breath. "You have absolutely nothing to apologize for."

"No," he paused as one who has to say something he wishes he did not. "I was on my way to the toilet."

Catherine had been ready to steer him to the couch just a few feet away.

"Oh."

They looked at each other, she determined and he humiliated.

"Then I will get you there," Catherine asserted and pressed him to step in that direction.

†

Over the weeks that Catherine had off work, they grew closer than they had been in the entire time since Winchester had taken in the orphaned little girl. It was precious time to Catherine, since she knew that her uncle would soon leave her, too. The time away from Radium Dial had turned out to be a blessing.

Her hip was feeling better as well. Even when she had to assist Winchester when he felt dizzy or weak, it did not pain her as much as it had before. Catherine decided that walking too much must inflame her arthritis. She would have to limit herself when the time came to return to work.

"Will you be alright without me here?" she asked a few days before her mandatory vacation time was over.

Winchester grumbled in his throat as if sorting out his words. "I will. If I am not stubborn and only do what I know I can do, you shouldn't have to pick me up off the floor again."

Catherine smiled and kissed his deeply lined cheek. "I will pick you up as often as necessary."

He took her hand, and she was surprised by how soft his was. When had it gone from being calloused and rough? She frowned and had to look away for a moment. When she turned back to him, she squeezed his hand and kissed his other cheek.

"I love you," she whispered.

"I love you, too, little Cat."

A sob caught in her throat as she remembered all the times through the years he had called her that. As a young girl, she had responded with enthusiastic meowing. Taking a deep breath, she asked him again, "You're sure you'll be alright?"

"You are just going to have to trust the Lord to watch over me when you're not here."

Winchester did not appear upset or anxious at the thought of her leaving, though she knew he depended increasingly upon her.

"Alright," she said. "If you can trust Him with your care, then I will too."

"That's all we can ever do. Whether we agree to it or not."

She smiled at him and wondered what she would do when he was gone.

The sun was already warm and inviting people out of doors when Catherine returned to Radium Dial. She had made sure that Winchester was as comfortable as possible with everything he might need within easy reach before she left, but knowing he needed her made her less eager to return to work than she had thought she would be.

A group of men who would normally be on their way to work had set up a card table under the drug store awning. Catherine wondered if they would be slipping inside for shots of moonshine throughout the day and she tried to increase her pace.

Some sciatic pain coursed up and down her leg, but her mind was too busy considering the unemployed men to notice. The stories about the stock market may not mean much to her, but breadwinners left with nothing better to occupy their time than card games concerned her. People from the countryside moved to Ottawa looking for work, while people from Ottawa tried their luck in Chicago. Catherine wondered if it was better anywhere.

When she marched up the concrete steps to enter Radium Dial, Catherine was less happy to be there than she had ever been. However, she felt the necessity of it with a new urgency.

Mrs Reed met her at the door of the studio.

"Catherine, it is lovely to have you back. I need your help in the mixing room."

She frowned but followed Mrs Reed, who gave her no other choice. Catherine had always been a dial painter. The only women who went to the mixing room were those unable to trace the tiny lines but who were good enough workers that Mr Reed hated to let them go. Why on earth was she being sent there, Catherine wondered.

"Since Mary Tonielli left our employment, we have been shorthanded in here," Mrs Reed explained, stretching her arms out to indicate the powders, mixing dishes, and dusty haze of the room. "We thought you wouldn't mind giving it a try."

"Alright," Catherine agreed in little more than a whisper. The only thing that she looked forward to about returning to work had been taken away. She would be trapped in this grimy storage room while her friends chatted and painted dials.

"The pay will be similar to what you are accustomed to," Mrs Reed assured her, assuming this was the reason for Catherine's reluctance. "It is more than we usually pay someone in this position," she added with a raised eyebrow.

"Thank you," Catherine murmured only because she could see she was expected to be grateful for this undeserved demotion.

"You can start with scraping out the remaining material in these dishes. We cannot afford to be wasteful." With those instructions, Mrs Reed left Catherine alone.

With a sigh, Catherine picked up a dish caked with dried paint and began scraping the material out into a bin. She had thought the room was dusty when she entered, but as soon as she began her work more dust from the dried paint filled the air. By lunch, she could feel a thin layer of it covering her skin and sticking to her hair. It was grubby, lonely work.

In this isolation, Catherine thought more about Charlotte and Pearl. They were married, and Catherine was dividing her time between Tom and work. Therefore, the friends had fallen somewhat out of touch. Catherine knew that Charlotte was due to have a baby soon, so she decided that a visit was in order. Pearl, although still longing for a child, continued to be occupied by her mother's poor health.

Catherine made up her mind as she scraped dried paint out of pots with her fingernails. She would see both of her old friends this coming weekend. It was the comforting thought she needed. Instead of seeing her depressing surroundings, she imagined what Charlotte would look like with a ripe belly and considered what she would tell Pearl about Tom.

At the end of the day, Catherine noticed that few of her coworkers spoke to her. They poured out of the studio, prattling and giggling as usual, but they took no notice of her. She was no longer one of them.

Until Marie walked out. She pulled Catherine into a firm embrace and asked how she was feeling. Catherine and Marie had little in common besides their tenure at Radium Dial, but at this moment Catherine felt like they were the best of friends. She told Marie that she was feeling better but that her uncle was feeling worse.

"That's a downright shame," Marie said, and Catherine knew that Marie didn't say anything unless she meant it.

"Thank you, but you needn't feel sorry for him. He is content with his lot and eager to be reunited with his wife."

Marie nodded thoughtfully. "Your Aunt Mary was a good woman. She was always nice to me, even when other mothers said I was a troublemaker."

Catherine couldn't help laughing at that. "Yes, she could see the good in everybody. Always told me to look at people the way God does. He loves them all."

Marie returned Catherine's smile but surprised her by not saying anything.

"Anyway," Catherine continued, "I do need to get home, but thank you for welcoming me back. It was odd to be away for so long."

"I missed you, Catherine. Too many new girls around here making me feel old." Marie gestured toward the stream of young women flowing out the doors to emphasize her point. "You and I need to be getting married and getting out of here."

For the first time, Catherine agreed. She wanted out of Radium Dial.

†

Catherine lavished affection on Charlotte's tiny daughter and offered all the expected praise. All the while, she was wondering if the undersized infant would survive. The child gurgled and cooed in Catherine's arms, and she had to admit that the baby appeared perfect, if far too small.

Charlotte did not seem to have concerns. Only love shone on her face as she reached out to take her daughter back from Catherine. She cradled the child and swayed as she walked, singing to the babe as she paced around the room.

"She is perfect," Catherine said, watching Charlotte and wondering how long it might be until she held her own child.

"Thank you," Charlotte whispered, although the child was not asleep. "Albert is just smitten."

Catherine grinned, picturing Albert with his daughter. He could probably fit her in the palm of one hand. "I'm sure he is just as devoted father as he is a husband."

This broadened Charlotte's smile, a feat Catherine would not have thought possible.

"It is wonderful to see you so happy."

"We are perfectly happy," Charlotte agreed. She stopped pacing and swayed in place. "Have you heard from Pearl?"

Catherine knew that Charlotte's unspoken question was

whether there was news of a baby on the way for Pearl, who had long desired a family. She simply shook her head. Poor Pearl had more clothes and furniture set aside for a baby than some of Catherine's friends with multiple children.

"The poor thing," Charlotte sighed. "Should I invite her to visit?"

"Oh, yes," Catherine quickly replied. "She loves being around little ones."

"It is not painful for her?"

Catherine tilted her head and considered this. "I believe it is painful, yes, but that she considers it worthwhile all the same."

Charlotte pursed her lips as she thought about this. "I will write to her and see how she responds."

"That is a good idea," Catherine agreed. "Pearl will want to shower you with gifts and hold this sweet thing," she said taking the babe once again into her arms. "Before we know it, she will be twice as big, and we won't believe she was ever this small."

"She's such a miracle, isn't she?" Charlotte asked, one arm around Catherine and the other encircling the infant.

"Indeed, she is," Catherine agreed. She would pray for this tiny miracle, that she would grow and thrive and be a joy to her mother always.

Charlotte moved her fond gaze from her daughter to her friend. "How are things with Tom?"

Blushing, Catherine murmured that she thought things were going quite well.

"It is wonderful to see you so well-matched and happy. Peg must be pleased with how her matchmaking has worked out."

Both girls smiled sadly, remembering Peg. The sweet, bookish redhead had been gone for over a year, and Chuck was not over losing her.

"Her family has filed suit against Radium Dial," Charlotte whispered.

Catherine was shocked. They continued to be assured that the paint at Radium Dial was not harmful.

Charlotte seemed to read her thoughts. "Apparently Peg's family does not believe the statements released by the company."

Shaking her head, Catherine said, "Well, who could blame them with the way poor Peg's illness was handled?"

"Indeed. Sometimes, I am glad I left when I did. Have you thought about leaving?"

Catherine swiftly denied having any such thoughts. "I need the job too badly. How else could I help my uncle and maintain the household?"

Charlotte didn't say anything, only pressed her lips together in a flat, sad smile that she hoped was encouraging. It reminded Catherine of how she used to look down on the underaged dial painters in quiet condescension.

"Am I making a mistake?" she asked in a low voice. Maybe Charlotte wouldn't hear. She wasn't sure she wanted an answer.

Looking at the baby instead of her friend, Charlotte thought for an uncharacteristically long time before responding. "I can't answer that for you, Catherine. These reports about radium are scary, but so is trying to get by without a job." She shrugged before moving the babe to her shoulder to pat lightly on her back. "I'm sorry, my dear friend, but I just don't know."

Catherine wasn't sure if she felt better knowing that her friend struggled with the same conflicting problems she did, or worse that no one could offer her a certain answer. She didn't know what to do, so she kept doing what she was doing. She was grateful when Charlotte changed the subject.

"What do you think of these people lobbying for an end of

Prohibition?"

Catherine shrugged. "I don't think about them much at all with everything else that's going on."

Nodding, Charlotte continued, "I can understand that. The one thing I find interesting is that they say it could help the economy – bring back jobs. They say that millions of dollars go to illegal businesses now instead of legitimate ones."

"Millions of dollars? I had no idea." Catherine's eyes widened in wonder. She couldn't fathom such a sum. "Do you think they're right?"

Charlotte laughed and lowered the baby between them where they could both gaze down in admiration. "I have to admit that I don't have many answers today."

"But you have her," Catherine said encouragingly, softly stroking the baby's soft head.

They smiled at each other and then down at Charlotte's daughter, and it was enough.

Chapter 10

*An industrial hazard does not exist in the
painting of luminous dials.*
Dr Frederick Flinn, 1926

The fragrance of simmering vegetable soup billowed through the door when Catherine entered the home that she now shared only with her Uncle Winchester. She stopped on the threshold, closed her eyes, and took a deep breath. Her stomach grumbled in response. Nobody needed to tell her that Shirley had been in the kitchen.

Before closing the front door, Catherine looked down the street toward Shirley's house. It was so kind of her to check on Winchester while Catherine was at work, and the soup would be a comfort to him. He might not be able to eat much, but the scents filling the house would remind him of the days when Mary spent much of her days in the kitchen and he was not quite so alone.

Catherine entered quietly in case he was asleep. She tip-toed into the living room, which was now set up as Winchester's bedroom. He could no longer traverse the steep steps to the second floor, so he was made comfortable here. Catherine didn't mind, and it made it easier for neighbors to check on him throughout the day as well.

Peeking around the corner, Catherine saw that he appeared to be dozing, but that is how he spent most of his days anymore. She slipped into the kitchen and ladled a bit of soup into a bowl before returning to the living room. This time, she did not attempt to be quiet. In fact, she made a show of clattering things around a bit so that Winchester would not be shocked by her appearance.

"Hello, uncle. How are you this afternoon?" Catherine asked as she entered the room and set a tray on the table at his bedside.

Winchester grunted but peered into the bowl. Catherine was cheered that he had some interest in food. The thin, grey man before her had little in common with the man who had raised her.

"I've brought you some of Shirley's delicious soup."

"I thought I recognized that smell. Did you know that Shirley always won prizes at the fair for her recipes? She was quite a catch when she was younger. When we were all younger." His eyes had that faraway look that overcame her uncle with increased frequency.

"Yes, I believe you have mentioned that," Catherine said with an encouraging smile as she offered a spoonful of soup. "I can imagine Shirley as a pretty, young girl, winning boys' hearts with delicacies of her own creation."

Winchester took the bite and nodded. "That she did. That she did." Then he looked ready for another bite, so Catherine obliged.

She did not say more while he was eating, allowing him to focus on the one simple task. When he had emptied the bowl, she praised his efforts. "And there is more - as much as you would like. Shirley has left an entire pot simmering for you."

Winchester wearily waved her off. "Not now. I am full, and I believe I'll take a nap."

"Of course," Catherine said, cleaning up the bedside table and carrying out the tray. "Just holler if you need me."

He appeared to be already sleeping. Catherine watched him for a few moments, wondering how many more days they had. She knew that one day soon she would believe him to be asleep but would find he had gone to his heavenly home. There would be tears, but she would also rejoice for him, knowing he would be free of his illness and surrounded by those he loved.

For the moment, Catherine chose not to think about what her life would look like when Winchester died. She knew the house would be left to her, but could she manage its upkeep all on her own? She sighed and scooped out more soup. It would be good for her soul too.

Catherine took her bowl into the living room and sipped her soup as she watched her uncle sleep. The slow, shallow rising of his chest told her that he would not likely last much longer, so she treasured this time in his presence, even if he was unaware of it. She memorized the lines of his face and thought about the joys that had left the deep creases at the corners of his eyes. Winchester had lived a good life and deserved his rest.

A soft knock at the door caused Catherine to swiftly set aside her bowl. Her heart lurched when she peeked through the window and saw Tom standing on the front porch. Smoothing her hair and skirt, she opened the door and greeted him with a smile. Catherine stepped outside, so that Winchester would not be disturbed.

"How is he?" Tom asked, leading her to the porch swing.

"The same. Slowly fading but not in pain."

"That is good."

They sat close together and pushed the swing only a few inches back and forth. Tom took her hand.

"How are you?"

She smiled at him. "I'm feeling quite fine right now."

He grinned back at her and kissed the top of her head.

After a few moments of quietly enjoying each other's

company, he asked her, "Can I take you out tonight?"

"That sounds lovely," Catherine tried to keep her voice casual, but her heart was leaping inside her chest.

"Will he be alright?"

She nodded. "I'll have a neighbor stop by. Everyone has been so helpful and thoughtful."

"Good. You deserve a treat." Tom squeezed her hand and moved to stand.

"Are you leaving already?" Catherine asked and was ashamed of how needy she sounded.

"Don't worry, my love," Tom said, placing a hand under her chin. "I have some things to take care of, but I'll be back in an hour."

She watched him walk away. He stopped and waved when he was partway down the block, just as she had known he would. After returning his wave, she went inside to prepare for the evening out. She wasn't quite as nervous preparing for a date with Tom as she once had been, but she still wanted to look nice for him. Tom was a good man and deserved a fine woman at his side. Catherine hoped that he was proud to have her on his arm.

By the time Tom returned, Catherine had convinced Winchester to have a few more bites of soup and arranged for a friend to check on him while she was gone. She had also curled her hair and put on a dress that Charlotte had helped her design and sew. Although she knew she was no particular beauty, Catherine felt pretty tonight.

Tom appeared to agree. His gaze was appreciative and his words kind. Catherine was sure she must be glowing, and not because of dust from the studio this time!

The only blemish on the evening was the pain in her hip. Catherine couldn't help limping, and she hoped that Tom hadn't had dancing in mind. It made her angry at herself – at her body for betraying her commands. How she would love to spend the evening dancing in Tom's arms, but simply walking was a chore.

Either Tom had known how Catherine felt or he had not felt like dancing, because he took her to a small restaurant with tables lit with candlelight and no dancefloor in sight.

"This is beautiful," Catherine sighed as Tom held her chair out for her. The scent of garlic and oregano hung in the air and made her stomach growl. "It smells wonderful, too."

"The aroma coming from this kitchen as I walked by is what made me want to try this place," Tom admitted, taking his own seat and placing the cloth napkin on his lap.

They ordered entrees and chatted about work and their families. Catherine thought Tom looked more handsome than ever in the candlelight and hoped that it had the same effect on her own features. Their dinners were as delicious as the fragrance had promised, and they lingered at the table not wanting the evening to end.

"Catherine, you know that I adore you," Tom said, setting his napkin on the table and looking at her with a very serious expression.

"Oh, Tom." She blushed and looked away, not knowing how to respond. He must know that she felt the same way.

Then he was at her side, kneeling and holding out a small but lovely diamond ring.

"Catherine," he had to pause and clear his throat. "Would you do me the honor of becoming my wife?"

Her heart burst and her jaw dropped. The uncertainty in his eyes tugged at his heartstrings. He must know what she would say. It was then that she realized she hadn't said anything.

"Oh, Tom! Yes, of course, I will marry you!"

He stood and pulled her from her chair and into his arms as the other restaurant patrons cheered and applauded.

Normally, Catherine would be appalled to be the center of attention this way, but she only had eyes for Tom as he placed the ring upon her finger and kissed her – right there in front of everyone!

"You've made me a happy man," Tom said when he released her. "I hope that I prove myself worthy of you."

Catherine put her hand on his cheek, savoring the feel of the short stubble. "You already have," she said before boldly kissing him again.

As they separated, Catherine began to feel embarrassed that they had put on such a scene. She smiled shyly at Tom as they retook their seats. Sensing her embarrassment, he promptly requested their bill and led her from the crowded dining room. Many congratulatory words were offered as they passed those who had shared their special moment.

Out on the street, Tom pulled Catherine into his arms, making her giggle and swat at him to no avail.

"You've already given your word, Catherine," he joked, holding her firmly. "This is the kind of thing you will have to put up with every day now."

"Is that so?" She relaxed against him. Her heart felt full. "Even in public, Mr Donohue?"

"Of course!" He nodded and looked up and down the street. "I'll want everyone to know that you're my girl."

Catherine buried her face in his chest to hide her blush. She felt like she had become the princess in a fairy tale. The scent of rosemary filled her nostrils, and she closed her eyes to relish the feeling of being in his arms. Every day. She prayed that they would have many days together.

†

The memories of that evening comforted Catherine as she struggled to walk the few blocks to work on Monday morning. Never before had her hip given her quite so much trouble, and she resigned herself to seeing the doctor. She wished she was still painting dials, so that working quickly for a day could earn a few extra cents to go toward the expense. She was glad the feeling of being in Tom's arms was so easy to remember and get lost in. The arthritis and other worries could be ignored, as long as she was his.

Then she came to the steps that led to Radium Dial's front door. Catherine eyed them warily, took a deep breath, and forced her feet to move forward. She had to take them slowly, one at a time, so that by the time she entered the storage closet where she now worked the bell had already rang.

Thankfully, neither Mr nor Mrs Reed was anywhere in sight. Catherine immediately began measuring out powder and water for the dial painters. She decided that when she did see Mrs Reed she would ask to return to dial painting and the opportunity to earn extra income.

However, it was Mr Reed, rather than his wife, who poked his head into Catherine's dust-filled domain. "Please, see me in my office," he requested before disappearing.

Catherine set aside the paint pots and moved to follow him. She had known Mr Reed for almost ten years, and he knew she was a dependable worker. Surely, he would approve her request.

It wasn't until Catherine stepped into Mr Reed's office that she wondered why it was that he wished to see her, but the look on his face was not encouraging.

"You wanted to see me, Mr Reed?"

"Yes, Miss Wolfe, please take a seat."

Catherine did so, mostly without wincing.

"Your sabbatical does not seem to have improved your health," Mr Reed observed.

"Oh, but it has," Catherine offered quick correction. "I am afflicted by some minor arthritis, but the vacation you so kindly offered allowed me much needed rest and restoration."

Mr Reed narrowed his eyes and chewed on the inside of his cheek. "I only wish that it had provided more complete healing."

Catherine did not think this conversation was going in the right direction, so she interjected, "I am glad you asked to see me, Mr Reed. I would like to request a dial painting position, as I had before." When Mr Reed only examined her without responding, she added, "I believe I am better suited to my original work."

Mr Reed slowly filled his lungs before almost sighing, "Is that so?"

Catherine only nodded.

"I am sorry, Miss Wolfe, but you seem to misunderstand why I have asked you here today." He moved some papers around on his desk but didn't seem to need any of them. "You see, your little problem," he looked down at her leg as he said this, "is quite disconcerting to the younger gals."

In confusion, Catherine remained silent.

"I'm sorry," Mr Reed repeated, "but I am going to have to terminate your employment. There are many healthy gals who are eager to work here."

This was the last thing Catherine expected, and she knew her surprise was painted all over her face. She tried to speak but didn't know what to say, so her jaw just moved noiselessly for a moment before she clamped it shut. Should she beg for her job? Would it make a difference?

She looked at Mr Reed. He was much the same as when she had started working at Radium Dial. His hair was greyer at the temples and his stomach softer and rounder, but he was the same friendly, fatherly man who had claimed Radium Dial was a family. The stoic expression on his face only made her feel worse. This moment was uncomfortable for him, but he would not miss her when she was gone. As he had said, there were dozens of girls waiting to take her place. She was a fool for believing that her employer cared for her.

Still, she could not form a response, so she only nodded and tried to keep tears from her eyes as she stood. Without saying a word, she left Mr Reed's office, collected her few belongings, and left Radium Dial for the last time.

She left without entering the studio. They would all hear soon enough, and those who were her true friends would reach out to her. She couldn't face the rest.

Tears sprang free of Catherine's control as soon as she crossed the threshold of her home. She heard Winchester's greeting and inquiry of what she was doing home but could not respond. Instead, Catherine shuffled to the makeshift bedroom at the center of the main floor and collapsed at his side, sobbing into his shrunken chest.

"What is it, dear one?" he asked as he gently patted her head with a bony hand. "What has happened, little Cat?"

Catherine managed a half-coherent explanation that was enough for Winchester to understand that she had lost her job. If he was worried about the loss of income, he didn't show it. He only continued to comfort her and shush her as he had when she was a child and suffered some minor injury.

"There, there. It will be alright."

But Catherine didn't know how. She wasn't sure what other

work could she find, but it certainly wouldn't be anything that paid like Radium Dial. How were they to survive?

Chapter 11

Complete information was not obtainable, and the firm protests against calling the diseased condition radium poisoning, but it seems well indicated by the test.
Swen Kjaer, 1929

One benefit of unemployment was that Catherine had plenty of time for visiting her friends, especially Charlotte and the new baby. Her friend had been sympathetic and encouraging about the loss of Catherine's job.

"I know it is a hardship, but I will rest easier knowing that you are no longer there," she had said. Since she had few other options, Catherine had decided to look upon her situation the same way. As long as nobody was sure about radium's impact upon people's health, maybe it was best that she was no longer around it, especially since she and Tom hoped to start a family as soon as they were married.

"Tell me about the wedding plans," Charlotte commanded, taking the opportunity to steer the conversation away from Radium Dial.

Catherine smiled and her face warmed at the thought of her upcoming nuptials. St Columba decked out in green and pink. Tom standing at the altar, watching her walk down the aisle to become his wife. Their friends gathered for the reception. The wedding night.

"I see you have plenty on your mind," Charlotte said with a

chuckle, drawing Catherine out of her daydream. "You will be a beautiful bride."

"I don't know about that," Catherine said, "but Tom loves me anyway, and that's all that matters."

"He's such a fine man. You will both be so happy."

"Thank you, Charlotte. My only concern is dear Uncle Winchester. He can no longer leave his bed, but I know it will break his heart to miss the ceremony." She did not add that she didn't know who else might walk her down the aisle, but Charlotte would perceive that issue without Catherine needing to say it.

"The solution will become clear. I'm sure of it."

Charlotte was right. Before Catherine's wedding, they all gathered at St Columba for Winchester's funeral. He had slipped away peacefully during the night, just the way he would have wished to, with no crying woman at his side or doctor poking and prodding. The scent of Shirley's vegetable soup still faintly swirling through the air.

Catherine had found him in the morning, and faithful neighbors had helped her lay him out in the room that had been his for the last several months. It would feel odd to convert it back to a family room, Catherine thought.

Now, the house on Superior Street was her own, until Tom shared it with her. Catherine had never lived alone, and she did not like it. For so many reasons, she was eager for her wedding day.

The same could not be said of her future in-laws. While Tom's parents had found her to be a nice girl, concerns that he was taking on an invalid for a wife caused them to raise objections. Word of Catherine's release from Radium Dial had coursed through town faster than the Fox River, and Tom's father was reasonably concerned that a woman not healthy enough to work would not be healthy enough to care for a household and bear children.

Catherine shared her future father-in-law's concerns, but nothing could make her give up Tom. She couldn't imagine her life without him, and he was adamant that he would not change his mind. As the wedding day approached, the objections of his family only made Catherine and Tom cling to each other more tightly.

Tom held her now. They sat close together on the sofa that had been returned to its place after Winchester's bed was removed from the living room. Some people might have found it scandalous that they were alone in the house, but Catherine didn't care. She had lost her parents and those who had taken their place, and she didn't want to be alone.

"Do you have any doubts?" she asked him, not daring to look up. If she did, she would examine his face for clues, and she wanted to accept his answer as he gave it.

"None," he stated simply and firmly.

Catherine tried to wriggle closer to his side, though there was no space between them.

"Do you?" Tom asked, and she was surprised to hear a sliver of fear in his voice.

"Of course not!" She pulled away enough to look up into his eyes. "I have been blessed with such a fine man and so much more than I deserve. How could I have doubts?"

"Then you know precisely how I feel," Tom said, drawing her back to his side.

They chatted about what their life would be like after the wedding. Just a few short weeks to go. Tom occasionally rose to tend the flames that were glowing warmly in the fireplace. It was easy to imagine that they were already married, until he had to leave and Catherine had to go to her cold bed alone.

As Catherine ascended the stairs, she envisioned Tom beside her. He soon would be every night. The idea no longer made her feel nervous and shy. She longed for him, his company and his warmth.

"It is not good for man to be alone," she murmured to herself. "Or woman either."

†

A letter from Pearl arrived the next day. Catherine squealed when she saw it and decided then and there that she would plan a visit to her dearest friend. Pearl was always full of news, and Catherine wondered how she had time to gather so much gossip while caring for her husband and mother.

Most of the letter was inconsequential. It was just seeing Pearl's writing and knowing that she had been thinking of Catherine that was important. One tidbit did cause Catherine to pause.

Ella Cruse's family had accepted a settlement of $250 from Radium Dial. Pearl quickly moved on to another topic, so Catherine lowered the pages to consider what this meant.

Did that mean that Radium Dial was accepting responsibility for Ella's illness and death? Or was it simply a kind gesture? The ache in Catherine's hip made her want more information. Was her rheumatism simply that, or had the radium that she worked with for nine years caused her injury?

Catherine dashed off a short note to Pearl, letting her know that she would visit in the next few days. Then she donned her coat and hat to make the slow, painful walk to her doctor's office.

As Catherine's unsteady gait carried her down the street, a memory of Peg came to mind. She was riding in a red wagon because it was too painful to walk, and strong, devoted Chuck pulled her along.

Catherine halted, gasping. Could the same thing be happening to her? She prodded her teeth with her tongue, remembering how Peg's had fallen out one by one. Catherine sighed in relief when all of her own teeth felt secure.

"I must stop worrying," Catherine admonished herself and she continued limping toward downtown.

"He assured me that I demonstrate no symptoms of radium poisoning," Catherine joyfully told Tom that evening. She had told him about her trip to the doctor's office but not her vision of Peg. There was no need since her news was reassuring.

"That is wonderful to hear," Tom agreed, hugging and kissing her enthusiastically.

"I know it was silly of me to worry," Catherine began, but Tom stopped her with another kiss.

"You are not a silly woman," he murmured once he had left her breathless, "and I am glad you went. It eases a burden that both of us were carrying, whether we cared to admit it or not."

"Now I can focus on the wedding." Catherine smiled. She felt happy and bold. Her hands glided smoothly over Tom's chest, and he raised his eyebrows at her.

"You have me thinking more of our honeymoon," he said in a voice raspy with desire.

"It will be worth the wait," she whispered. "Not too much longer."

Tom groaned. "Thank goodness for that!"

Catherine laughed and kissed him brazenly. It was the first time she had allowed him to see that she desired him in that way, and she hoped that he did not think her unrespectable. He held her as if he would never let go, and Catherine decided that he was not disappointed in her.

†

The church was mostly empty with only a few pews in the front filled with close family and friends. A large gathering was not affordable or desired. Tom and Catherine only needed those they loved most to share their special day with them.

Catherine's light green dress had been taken in to emphasize her tiny waist. The excitement of wedding preparations had taken away her appetite, but she was certain that she would grow more plump when she was making meals for Tom each day. It was easy to skip supper when living alone.

She held a bouquet of perfect, tiny tea roses. They matched the pink streamers that decorated the front of the church. A single matching flower was pinned into Tom's suit pocket.

Charlotte and Pearl were there for her in the absence of female family to attend Catherine on her big day. Tom had his brother, Matthew. Catherine was so thankful that Tom's family had given their blessing once Tom had made it clear he would choose Catherine over them if they forced him to make the choice.

Matthew smiled and winked at her as she began her procession down the aisle, and Catherine chose to believe that he, at least, had always been on her side. If the smile of Tom's sister was a bit more forced, Catherine was prepared to pretend that it wasn't. After all, she was only trying to watch out for Tom, and how could Catherine fault her for that?

These thoughts were shoved aside as Catherine concentrated on minimizing her limp as she slowly approached the altar, and Tom, and her future. She scarcely felt the pain in her hip due to the ache in her chest. Before this day, Catherine had not realized that you could love someone so much that it physically hurt.

Tom was so handsome, standing there ready to proudly claim her, his eyes bright and smile broad. Catherine grinned so wide she thought her face might split in two. And then she was at his side, releasing the breath she had been holding and attempting to listen to the words of their priest. Tom tried to remain solemn, but his eyes danced and crinkled at the corners when Catherine looked at him.

During the mass, Catherine felt the hand of God upon them and took comfort in it. He would bless their marriage with love, joy, and children. She did not doubt it for a second. At the same time, she felt surrounded by the great cloud of witnesses that included her father, mother, aunt, and uncle. Catherine hoped they were pleased with the woman she had become.

Although she knew the wedding mass was not brief, Catherine felt that it was quickly over. Suddenly, their friends were showering them with rice as they descended the front steps of St Columba.

"This is the happiest day of my life!" Catherine almost shouted to Tom to be heard over their small crowd of guests.

He leaned down so that his lips brushed against her ear, making her knees go weak. "I aim to fill all of your days with joy, my love." Then he straightened and looked down at her and cried, "My wife!"

Everyone around them laughed at his sudden realization. They were indeed now husband and wife.

Chapter 12

*God has sure blessed me with a grand husband
and lovely child.*
Catherine Donohue, 1933

Sunlight danced on the golden surface of Catherine's watch as she slowly turned her arm to observe the shimmering light. The watch was her most prized possession, and she had rarely taken it off since Tom had placed it on her wrist the morning after their wedding.

He had left for work that morning, so Catherine was alone in the house again but did not feel as alone as she had before. Knowing that Tom would come home to her at the end of the day made the house feel less empty. Her dream, as simple as it was, had come true. She would spend her day keeping house while Tom went to work. The only thing missing was children, but Catherine felt in her heart that she would not have long to wait.

As Catherine chopped vegetables, she thought of Tom and how he was spending his day. The glass factory was not the most fulfilling work, but she was grateful that Tom had a job when so many others did not. She had already set aside some of the produce from Aunt Mary's garden, for Aunt Mary's garden is what it would always be to her, for her less fortunate neighbors.

Only once the responsibility was passed on to her did Catherine realize how difficult it was to stand in the kitchen all day. By midday, she was in agony, the pain centered in her hip radiating up and down her body. She decided to rest and use the time to finish a letter to Pearl.

Pearl was the sole friend that Catherine felt she could confide in completely, and she scribbled passionately onto the page. Catherine had tried to reach out to a few of her former coworkers. Her objective had been to warn them and protect them from the damage that radium exposure could cause, but Catherine had been shocked by the negative reaction she had received.

Women she had thought of as friends had not only refused to listen, they became angry when Catherine insisted that something was wrong. Sharing the stories of women who snubbed her at the grocer or turned away when she approached them at church didn't take away the sting of their rebuke, but it was a small comfort to know that Pearl would be on her side.

"Radium Dial is one of the biggest and best employers in this town – one of the things keeping us all alive," one angry neighbor had shouted. "How dare you speak out against them just because you got the rheumatism!"

Catherine hoped – much more so than her neighbors – that her ailment would ease the longer she was away from the studio and whatever was causing women to sicken. Not a word had she spoken about radium poisoning until her condition far outlasted her employment. Of course, she hadn't wanted to speak out against one of the best paying employers in town.

But now, she no longer wondered if it was true. Peg's case convinced her thoroughly, and she was glad she was forced to leave before anything like that happened to her. She shook her head at how stupidly stubborn she had been, not wanting to leave a job that was making her ill. Even less could she understand those who were angry that she attempted to warn others.

She would have to keep it to herself from now on. Those who still worked there didn't want to hear it, and those who hoped to work there, or anywhere, wanted to hear it less. Sighing, Catherine wrote to Pearl of other things, happier things.

†

Catherine couldn't believe she hadn't noticed earlier. With all of the changes in her body and stress that she was under, it had taken her weeks to realize that she must be pregnant. She was ecstatic and scared, praying fervently that her body was healthy enough to nourish a precious new life.

The doctor appointment that she had scheduled to confirm her suspicion had been little help on that front. He had been happy to congratulate her on her pregnancy but scoffed at the idea that she suffered from radium poisoning.

"No need to worry, little lady. There is no such thing. Now, you make sure you are eating for two, because you look like you've not even been eating for one!" he had joked as he left the room, leaving his nurse to complete the paperwork and usher Catherine out the door.

Despite her concerns, Catherine was overjoyed. She had overcome hardship, and they would be blessed with a baby. Tom would be thrilled, and now she felt confident enough to tell him. Such a fine husband; he deserved some happy news.

Catherine was giddy by the time evening came. Her concerns faded as she envisioned their future with the family that would begin with this tiny life growing inside her. She couldn't wait for Tom to get home from work.

When he did, all of Catherine's plans for how she might present the news flew from her mind. He hadn't even closed the door yet when she happily exclaimed, "Tom, I am pregnant! We are going to have a baby!"

The door remained open as Tom dropped his lunch box and swept her up into his arms. He twirled her around, and they both laughed with joy. When he finally placed her on her feet, he asked, "Are you sure?"

Her heart broke at the boyish doubt on his face. He was so unsure that something truly good could be happening to them.

"I've confirmed it with the doctor just this afternoon," she was proud to be able to tell him.

"Why, Catherine, this is just wonderful!" he exclaimed, taking her into his arms again. "God is so good," he said, not completely releasing her.

"Yes, He is," she agreed. "We are so blessed."

When they laid side by side that night, Catherine didn't fall asleep right away. She looked toward the window, smiling at the stars. They hadn't gone to bed so filled with utter joy since they were newlyweds. She placed her hands on her still-flat stomach and whispered, "Thank you, God. You always know just what we need."

†

As the weeks passed, Catherine's stomach rounded, and she felt healthier than she had in quite some time. She stopped worrying about radium poisoning as her mind was consumed by thoughts of the little one that would soon join them. Holding Charlotte's newest babe gave her especial joy, knowing that her own child was on its way.

Tom was a perfect gentleman. He asked how she was feeling the moment he walked through the door and offered to run to the store for any food that sounded tempting. Catherine never sent him for anything though. She had never felt more sure that she already had everything she needed.

Little Tommy was born with spring in the air, and Catherine was in awe of the fact that she was part of the miracle of new life as the flowers began to bloom and the sun shone down on the town of Ottawa. Her pregnancy had been blessedly free of complications, and her son was perfect in every way.

The first time she lay him down in the nursery, which was filled with gifts from their friends, Catherine thought her heart might burst. She watched Tommy's lips move as though he was still at her breast and felt her body respond with the milk he needed. It was all such a wonder.

Tom tiptoed in and wrapped his arms around her.

"It is difficult to believe that he is ours, equal parts of you and me."

She smiled and turned to face him. "I pray that he will be just like his father."

Tom grinned playfully. "His mother isn't so bad herself."

Catherine swatted at him, and then put a finger to her lips when Tom's laughter made the baby stir. They left the nursery hand-in-hand.

Chapter 13

*I was only twenty-two years old, with youth on my side,
and yet no one was able to help me.*
Katherine Schaub, 1925

"This pain in my arm just won't let up," Charlotte said. She stretched and moved her left arm in every which way in an attempt to alleviate the pain. "I actually dropped my shopping bags just the other day. I wonder if it could be a pinched nerve."

"I'm sorry to hear that, Charlotte." Catherine placed a tray of tea and cookies on the table and sat across from her friend. "Have you been to the doctor?"

"No, not yet." Charlotte helped herself to one of the oatmeal cookies that Catherine made every bit as well as her Aunt Mary had. "We might have the money next month, but hopefully I'll feel better by then."

"I will pray that you do."

"What about you? Has your limp improved?"

"No," Catherine sighed. She had hoped that it would once she was away from Radium Dial. "It didn't bother me as much while I was pregnant, but it's back just the same as before now. Maybe it is just plain old rheumatism after all."

"Maybe," Charlotte muttered.

Catherine could tell she was distracted by her own pain by the way she constantly repositioned her arm. "I haven't seen our little bird," she said to put them in mind of pleasanter things.

Charlotte laughed. "It's a bit too cold out for him, isn't it?"

"It's too cold for me," Catherine agreed, sipping her tea and gazing gratefully at the fireplace.

"One thing about winter though, it keeps us cozy inside."

"And no work in the garden."

"There are blessings to every season."

On this they agreed. The remainder of the tea and cookies were consumed in companionable silence except for the sound of the fire crackling and popping and children playing.

†

That Sunday, Catherine prepared for church with a smile on her face. Although they had been married for over a year, it still felt exciting and new to attend worship as husband and wife. Butterflies filled her stomach at the sight of Tom in his Sunday best, and Catherine wondered if they always would.

They slipped into their pew at St Columba as the service began, so they nodded and smiled at friends who would have to wait until afterward for proper greetings. Some smiled knowingly in return, as if they knew exactly what had made the young couple tardy. The familiar sensation of a blush crossed Catherine's cheeks, but she willed it away. Tom was her husband and she had nothing to be ashamed of.

The flush of her cheeks disappeared as the blood drained from her face when Catherine attempted to kneel for prayer. Pain as she had never felt before radiated from her hip, and she almost cried out. Tom took the baby from her and kept his free arm around her, sensing her distress.

"Are you alright?" he whispered.

She struggled to keep her face neutral. "Of course, just a pinch," she lied, wondering if she would be able to stand. Her prayer was fervent. Would God take the pain away? Was it a punishment? A trial sent to draw her closer to Him? Maybe if she knew the purpose of her pain, she could endure it.

Thankfully, she was able to stand when prayers were complete, and the pain lessened when she did. Tom's eyes found hers, and she smiled encouragingly in answer to his unasked question.

"I'm alright," she insisted, holding her hands out to receive little Tommy, but she was glad that Tom kept his arm around her for the remainder of the service.

The congregation lingered after the priest ended the final blessing. Friends were greeted and tittle-tattle was shared. It was a whisper of an acquaintance that informed Catherine of the news she shared with Tom once they returned home.

"Helen Munch's husband is divorcing her."

"What? On what grounds?" Tom's surprise was as great as her own. Catherine watched him to gauge his feelings on the rest of the story.

"It is due to her illness. He told the priest he does not wish to have an invalid wife."

Tom scoffed. "Did their vows not include the promise to love each other in sickness and in health?"

Catherine could only sadly shake her head. "The promise was easier to make than to fulfill."

"Poor Helen. What will she do?" Tom asked.

"I'm not sure. Return to her parents? She is not well enough to work and live on her own. That much of what he says is true."

"He should be ashamed of himself. It is a husband's calling to provide and care for his family, especially his wife."

Catherine went to him and placed her hands on his cheeks. "I am so blessed that you are mine," she whispered with tears in her eyes.

"You are tenderhearted, my love."

Catherine knew that Tom believed her tears were for Helen, and she did not correct him. However, she did wonder if Tom's principles would be tested and what the result would be.

The next day, Catherine contacted the local doctor that Aunt Mary and Uncle Winchester had trusted most. Without revealing to Tom just how worried she was about the pain she had experienced at church, she let him know that her hip bothered her enough that she felt an appointment was necessary. Catherine was thankful when he had wholeheartedly agreed and expressed no concern regarding the expense that they could scarcely spare.

Leaving Tommy with a neighbor, Catherine walked to the doctor's office, considering what she would say as she strode down the street. Should she mention that she was concerned about radium poisoning or simply wait to see what conclusion the doctor came to? It seemed dishonest to leave out that she had worked at Radium Dial. However, she also didn't want to set the doctor against her from the start if he was one of the company's supporters.

Pausing before the medical office, Catherine took a deep breath before she went inside. For once, she was thankful for the time spent in the waiting room. It helped her to calm her nerves and work out what she was going to say. When she was called back to an examining room, she was ready.

"I have a pain in my hip," she explained. "I've developed a limp, and it is becoming difficult to kneel." She was proud of how emotionless her voice remained.

The doctor took some notes and made some noncommittal sounds before asking, "How long has this been happening?"

Catherine took a deep breath. "It started when I was

working at Radium Dial and has steadily worsened, even after I left." There. That included that radium might be a concern but admitted that discontinued exposure hadn't helped. She couldn't meet the doctor's eye.

"Is there a history of arthritis in your family?"

She frowned. "I don't believe so. My parents died young, but, as you know, my aunt and uncle were both a ripe, old age and did not suffer like this."

"Mmmmm...Hmmmmm...."

Was he thoughtful? Dismissive? Catherine's carefully made plans were not getting her the answers she wanted.

"Is there a chance that this is caused by radium poisoning?" she asked, knowing that she would regret not directly addressing her biggest fear.

The doctor looked at her in surprise as if the thought hadn't crossed his mind. "Oh no, of course not. There's no such thing as radium poisoning." Seeing the doubt on Catherine's face, he continued, "With a big company like Radium Dial in Ottawa, don't you think we'd know if radium poisoning was real?"

"But the girls in New Jersey," Catherine couldn't stop herself from saying.

He was shaking his head. "Entirely unrelated. Radium does not cause the illnesses they suffered. But don't worry." He was writing out a prescription. "I will give you something for rheumatism. It should make a world of difference."

Catherine remained quiet through the remainder of the visit. Rather than dispel her fears, the doctor's dismissive attitude had only increased them. If radium poisoning wasn't real, what had killed Peg Looney?

She tried another doctor a month later. And then another a few months later when she thought they could afford it, but it was no use. There wasn't a doctor in Ottawa that was going to accuse Radium Dial of poisoning its employees.

"I am going to Chicago," Tom announced. He was already pulling clothes from their closet and a suitcase was open on the bed.

Catherine was speechless. A million questions were on the tip of her tongue, including how they could possibly afford it. She was still standing there with her mouth hanging open when Tom offered an explanation.

"The doctors here are not making you better. They're not even taking you seriously. I am going to find someone else."

"Oh," Catherine whispered. Had she been expecting a romantic weekend on the town? She gazed dumbly at the suitcase as Tom neatly folded his clothes and piled them inside. He was not leaving any space ready to receive whatever Catherine would take.

"You are going by yourself?"

"Only overnight," he said, as if this was the only thing she needed to know.

Propelling herself forward, Catherine only said, "Alright," as she lowered herself onto the edge of the bed.

Tom halted his frantic activity and went to her. He lifted up her chin and gazed into her eyes. "Tommy needs you here, and the trip would be difficult for you. You would be terribly uncomfortable on the train. I will bring a doctor back to you."

"Oh, Tom." Her heart swelled and eyes burned. It was as if she was realizing for the first time how much he loved her. As she knew from Helen Munch's situation, this kind of devotion could not be taken for granted. They held each other tight for a moment before Tom returned to his task. He was single-minded and gone within the hour.

Catherine imagined him sitting there alone as the train rattled its way across the Illinois countryside. Questions still swirled in her mind, but some of them she had managed to answer for herself.

Tom's father must have lent him money for this trip. The thought warmed her slightly. The Donohues had warned their son not to marry an ill woman, so it was meaningful that they would continue to offer their support. Catherine would find a way to show her gratitude without going so far as letting them know that she knew.

Other questions continued to baffle her. How had Tom found a Chicago doctor to see her? How would he get one to Ottawa? What difference would it make? She could only turn her worries into prayer and take comfort in the fact that there was a plan for her life.

The next day, Tom returned and instructed Catherine to ready herself. He was taking her to Dr Loffler, who had allowed himself to be convinced that the women of Ottawa needed him.

Charles Loffler was in the process of setting up a makeshift clinic in a small hotel room when Tom introduced him to his wife. Catherine felt like her examination began immediately due to the way the doctor's eyes analyzed her face and figure.

"You are thin for a new mother," he observed.

"Um, I suppose," Catherine stuttered. "It is sometimes painful to eat." She hated confessing this, remembering Peg – her teeth falling out, her inability to eat, her body withering away.

"You have pain in your jaw?" Dr Loffler asked, bringing her back to the present.

She just nodded.

"Anywhere else?"

Catherine almost laughed. It might be a shorter list to tell him where she never felt pain, but she tried to be precise. "My hip, knees, fingers, especially after spending a few hours in the kitchen."

"Activity inflames your joints."

"I guess so."

Dr Loffler had kind, intelligent eyes, and Catherine was glad. It was difficult to be examined so closely. His ears stuck out a little too far below his fringe of grey hair, and that somehow made him more approachable.

"Have you formed any opinions?" Catherine couldn't help asking after he had examined her.

He took a deep breath before answering. "Your symptoms could be attributable to several conditions. I think it would be better if I waited for your bloodwork before attempting to come to any conclusions."

Catherine suppressed a sigh and said, "Of course." He was correct, but she felt deflated leaving without answers.

"He will be in touch as soon as he knows something," Tom tried to reassure her.

Catherine knew that she should be grateful. Tom had gone all the way to Chicago and found a doctor willing to return with him just to see her, but she couldn't help feeling disappointed and ornery. Why couldn't anyone determine what was wrong with her?

She said little to Tom for the rest of the day, but he tried to please her all the same, bringing her tea and plumping a pillow to set behind her back. Part of her wanted to tell him what a fine man he was, but the part of her that hated the fact that she couldn't do more for herself won, so she just grunted at his efforts instead of thanking him.

The next morning dawned cold and bright, and Catherine woke with a half-frozen nose despite the sun shining into the room. The fragrance of coffee floated up from the kitchen, and she could hear pots and utensils clattering. Curious, Catherine rose and pulled on a robe to venture down to the kitchen.

Tom had coffee bubbling and French toast crisping on the stovetop. He had Tommy balanced on his hip, and Catherine took the baby into her own arms before he could make a mess of his father's vest.

"It smells heavenly in here," Catherine sighed with her eyes shut to breathe in the scents.

"Good morning. How are you feeling?" Tom set aside his spatula only long enough to kiss her on the cheek. He gestured toward the table. "Have a seat. It's almost ready."

"You spoil me, Tom."

"No more than you deserve," he said, placing a plate full of French toast and sausage in front of her.

Catherine considered apologizing for the previous day's behavior but decided it was best not to bring it up. Instead, she picked up her fork and exclaimed, "This looks delicious, but I don't think I can eat so much!"

"You just eat as much as you can," Tom replied while placing another kiss on her forehead.

She took a bite and fed one to Tommy before she smiled up at him. "You are a mighty fine husband, Tom Donohue."

He nodded in acceptance of the compliment and sat down with an overflowing plate of his own.

They were content not to speak for a few minutes, but Catherine couldn't stay silent for long.

"When do you think we will hear from Dr Loffler?"

Tom stopped chewing and peered at the ceiling as though he might find the answer written there, but then he just shrugged and continued eating.

Catherine tried not to sigh. "I'm sorry. I suppose I'm anxious instead of grateful for all you've done for me."

"Nonsense," Tom said around a large bite of French toast. When he swallowed, he continued, "I've done nothing any man wouldn't do for his wife, and you've a right to be anxious. I've prayed so many times for God to ease your burden, Catherine, since I cannot."

She went to him then, and he cradled her and the baby in his arms. They were like this when a knock came at the door.

Tom eased her aside, saying, "I'll get it. You finish your breakfast.

Although Catherine didn't think she could eat another bite, she obediently retook her seat. She immediately recognized Dr Loffler's voice in conversation with Tom's, so she was prepared when they entered the kitchen together.

"Can I get you a plate? Have you had your breakfast?" she asked.

"I, um . . ." The doctor seemed surprised to be offered hospitality, but, glancing at Tom, he nodded and said, "That would be nice. Thank you."

He took the spot at the table that Catherine still thought of as Aunt Mary's, and she set a heaping plate before him.

"Tom made it," Catherine said, although she wasn't sure why she felt that it was necessary for Tom to receive credit for his cooking.

Dr Loffler nodded again. "He is a good man."

Catherine smiled, happy to know that they agreed on this important point. Then she sat down again and waited. She pushed food around on her plate, taking only a few more bites, while the men made small talk until the plates were cleared.

At that point, Dr Loffler cleared his throat to announce that he was ready to attend to his reason for being there.

"I have the results of your blood tests."

Catherine wished she was not across the table from Tom. She wanted him to hold her or, at least, take her hand. Instead, she grasped her hands in her lap and clenched her jaw, nodding for the doctor to continue.

"I am very sorry to say that you are suffering from radium poisoning."

In all the years Catherine had lived in the house on Superior Street, it had never fallen as silent as it did after that pronouncement. Not after Aunt Mary or Uncle Winchester died. Not during her nights that she spent all alone. Only now was the silence painful in its completeness.

"I'm so sorry," the doctor finally repeated.

This nudged Tom into action. He put his hand out to shake Dr Loffler's. "I want to thank you for all you've done. While it is not the news we hoped for, I am thankful to have a diagnosis to work with."

Catherine also perked up. "What is the next step?"

Her eyes locked on Tom's. Whatever it was, she would get better.

However, Dr Loffler was shaking his head. "I don't think you understand." He cleared his throat again. "This condition is rather new and unknown. I will, of course, research any techniques that we might try, but I cannot guarantee a cure."

Incurable? The word bounced painfully around Catherine's mind. She wondered if she was going to die, and almost asked. Then she stopped herself, uncertain if she desired an honest answer.

"I will have to return to my office and perform some research," the doctor said. He continued talking about experimental treatments they might try and how important it was for Catherine to get plenty of rest, but she could not focus on his words. The room was a blur, and Catherine started to panic. Was blindness a symptom of radium poisoning?

Then she realized that her eyes were full of tears. Embarrassed, she mumbled an apology as she hobbled from the room. She could trust Tom to say what needed to be said to the doctor, just as she could trust him to cope with anything she could not. Catherine reached her bed and sobbed, thinking of the life she and Tom were meant to have, now blemished with illness and experimental medical treatments.

Tom soon found her there and collected her into his arms. He didn't offer any empty platitudes or words of comfort. He just held her in his strong arms and loved her.

Chapter 14

I see no hope for them.
Marie Curie, 1927

A knock on the door brought Catherine painfully to her feet. She wondered if it was another neighbor, trying to make silent apology for the way they had treated her with a casserole or cake. Several had arrived at their door since Catherine's diagnosis. She tried to be forgiving, but many of those who now pitied her kept their distance as if radium poisoning was contagious. Catherine wasn't sure which was worse, for people to think she was lying or that they were afraid of her.

When she opened the door, she was surprised to find a police officer standing on the front porch.

"Can I help you?"

His face was stern and unreadable. He was young and unfamiliar to Catherine. His words were clipped. "Catherine Donohue?"

"Yes."

"I am here to inform you that your husband, Thomas Donohue is being held at the Ottawa Jail."

A fist tightened around Catherine's heart, and she reached for the door frame as her world spun around her. By the time the regained control of herself, she realized the police officer had already turned to leave.

"Wait!" she cried. "What has happened? What am I to do?"

He shrugged, making it clear that it was not his problem.

He had performed his duty and had no pity on the wife of a criminal. "You may obtain more information down at the courthouse."

Catherine closed the door and leaned against it. She would have slid down to the floor but for her fear that she would not be able to stand again on her own. She couldn't imagine what could have happened. Tom rarely even sipped on moonshine. What could he have possibly done to end up in one of the little cells in the basement of the courthouse?

She would have to go there and find out. Although the walk was only a few blocks, Catherine's hip throbbed at the thought of it. She took one of the painkillers that Dr Loffler had left for her, knowing it was too early for her next dose but also knowing she would never make it without it.

Then she donned her hat and coat and began limping toward Columbus Street, stopping briefly at a friendly neighbor's home to arrange for someone to watch Tommy. She had considering having him toddle along next to her, but she couldn't carry him so far if he threw a tantrum or grew tired. He still thought it was an adventure to get to play somewhere other than at home.

Catherine refused to look toward Radium Dial, just down the street from the courthouse. It would only upset her more. She paused before the limestone structure and wished that she could purposely stride in and demand to be told what was going on. She knew that she was a frail figure whose voice did not command attention, but she hoped to find someone more sympathetic than the informing officer had been.

Pain made her body tense, which also caused her to have a headache by the time she reached the courthouse lobby. Catherine looked around, wondering where she should go and who would help her.

She almost cried in gratitude when she saw a friendly familiar face.

"Oh, Robert. I know you can help me," Catherine said, trying to keep the panic from her voice. "I was told that my Tom is here."

Robert, a tall, heavily muscled man who looked like a police officer even when not in uniform, looked down at Catherine with a deeply furrowed brow. "Thomas Donohue?" he asked, though he knew very well who Catherine's husband was.

She only nodded and gazed back up at him as if he were her guardian angel.

"Well, let's find out what this is about."

He led her through a door marked, *Officials Only. Not Open to the Public.*

Catherine was glad she had taken the extra pain pill. She would not have been able to keep up with Robert's long strides otherwise. He went to a desk and murmured quietly with its occupant before gesturing for her to follow him again. Catherine gulped when she saw that they were headed down steps.

Steeling herself for the pain that would come, she followed. Nothing would keep her from Tom. The row of basement cells brought tears to her eyes. Poor Tom. She wanted to ask Robert for information before she faced her husband, but she was too out of breath and Robert's pace did not slacken.

When they arrived at the small cinderblock cell holding Tom, Catherine was surprised that Robert immediately opened the door and indicated that Tom should come out.

Tom's head hung low, and he did not speak. His rounded shoulders and lack of eye contact told Catherine that he was humiliated. How many of their friends would hear that he had spent time, even if less than a day, in Ottawa's jail?

"I will come by your house later with some paperwork," Robert said after they had followed him to an exit away from the street where Catherine had initially entered the building. "I know you're not going to run from justice, Tom." An ironic grin was on Robert's face. "I'm going to do my best to see that no charges are pressed against you."

Catherine's mind was a whirlwind, but Tom simply dipped his head to Robert and murmured his humble thanks. Only then did Robert realize how much this incident had taken out of Catherine. He seemed to notice her shrunken frame and weary eyes, and it made him want to do more.

"Let me give you two a ride home."

Tom started to shake his head, still too overwhelmed by his own predicament to realize Catherine's need. Catherine spoke first. "Thank you, Robert. I would appreciate that more than you know."

Tom finally looked at her, and his eyes pleaded for forgiveness. She saw his expression shift to surprise when he did not find anger in her countenance.

"Let's get you home," she said, touching his cheek and noticing a cut above his eye. "Then you can tell me what happened."

"Yes, ma'am," Tom agreed with a bow. Then to Robert, "Thank you. You are a true friend."

Robert smiled and gave a perfunctory tip of his head. "Just doing my job." That wasn't entirely true, but neither of the Donohues pressed him further.

The few blocks to their house did not take long enough for conversation, so Tom and Catherine were quiet until they entered their home and she asked if he wanted something to drink. Tom only shook his head and walked to the living room where he threw himself down on the sofa.

Catherine followed him, watching his defeated movements. Finally, she asked in a low, neutral voice, "Tom, what happened?"

Tom shook his head and covered his face with his hands, as if he couldn't quite believe what he had done either. However, after a moment, he took a deep breath, dropped his hands, and looked at her.

"I decided to confront Mr Reed about your test results."

Catherine's eyes widened. "What did he say?"

"Told me it was none of my business. That's what he said." Tom's face reddened and the muscles of his arms looked tense, as if it was taking all of his self-control to remain still.

"He tried to brush past me in the street. I grabbed him. He took a swing at me. I returned the favor."

Now, Catherine's jaw dropped to the floor. She didn't believe Tom had ever been in a fight.

"It wasn't much of a fight," Tom continued ruefully, admitting, "Nether one of us really knew what we were doing." He shrugged and relaxed back into the cushions.

"Is Mr Reed in jail too?" Catherine couldn't help but ask.

One short, humorless laugh escaped Tom's throat. "No, of course not," he said. "Only me. He told the police that I had attacked him."

Tom rolled his eyes, but Catherine went to him and sat closely by his side. "I'm sorry that I've brought you to this."

"Don't be ridiculous."

"It's not ridiculous," Catherine insisted. "If it weren't for all my problems, you wouldn't have any.

"Well, I guess that's why the Lord wants me to help you with yours," he said, pulling her close.

†

The next day, Catherine still felt bleary and sore from the courthouse drama, but she forced herself to rise from her bed and dress. If it weren't for dear little Tommy and the fact that Charlotte was planning to visit, she might have remained in bed all day. She was exhausted by the time she had completed her minimal toilet and decided to rest on the sofa until Charlotte's arrival.

Tom often saw to Tommy's care in the morning. It was little enough that he could do before he had to leave for work, knowing that Catherine would struggle to keep up with the rambunctious little boy all day.

It wasn't until her friend walked in without knocking that Catherine realized she had neither eaten nor prepared snacks for their time together. After greeting Charlotte warmly, Catherine apologized for her error.

"Don't you worry about that, Catherine. I have come prepared." Charlotte reached into a large bag that Catherine had somehow not noticed. From it, she pulled a box of cookies that looked like they came straight from heaven. "And I will just go get the tea started."

Charlotte was in the kitchen before Catherine could protest that she should be doing that. She had left the box of cookies open and their sweet scent tantalized Catherine in a way that food rarely did anymore. She fidgeted with the loose gold watch on her wrist as she wondered how much weight she must have lost since her position had been terminated at Radium Dial.

Teapot in hand, Charlotte returned and distracted Catherine from her worries. Catherine found herself relaxing as she listened to Charlotte's stories of her children's antics while dipping her cookie in tea before taking a soft, warm bite. She gratefully released her concerns for a little while, enjoying the companionship and sweet snacks.

And then Charlotte dropped her teacup.

"Oh, Catherine! I'm so sorry," she cried, rushing to the kitchen for a towel and trash can for the broken pieces. "I hope that it wasn't a precious piece."

Catherine shook her head and felt the weight of her worries settle back onto her slender shoulders. She watched Charlotte clean up the mess for a moment but couldn't stop herself from asking, "Are you alright?"

Her shoulders visibly drooped and Charlotte's movements came to a sudden halt.

"No," was all she said at first, but Catherine waited. "I didn't want to burden you."

Catherine could hear the sob fighting for release in Charlotte's voice.

"What is it, my dear? I would not be a very good friend if I only shared my burdens without helping you carry yours."

Charlotte returned to cleaning up the broken teacup and soaking up the spilled tea. Catherine began to worry that she would not tell her what was bothering her, but, once she had completely cleaned up and returned from the kitchen with a new teacup in hand, Charlotte took a deep breath and spoke.

"It is my arm."

"You have had pain in it for some time, haven't you?"

Charlotte nodded sadly. "Yes, but it is worse than that. Al is taking me to Chicago to see a specialist next week. That is why I wanted to visit today, to let you know."

Fear twisted in Catherine's gut, and she couldn't help but think about her own recent diagnosis. But Charlotte had worked at Radium Dial for only a year. Surely, this trouble with her arm couldn't be related. Could it?

"We must make you an appointment with Dr Loffler the next time he is in town as well," Catherine said instead of giving voice to any of the questions and fears plaguing her.

"Thank you," Charlotte said, taking her hand and squeezing it hard enough to cause Catherine some pain.

"Have Albert write to us from Chicago. I must know how you are doing."

Charlotte nodded and took a deep breath. "I will. Now, I think we both deserve another cookie."

They smiled at each other, refusing to give power to the unknown demons stalking them. They would enjoy their time together as much as they could. Charlotte poured more tea, and Catherine prayed that Charlotte would be healthy and whole and that she would never experience any of the pain that kept Catherine in bed instead of doing the things other young mothers were doing.

A week later, a letter arrived in Albert Purcell's fine script. As much as Catherine longed to know what it said, she waited for Tom to get home from work. In the case that the missive held any bad news, Catherine wasn't sure that she could cope on her own. It took her last reserve of self-control to wait until Tom had changed his clothes and had a moment to relax before she thrust the envelope into his hands.

"Can you please read it to me?"

Tom squinted at the return address, and then raised his eyebrows at his wife. He did not answer but began carefully breaking the seal. Catherine was losing patience when he scanned the letter before beginning to read aloud.

Then came the words that Catherine had been afraid of.

We are sad to tell you that Charlotte has had her arm amputated. The doctors believe that radium caused the tumor that grows there. Charlotte was quite insistent that drastic measures be taken in the hope that the damage would not spread to the rest of her body. Please, pray that we have made the right decision.

Albert's words carried on in Tom's voice, but Catherine couldn't concentrate. She would have to reread the letter later. For now, she could only wonder what agony Charlotte was in, how she would appear with only one arm, and how she would care for her children.

Tom's own words broke in. "I'm so sorry, Catherine. Let's pray that this surgery will ensure Charlotte's good health from now onward."

Catherine sniffed and nodded quickly. She no longer attempted to kneel on the floor next to Tom for their prayers at home. Instead, he knelt in front of her while she sat with her head bowed. Leaning into each other this way, they offered up their prayers to God.

†

Tom led Catherine into church, and she was suddenly reminded of her dear Uncle Winchester and how he would lean on her in his later years. Catherine was in her early thirties, but she felt as weary as the elderly folk who had to be coaxed into activity and then moved stiffly and slowly. She shook her head. She could not allow these ungrateful thoughts to overtake her, not within the walls of her beloved St Columba.

She struggled to kneel as they entered their pew. Tom kept his hand on her elbow.

"Catherine, don't," he urged her toward the seat. "Everyone

understands. Your prayers are not of lesser worth if offered while seated."

She refused to meet his eye, pulling her thin arm from his grasp and forcing her body to obey. Daggers of pain shot through her hips and her knees creaked like the old plank flooring, but Catherine managed to arrange her aching body into the prayerful position she desired. Once there though, the pain was so overwhelming that prayers flew from Catherine's mind. The only one she could capture was, "Please, take this pain away."

Her eyes filled with tears. Tom deserved better than this. Why was he so burdened with hardship and an incapacitated wife? "Lord, show me the meaning of our suffering. What would you have us learn from these tribulations?" she quietly begged.

When she moved to rise, Tom's strong arm was around her waist, easily lifting her and gently depositing her onto the pew. The wooden seat that had never bothered Catherine before rubbed painfully on her unprotected bones. The complaint in her hips did not ease in this position, and Catherine struggled not to cry. Or scream.

Tom understood. She could tell by the watery sympathy in his eyes. Catherine knew that he would do anything to take her pain onto himself, but he could not. She concentrated on relaxing the muscles in her face and neck, so that he would think her discomfort had lessened. She could give him that much at least, and she did feel a tiny bit better when he smiled and leaned back to look at the hymns that they would sing that morning.

Catherine knew she was being stubborn. Maybe God was trying to rid her of her pride or vanity, but when the time came to kneel again, she slid forward on her seat and took a deep breath in preparation. Tom did not try to dissuade her but put a helpful arm around her instead.

But when Catherine urged her body forward, it didn't move. Her hips locked and pain struck like lightening through her entire body. She gasped and looked pleadingly at Tom. She tried again. Maybe the pain would ease if she knelt in prayer. But she couldn't. She was entirely immobile and wracked with pain that exploded anew with each attempt to move.

Unable even to pray, Catherine forgot they were surrounded by people and sobbed against Tom's chest. He lifted her and moved as though he would carry her out of the church, then and there, with everyone's eyes upon her.

"No, Tom, please."

He sighed but sat down with Catherine wrapped firmly in his arms. Catherine could not participate for the remainder of the service. She could only silently pray that God would see her and have pity. When the final hymn began, Tom lifted her up and carried her home.

Chapter 15

*I am now of the opinion that the normal radioactivity
of the human body should not be increased.*
Dr Martland, 1931

The incident at church spurred the Donohues into action. The next time Dr Loffler came to Ottawa for the clinic hours that he regularly offered to former Radium Dial employees, Tom asked him if he could recommend a lawyer. Medical expenses had drained their savings, and they were thankful that Catherine's uncle had left them the Superior Street house free of debt. They were struggling in more ways than one, and Tom thought Radium Dial should be held accountable.

Loffler had been a godsend to his suffering patients. He charged barely enough to cover his expenses and gave them the name of Jay Cook, a former Illinois Industrial Commission attorney with a taste for justice. Tom wrote to him the same day and received a prompt reply.

"He suggests that we contact Radium Dial to notify them of your condition," Tom said to Catherine, the letter from Jay Cook still in his hand.

"They know of my condition," she responded reasonably. "They fired me for it."

Tom's lips pressed together in anger. He nodded but insisted, "It is the first step. If we hope to be awarded any compensation, we have to be able to prove that we have made them aware of your diagnosis."

So, Catherine did. She wrote a letter to Radium Dial and tried to imagine Mr Reed reading it. Would he think of her with the fatherly affection that she once believed he had for her, or would he disdain her the way he had when he terminated her employment? It no longer mattered. Her family was what was important.

Catherine glanced at baby Tommy happily exploring and examining anything he could get his hands on, and she took up her pen.

Tom inquired each day when he got home, but her answer was always the same. Radium Dial had not responded. She had worked there for nine years and was in constant pain because of it, but they couldn't even take the time to respond to her letter.

Once two weeks had passed, Tom and Catherine were sure that Radium Dial had no intention to recognize the women's claims, so they moved on to the next step.

"We will go together," Catherine said.

Tom gave her a look full of doubt. "I should be there."

Catherine was already shaking her head. "Charlotte and I can do this. It will show that we are willing to fight our own battle, not simply hide behind others."

Tom took a deep breath, as he always did when he wanted to take time to consider his next words. Then he nodded. "Alright, Catherine, but you go, present another copy of the letter, and leave. Nothing more."

Catherine laughed. "What do you think they're going to do?"

Tom didn't say anything, but he didn't need to. Written on his countenance was his anger at what Radium Dial had done to her and his doubt that they would suddenly play nicely.

"I promise," she said, no longer laughing.

She and Charlotte walked the short distance between Catherine's house and Radium Dial the next day.

"What a pair we are," Catherine said as she limped along and Charlotte swayed awkwardly, still adjusting to her missing arm.

"You never realize how you use your arms for balance until someone takes one away."

Catherine pursed her lips and forged forward. When she watched her friend struggle, she understood Tom's anger. It was so much more upsetting to see one you loved mistreated than to suffer yourself.

"How are you coping?" Catherine asked after she had managed to reign in the worst of her anger.

"Oh, I do alright. I've figured out new ways to change the baby's diaper and get the dishes washed up. Al helps with some things."

Catherine could hear the shame in her friend's voice, and she understood it. "It is difficult to watch your husband do things that you wish you could do yourself, especially after he has already worked hard all day."

Charlotte nodded. "But we manage."

"Us too."

Then they were in front of Radium Dial, and they paused before the steps leading up to the door. Catherine was remembering how she had skipped up them on the first day of work and wondered if Charlotte was lost in a similar memory. Charlotte reached out and took her hand. Catherine was sure it was in part to ensure her balance as they made their way up those stairs that used to pose no challenge to either of them.

Inside, little was changed. Dust floated through the air, sparkling in the sunlight that shone through the oversized windows. Catherine remembered when she thought it was magical. Now she wondered what evil was contained within that dust and cringed at how many days she had spent coated in it.

Charlotte pulled her forward, still holding her hand. They would start at Mr Reed's office and hope to avoid the painting studio. Catherine's uneven stride echoed down the hall and fueled her anger at this place and the man they were about to face.

Mr Reed was in his office, and he glanced at them in surprise before hardening his features. He did not greet them, so Catherine took the lead.

"I have received a letter from my doctor, who has been treating me for weeks. He has come to the definite conclusion that my blood shows radioactive substance. We have radium poisoning."

At that point, she realized that they were still holding hands. She didn't know if it made them appear weak or strong, but, being done, she took strength from Charlotte's presence. Still, Mr Reed said nothing. He gazed at them in disinterest.

"I have a similar letter from my doctor," Charlotte added. "And the company has been notified of our condition."

Catherine was certain that Mr Reed rolled his eyes, and she blinked, hoping that it was a trick her vision had played on her.

"Having consulted legal advice," Catherine stated, proud of the confidence in her voice, "we have been advised to ask the company for compensation and medical care."

"We are entitled to compensation," Charlotte added, shifting her shoulder to emphasize the lack of arm that should have been attached.

Mr Reed sighed as he looked them over. "I don't think there is anything wrong with you."

Catherine fought to keep her face free of emotion. She

didn't look at Charlotte. She couldn't.

"There is nothing to it at all," Mr Reed continued, gesturing toward the door.

"It is not only Charlotte and I," Catherine cried in a final attempt to appeal to his Christian mercy. "Mary Robinson, Marie Rossiter, Inez Vallat . . . . and what about what happened to Peg Looney?"

Now Mr Reed looked angry. Instead of pitying them, he hated them and what they represented. "You must leave now," he said. He stood and walked around his desk, looking down at them in a way that made the women feel very small and vulnerable.

"We had no choice but to leave," Catherine said to Tom when he got home that evening. "He wouldn't respond to our presence any more than the company would respond to our letter."

"You did the right thing," Tom said, and she could hear the control he kept his voice under. He was trying to not let her see how angry he was.

"How can he not believe us? How does anyone not believe us?" Catherine cried, losing control and allowing tears to stream down her face. "Charlotte is standing there missing an arm . . ."

She couldn't continue. She dropped her head into her hands and sobbed.

†

Catherine's stomach turned as she added her signature to the paperwork contracting Mr Cook to pursue her lawsuit against Radium Dial. How had it come to this, she wondered as she watched the other women do the same. They had been happy, healthy, and young. Radium Dial had taken that away, and they just didn't care.

When she looked at Charlotte's empty sleeve, Catherine felt her face grow warm in anger. Her friend signed the contract with the only hand remaining available to her. Catherine had spent some time in doubt, wondering if it was the Christian thing to do to sue the company for compensation. When she looked at her own unfilled pantry and drained bank account, she wasn't sure. But when the sleeve of Charlotte's dress hung loose and pointless, Catherine's resolve hardened.

Her days were now filled with taking pills, drinking tonics, and attempting to perform the exercises that Dr Loffler prescribed. The only thing that made her feel better was spending time with Tommy. Without him and Tom, Catherine would give in to despair.

Watching Tommy grow strong and learn new skills was such a comfort to Catherine. Her own body may be withering away, but this perfect, little boy had come from it somehow. She was so proud to be his mother, even if she never would have a house overflowing with children and love like the Looney home.

During her next visit to Dr Loffler, Catherine felt he was taking unusually long with her exam. Worry wormed through her, and she fidgeted with her watch, which fit more like a loose bracelet these days. She bit her tongue to keep from asking what new problem he had discovered.

At the end of the exam, she could not interpret the mixed emotions on Dr Loffler's face. She decided to wait for him to speak instead of trying to guess.

Dr Loffler sighed deeply before he began. "Catherine, have you noticed any changes in your health?"

She couldn't hold in a bark of laughter. "It is ever changing, if not for the better. Some days, I can get around quite well. Other days I have to force myself to get out of bed for Tommy's sake."

Dr Loffler nodded and sighed again. "You are pregnant."

He watched her as if the statement was some sort of experiment. Catherine's mouth fell open and her mind went blank. Her cycle had become so irregular that she no longer tried to track it. She didn't think she was capable of becoming pregnant. Then she felt the whisper of joy in her heart.

"Another baby?" she whispered as though afraid to ask, sure that he was going to take away this gift as soon as it had been offered.

Dr Loffler frowned. "Yes, but, Catherine, I am afraid you are too weak. I'm not sure you can survive another pregnancy."

She looked at him, realization dawning of what he was suggesting that she might choose to do. Her head was already shaking adamantly.

"This child is a gift from God. If it is His will that I die in order to give it life, then so be it."

The good doctor nodded, knowing that she would feel this way. "Then I will do everything I can for you, but please make sure your husband feels the same way."

"He will," Catherine said, taking up her coat and hat. She turned to leave, but then realized how ungrateful she was being. Dr Loffler was one of the few people supporting her and caring for her. She turned back to him and took his hand. "Thank you so much, for everything."

He met her eye and nodded gravely.

Then she left, filled with mixed emotions but the greatest of them was joy like she hadn't felt since Tommy's birth.

If Tom had any of Dr Loffler's doubts, he did not let Catherine see them. His happiness matched her own, and they basked in this unexpected blessing.

As the weeks went on, Catherine soon learned that this

pregnancy was not going to be as easy as her first. Her body ached and she couldn't eat enough to gain weight the way she should.

Dr Loffler gave her powders to add to her food and drinks, adding calories to her diet in every way he could. He had changed her regimen of pills and tonics, removing anything that might impact the development of the new life inside her. However, there was nothing he could do about the radium trapped within her body. They could only pray that the baby would be born healthy, as Tommy had been.

Catherine did not leave the house often, but when she did she felt the town's eyes upon her. It was clear that word about the women's lawsuit had been spread far and wide, and that the townspeople were not pleased. Catherine wondered how they could look at the evidence of the dial painters' failing health and continue to rally behind Radium Dial.

Then she saw the soup line, with formerly proud men standing in its ranks, and homeless people on the streets of Ottawa where none had been found before, and she understood just a little bit. In this time of struggle, any work was seen as a blessing, even if it were work that one knew might kill them.

Catherine ventured out to the grocer, feeling guilty for how often she asked Tom to stop on his way home from work. She was weighing a small cabbage in her hands when she overheard words clearly intended for her ears.

"Well, they're just trying to get something not owed to them. Anyone could see that Peg Looney was sick long before she started working at Radium Dial."

Feeling her face grow warm, Catherine refused to turn around to see who the speaker was, even when that lady's friend agreed and added that Charlotte had cancer in her arm that had nothing to do with radium.

"Everyone knows radium is good for you," the first speaker agreed.

Catherine took her cabbage and other small purchases to the counter, forcing herself to keep her eyes forward like a horse with blinders on. She would not give them the satisfaction of knowing that they wounded her.

Adding up her items, the grocer was kinder. He gestured to her swollen belly. "Grab yourself a couple potatoes. I've got extra and you need to eat more."

A protest rising in her throat, Catherine squashed it. She said, "Thank you," in a low voice, adding the potatoes to her bag. Pride was a luxury she could no longer afford. The potatoes would make up the bulk of her little family's dinner that night.

The women's cruel words still swirling through her mind, Catherine placed a plate of mashed potatoes, accompanied by just two tiny sausage links, in front of Tom that evening. It wasn't her auntie's bangers and mash that had always included more sausage than Catherine could imagine eating now, but Tom said thank you and dug in enthusiastically after saying grace.

"You forgot to pick up the mail," he said midway through their meager meal. He set an envelope in front of her, already grinning in anticipation of her response.

"Pearl! Oh, it's been ages since I've heard from her."

Catherine's food was forgotten as she scanned the words, written in familiar, beloved script. The missive was filled with congratulations on her pregnancy and concern for her health, but the best was saved for last.

"She's coming to visit!"

"That's mighty fine of her," said Tom, finishing off his last bite. "I hope I don't have to tell her that my wife isn't eating her dinner as she should," he teased, and Catherine set the letter aside to finish her own food.

"Oh, Tom," she said between bites, "it just warms my heart to think of seeing dear Pearl again. God is good."

"Indeed, He is."

Pearl's upcoming visit invigorated Catherine, making her feel healthier than she had in several months. Guilt pestered her, but she had her excuses ready. She would have kept in touch with Pearl better if it hadn't been for caring for Tommy and dealing with her own poor health. She hoped the fact that Pearl was coming was proof that she was forgiven.

Catherine had busied herself with some housekeeping that she hadn't previously had the energy for. Little Tommy was recruited to help, and he was the ideal assistant for performing the tasks that Catherine could not stoop or kneel to do. His proud smile whenever Catherine praised his efforts made her heart swell.

"You are such a good helper, Tommy. Can you reach those dust bunnies under the sofa?"

He quickly scrambled across the floor, collecting every bit, some in his hands and the rest stuck to his clothes.

Catherine grinned as she wiped his grimy face. "Good work. It is much easier for mama to wash your clothes than get under that sofa."

He scampered away to play outside, and Catherine agreed that it was a good time for a break. She placed lemonade and cookies on a tray and followed her son outside.

They relaxed in the sunshine. Catherine almost dozed off while Tommy played with his imaginary friends. Soon he would have a real friend to play with, Catherine thought as her hand rested upon the mound of her stomach. For now, she would not worry about how she would find the energy to care for them both.

The house was sparkling clean when the day of Pearl's visit

arrived. Catherine rose before the sun, unable to sleep in her excitement. She took the time to carefully curl her hair and apply some rarely worn cosmetics. She wondered how she would appear to someone who had not seen her since her health started its greatest decline.

The thought made Catherine sigh and fidget with her loose watch. When Pearl had last seen her, it had fit properly. She shoved the discouraging thoughts aside. Pearl would be here today and that was all that mattered.

By the time she was dressed and ready, Tom was up as well. He had Tommy dressed and had given him his breakfast, knowing how these seemingly simple tasks tired Catherine. She thanked him with a kiss and packed his lunch box.

"You and Pearl have a good visit," he said before kissing her goodbye.

Catherine wasn't sure what to do while she waited, since she had already completed everything that needed to be done. She picked up a newspaper and sat at the kitchen table while Tommy played with measuring cups.

She didn't always read the news anymore. She hated to seem uncaring, but she couldn't read all those articles about the poor girls in New Jersey. Women who were suffering from radium poisoning, just like she was. Women who were dying. Grace Fryer and Katherine Schaub, two women whose stories had inspired Catherine to file her own lawsuit, had died recently.

Mercifully, there were no stories about radium in today's newspaper. Catherine paged through it, not really absorbing anything from its pages. She took note of what was on sale at the grocer this week but little else.

When Pearl finally arrived, it was Catherine who was shocked by her friend's appearance. Rather, they were surprised to see each other looking weaker and older than they should. Pearl was not as bone thin as Catherine, but her face was drawn and grey. The bright light gone from her eyes.

"Oh, my dear Pearl," Catherine cried, embracing her as if no time at all had gone by, and indeed it felt as though it had not. "You must tell me how you have been and about little Lotte."

Some of Pearl's former joy brightened her countenance. "My daughter is just as perfect and wonderful as could be," she said, "as must be your little Tommy. And you have another child on the way," she exclaimed.

"Yes," Catherine said, unnecessarily framing her bulging stomach with her hands. "We are blessed."

"Indeed," Pearl agreed as they slowly progressed into the house. "You have made it your own," Pearl observed, noting a few changes that Catherine had made since inheriting her aunt and uncle's house.

"In a few small ways," Catherine agreed. "Of course, there is always more we wish we could do."

"That is the way of things." A faint smile was fixed on Pearl's face as she took in her surroundings that were only negligibly different than when they had been little more than children here.

"Please, sit." Catherine gestured to the dust-free sofa and rushed to the kitchen as quickly as her limp would allow. She returned slowly, balancing a tray and not wishing to spill any lemonade.

Pearl had taken the offered seat and was also happy to accept a glass. "Thank you."

"How is Hobart?"

"He's as fine as ever," Pearl said, her dimple forming and softening her haggard appearance. "And Tom?"

"At work. Thankfully."

"Yes, so many are out of work," Pearl sighed and gazed far away.

"The two of you are doing well though?" Catherine couldn't help but ask as fear began to niggle.

"As well as anyone else," Pearl said, sighing again. She told Catherine of Hobart's struggle to find and keep work, and Catherine knew that Pearl must also feel that their friendship was as true as ever to be confiding such things.

"I'm so glad you decided to visit today, and I must apologize for my lack of letters."

"It was no greater lack than my own," Pearl said. "As wonderful as it is to see you, I do have a less personal reason for being here." Catherine looked at Pearl in open curiosity, and Pearl forged ahead. "I wanted to ask you about your lawsuit in hope that you might advise me in my own."

Catherine's face fell in dread, but it was more than that. Her entire body slackened, and Pearl appeared afraid that she might faint. She only whispered a horrified, "No." She shook her head as if hoping she might have heard wrong. "No, Pearl, you cannot be sick."

Pearl laughed humorlessly. "I can assure you that I have been quite ill, but, despite my warnings to you, it took me ridiculously long to realize why."

Still, Catherine could only look at her, the sagging skin and fine lines taking on a new, darker significance.

"I have had surgeries to remove tumors, but that is not the worst of it." Tears pooled in Pearl's eyes, and she took a moment before continuing. "I had to have a hysterectomy. I'm entirely infertile."

Catherine didn't know she could feel worse after her initial shock, but she did. There was nothing in this world that Pearl had wanted more than a large family. It was a dream that would never come true. Instead, Pearl was fighting for her life like the rest of them. "But you only worked at Radium Dial for a few months."

The angry smirk on Pearl's face was the only response to Catherine's remark.

"Oh, Pearl, I'm ever so sorry," Catherine cried, wishing she still had the ability to fling herself at her friend's feet. "That company has taken away so much from so many of us." She felt her unborn babe move under her hand and prayed that this, too, would not be taken from her as the children she should have borne had been taken from Pearl.

Pearl's features softened at the sight of Catherine's agony. "Do not apologize, love. I came here to ask for help, but not because I blame you. Let me join you in making them confess what they have done."

"Yes," Catherine firmly stated. "We will expose this injustice."

Catherine and Pearl tried to talk about their children and other parts of their lives, but the conversation inevitably returned to Radium Dial.

"You'd think that I would be done being naive, but when they closed the studio I actually believed we had won a victory. Imagine how stupid I felt when Luminous Processes opened just a few blocks away!" Catherine hid her face in her hands, remembering her frustration and anger. "Do you know what they're telling the young women who work there?" She continued without waiting for Pearl to guess. "They tell them that we got sick because we put the brushes in our mouths, so they are not allowed to."

"But that's how they told us to do it!" Pearl was every bit as angry as Catherine at the deception.

"You weren't there when they gave us glass pens to paint with. It was a disaster, and they gave us back our brushes. Now I realize that they must have known even then."

Pearl clamped her lips tightly together, her face pink with fury. "How could they?" she murmured through clenched teeth.

Catherine shrugged. "I guess they thought our lives had no value." Her voice grew soft as she thought of Peg and others whom she now firmly believed had died of radium poisoning, whatever their death certificates said.

"We will fight this together," Pearl asserted, and Catherine felt stronger just having her at her side. "God will not allow this injustice to continue. He is using us to stop it."

A sense of purpose flooded through Catherine. It wasn't that she hadn't felt fulfilled by her life. She loved Tom and their family more than anything, and a large part of her still wished that they could just have their happy little household. However, was that part of her plan? Just as Pearl's destiny did not include the large family that was her desire, Catherine's life would not be lived out in quiet normalcy.

"We will fight Radium Dial, and we will win."

"We are David and they are Goliath," Pearl said with a smirk.

Catherine's smile was determined. "And we know who won that battle."

Chapter 16

*I'll tell you how I feel. I'm just thirty-six,
but I live like an old woman of seventy-five.*
Olive West Witt, 1934

Catherine was awoken by sharp, stabbing pains in her abdomen. Since she now lived with pain every day, her labor was well progressed before her pain reached a point that it woke her. She stumbled to the bathroom, where her water broke as soon as she sat on the toilet. The next contraction sent her pain like she had never felt before.

For the first time, Catherine wondered if she was going to die giving birth to this child. She had been so certain, less than twenty-four hours earlier that her life had a different calling, but she felt like she was being torn in two.

She cried out for Tom, not in words but in a guttural scream that would have embarrassed Catherine in any other circumstance. He was at her side in an instant.

"Is there anything I can do, or should I fetch Marie?"

Despite her agony, Catherine gave him a weak smile.

"Stay with me for a moment first, but I think I will be needing her shortly."

Tom nodded and held Catherine as best he could while kneeling next to the toilet. He could feel the strength of the contractions tearing through her body.

When she was given a moment of respite, Catherine nodded to him. "Help me back to bed and then go fetch her."

So much more was going through her mind. She was scared and hated for him to leave, but the baby was coming fast. It was too soon. She would need help.

Tom did as he was instructed and paused only a second at the door, long enough for Catherine to gain comfort from the fact that he did not want to leave her any more than she wanted him to go. He would be back as quickly as humanly possible.

In the meantime, Catherine tried to slow her breathing and relax the tension in her muscles. She prayed for strength and the health of her babe, which should not be entering the world just yet. Murmuring to herself, she wished she had thought to have Tom retrieve her rosary before he had left. It would be soothing to run the beads through the fingers.

As each new contraction took hold of her, Catherine watched the door, hoping for Tom and Marie to appear. It felt like he left a lifetime ago, though Catherine knew it couldn't have been more than a few minutes. She felt tears begin to roll down her cheeks, but she determinedly wiped them away. Catherine refused to be defeated, regardless of what weakened state radium poisoning had left her body in. She sat up and concentrated on relaxation, willing her body to slow this process until help arrived.

In the midst of another earth-shattering contraction, Catherine glanced up to see Tom and Marie hurrying into the room. "Thank God," she whispered through clenched teeth.

"Tom, go heat some water and bring towels." Marie put Tom to work right away, sending him from the room. "How do you feel?" she asked Catherine once it was clear the worst of the contraction had passed.

"Much harder than before," Catherine groaned, and Marie pursed her lips. She didn't give voice to her concerns, but Catherine could see them all over her face. "You don't think I can do it," she said weakly.

Determination took over Marie's countenance. "Of course, you can. Now, let me get a look at you."

Marie refused to offer an opinion as she examined Catherine's tiny body. She only said, "It looks like you are ready to push." If she had fears that Catherine's pelvis might break into pieces the way Peg Looney's jaw had, she kept them to herself. Catherine refused to admit that the thought had crossed her mind.

Maybe it was a blessing that the baby was coming early, Catherine thought as she braced herself to bear down and push. A smaller babe would be easier to birth, she hoped. Whether it was better or not, it was happening.

She pushed.

This pushing, the part of labor that was all men thought of when they thought of labor, was over mercifully quickly. After the agony Catherine had endured, the tiny baby girl was delivered with relative ease.

Marie took care to clean the babe and swaddle her quickly against the cold draft. Although she was small, no defects were evident.

"Mary Jane," Catherine murmured when Marie handed the child over to be nursed. "She is perfect."

Marie nodded and smiled at Catherine, who was now glowing happily, the pain all but forgotten. As she breastfed little Mary Jane, Marie picked up the bloody towels and put the bedroom back in order. As Catherine and the baby dozed off, Marie remained on duty, monitoring Catherine for any signs that anything had gone wrong. Thankfully, mother and child blissfully slept.

The next time Catherine was drawn out of her sleep, it was the sound of voices that stirred her. Marie could be heard offering instructions and advice to Tom. They must have been standing just outside the bedroom door, because their voices carried to Catherine just as though they were in the room.

"She appears to be doing well. I will come check tomorrow, and it would be best if someone stayed with her for a few days. Let me know or send for the doctor if there are any changes." There was an urgency in Marie's voice that Catherine wasn't sure she had heard before. "She has done well, but her body is not strong. If anything concerns you, get the doctor without delay."

"I will." Tom's voice was a low grumble. "Thank you, Marie."

Their conversation faded as Tom walked Marie to the front door. Catherine imagined him saying thank you, and Marie offering a single nod before donning her hat and striding away. Marie's words caused Catherine to consider if anything felt wrong. It was so difficult to tell after childbirth. Of course, she felt tired and sore, but nothing seemed out of the ordinary. Catherine gave thanks for her sweet daughter and prayed for continued good health. She felt secure in the arms of the Great Physician.

Catherine's healing was also encouraged by the constant presence of friends. Marie's orders ensured that she was never alone for more than a few minutes. While Catherine did not experience any additional complications from the birth, having these friends at her side brightened her mood almost as much as little Mary Jane.

It was only after a few days had passed that Catherine noticed that most of the friends visiting, besides Tom and his sister, were former co-workers.

"Now, why do you think that is?" Catherine posed the question to Pearl once the realization had struck her.

Pearl sighed and paused in her knitting. She looked at

Catherine and responded as though there was no good in keeping it to herself. "Some of the neighbors that Tom asked to stop in had . . . other obligations."

"All of them? How odd."

Pearl gazed at Catherine, willing for her to understand. Failing that she sighed again and admitted, "People seem hesitant to spend time with those of us who . . . are ill."

"What do you...." And then Catherine understood. "The radium poisoning." She laughed at the irony of the same townspeople who refused to believe in radium poisoning now being afraid that it might be contagious. The more she thought about it, the more deliriously she laughed, until her laughter turned to tears. "It's just so unfair," she sobbed.

Pearl set her knitting aside and stroked Catherine's arm, saying softly, "Yes, it is, but you still have your very best friends at your side, and we will not be leaving."

Catherine sniffed and blinked to dry her eyes. "Forgive me, dear Pearl. I must sound terribly ungrateful."

Now it was Pearl's turn to laugh. "You have been many things over our years of friendship, but I do not believe that ungrateful has ever been one of them." She gently embraced her friend before returning to her knitting. "I believe Marie is coming in an hour," she said as though nothing was at all amiss.

With a smile, Catherine was thankful for the friends who remained at her side, whatever happened.

†

After recovering for a few days, Catherine was eager to be out of bed. With Mary Jane snugly swaddled in her arms, she shuffled to the kitchen, where Tom had already placed the small cradle. Mary Jane looked like a doll placed there, not filling it at all the way Tommy had.

The thought of Tommy seemed to conjure him, and he came running into the kitchen with all the enthusiasm of a three-year-old anxious to teach his younger sibling everything he has learned. Tommy peered down into the cradle for a moment before looking up at Catherine with a bit of disappointment creasing his features.

"When can she play?"

Catherine laughed. "Not for a few weeks yet." She tousled his hair and resisted the urge to take him into her arms. Much as she wanted to, the doctor had insisted that she not lift anything heavier than Mary Jane.

"Weeks?" he moaned, no longer attempting to hide his dismay.

"Yes. Until then, maybe you can help me in the kitchen."

"I guess so," Tommy acquiesced with his bottom lip thrust forward.

"I was thinking about making apple turnovers," Catherine added with a wink.

"Oh, yes! I'll help!" Tommy was suddenly a happy helper, pulling out the stool that Tom had built so that the boy could reach the counter. "I want to mix!"

Catherine laughed and began assembling the required ingredients. This was the way life was supposed to be, she thought with glimpses at her children. She tried not to wonder how long it would last.

†

The first time Catherine was forced to leave Mary Jane was

the day of her hearing in the Ottawa courthouse. She had not set foot there since the day she went to have Tom released after his incident with Mr Reed. This time, she was supported by Tom and Mr Cook, the lawyer Dr Loffler had secured for them.

Catherine tried to set aside thoughts of her children and focus on the issue at hand. She squeezed Tom's hand and stepped forward.

Inez Vallat was the first litigant listed in their lawsuit. Catherine's heart broke when she watched the formerly vivacious young woman hobble about like a grandmother. This is why Mr Cook had put Inez first. Her condition was the worst, and everyone secretly wondered when she would die.

Unable to pull her gaze from Inez, Catherine remembered comforting her a few short years ago when Della was dying of tuberculosis. No, Inez had been sure that it wasn't tuberculosis. How different would their lives be today if they had realized what was happening? Would they have had the courage then to take the stand they were making now?

When the testimonies began, it didn't take long for Catherine's mind to swim in the legalese and twisting of words. She was frustrated that she couldn't follow what was happening, but it certainly didn't sound like things were going well.

The team of lawyers that faced Mr Cook appeared confident from the moment they walked in. They wore three-piece suits that probably cost more than Catherine's entire wardrobe. Their hair was stylishly slicked back, and Catherine couldn't imagine what was contained in the reams of documents that they carried.

The first objection she had understood. Inez had filed suit years after leaving Radium Dial.

"We are far outside the statute of limitations, your honor," one of the big-city lawyers had said in exasperation, giving the judge a look that insinuated they were enduring this ridiculous exercise together. "Even if we were not, injuries caused by poison are not included in the Occupational Diseases Act."

That was where he lost Catherine, and she resisted the urge to lean over and whisper to Tom because she didn't want to miss anything.

"Furthermore, the law itself is so vague it is impossible to discern what conduct is required of Radium Dial."

The judge frowned throughout this statement, but Catherine wondered if he didn't always frown, for the lines of his face seemed deeply set in their places. It did not take long for the hearing to end and the judge to rule on the side of the team of corporate lawyers.

"The legislature has failed to establish any standards by which compliance with the law could be measured," he stated. "Without an intelligible standard of conduct, I can do naught but rule in favor of Radium Dial."

Mr Cook appeared as devastated as his clients as they filed out of the courtroom. He hung his head, while his opponents joked about what they were doing that evening and how quickly they could be back in Chicago.

"You've done your best, Mr Cook, and we thank you," Inez said in a weak voice. He seemed about to counter her, but she insisted, "You are the only one who would take on our case, and it is not your fault if the law itself is against us."

He pressed his lips into a line so thin they almost disappeared. "I am going to fight this. All the way to the Supreme Court if I have to," he insisted.

And he did. However, the state law was, indeed, declared invalid, putting the women right back where they had started. State legislators went to work on a new law, but Mr Cook had done all he could for the time being.

"I'm sorry, ladies," he apologized at their final meeting. "If I could afford it, I would keep you on as clients until you have the victory you deserve . . . . but I just can't." His entire body sagged, and Catherine knew he was disappointed in himself.

"We appreciate everything you have done for us," she said, placing a thin hand on his. Despite everything else going on, she noticed that hers looked aged and haggard compared to his, though she was actually younger than the middle-aged lawyer.

"I hope and pray that you are able to find another lawyer – a better lawyer – one able to stick with you through to the end."

Catherine patted his hand before withdrawing her own. "God has a plan for us," she said, and was pleased with the confidence she heard in her voice and the whisper of reassurance she could see in Mr Cook's eyes.

That confidence was gone by the time Tom and Catherine returned home. She felt weary and worn, her mind too overwhelmed to consider what the next step might be. Tom's sister met them at the door, Tommy in one arm and Mary Jane in the other.

"What would we do without you, Margaret?" Catherine sighed, taking Mary Jane into her own arms. The child was still tiny, and Catherine had been forced to admit defeat in nourishing her through breastfeeding. Her body was scarcely strong enough for one. She was not able to feed her child, but counted her blessings that Mary Jane was healthy otherwise.

Margaret was a strong, no nonsense woman. "You would likely struggle even more than you already do," she stated in response to Catherine's rhetorical question as she deposited Tommy into his father's arms. "Dinner is ready but not getting any warmer." Her coat and hat appeared in her arms as soon as they were free of children. "I will see you on Sunday."

Like a whirlwind, she was gone. The little family shuffled into the kitchen. Only Tommy chattered happily, oblivious to his parents' aura of despair.

When Tommy had eaten his fill and begged to be freed from the table, Catherine finally asked, "Tom, whatever will we do?"

He took a bracing breath before taking her hand and saying, "We will do what we always do. We will pray and trust our future to God."

Tears flooded Catherine's eyes. "But, Tom…"

He didn't let her finish. "For tonight," he insisted, "it is enough."

She nodded as a single tear tracked down her cheek. Tomorrow they would have to face the fact that they had to start all over with no sign of assistance in sight. For tonight, they would pretend to be a normal, healthy family with everyday concerns and problems.

Picking up the baby, Tom said more cheerily, "Come, let's find our Tommy and see what trouble he's up to."

Catherine smiled up at him, happy to get lost in the charade for a few hours. Hand in hand, they left their little kitchen to find their son.

The next day, they were forced to set aside their attempt at normalcy and take out a mortgage on the Superior Street house. Catherine was proud that she kept her eyes dry, even as she cursed herself for being the reason for their predicament. The medicine she required and her inability to work had caused them to drain every bit of the money she had saved from her years of work and every penny that Uncle Winchester had left to her.

"It is only money," Tom whispered as they slowly walked

home from the bank.

"Are you a mind reader, Tom Donohue?" she asked with a shadow of a smile.

"Only yours." He grinned. "We have been blessed us with so much, I cannot mourn our financial situation." With a glance toward the soup kitchen line, he added, "We are still far better off than some."

Catherine nodded. "You are right, of course. And we have two healthy, happy children."

With Tom's arm around her and the image of her children in her mind, the thought of a bank mortgage seemed only a minor setback. They would find a way, together.

Chapter 17

An almost unbelievable miscarriage of justice.
Chicago Daily Times, 1935

Inez Vallat had not been a close friend of Catherine's, but they had been co-workers at Radium Dial and crusaders in the battle against them. That was almost a closer bond than friendship now that the town was turning against anyone who spoke out against Ottawa's largest employer. Inez had faced Radium Dial in court with Catherine and Charlotte in their failed lawsuit.

Today she would be buried in St Columba Cemetery, before her case had even been heard under the new laws written in response to their situation. Catherine tried to shut out the whispers of how horribly Inez had died. Instead of envisioning her thin and weak, bleeding out where her mouth and nose had so thoroughly wasted away, Catherine thought of her friend the way she had been before radium had devastated her body.

The funeral was somber and poorly attended. Even in death, the dial painters did not have the support of their neighbors. Catherine wondered if it would it someday be the same for her.

A few days later, Pearl brought Catherine a copy of the *Chicago Tribune*. A photo of Inez's funeral appeared in grainy shades of grey. Catherine's heart fluttered at the sight of it. She wasn't sure whether to be happy that their problems were gaining attention or angry that Inez couldn't be respectfully laid to rest. Then she saw it.

Ottawa's Suicide Club.

What odd terminology to use for a group of women with no desire to die, Catherine thought with a strange feeling of detachment. She was in the picture, along with the other women who had filed suit against Radium Dial. Charlotte with only one arm. Marie painfully hunched over, and herself looking as though a stiff breeze could knock her over. But none of them asked for this. They didn't want to die.

The news story was still on Catherine's mind when there was a knock at the door. She wasn't expecting anyone, but several of her friends continued checking up on her, a habit begun after Mary Jane's birth but not given up almost a year later.

Catherine was shocked to find a young, well-dressed woman on the front porch. From her smart hat to her grey suede shoes, not a hair or fold was out of place. Catherine felt frazzled and messy in comparison, but the woman's smile was friendly.

"Hello," she said in a pleasant voice. "My name is Mary Doty, and you must be Catherine Donohue."

"Why, yes. I am."

"I am a reporter with the *Chicago Daily Times*, and I would like to help you tell your story."

Catherine was at a loss for words. A reporter from Chicago was standing on her doorstep, and she could only stare in wonder.

Miss Mary Doty seemed accustomed to this reaction. She waited a moment before peeking around Catherine at the inside of her home. "Would it be alright if I came in?"

"Of course," Catherine said, awkwardly holding the door open, as though she had never invited a guest in before. She shook her head to clear it. "How can I help you, Miss Doty?"

Miss Doty had only taken a few steps inside, but she quickly took in all she needed to see. Her eyes seemed to memorize

Catherine's drooping hairdo, loose watch, and tired eyes. She said, "I think the question is how I may help you."

It took almost no time for Miss Doty to make Catherine feel enough at ease to confide in her. Some small talk and a few compliments directed at her children were all it took. Or maybe Catherine had been subconsciously awaiting this opportunity to take her complaints public. Whatever the reasons, she found it quite easy to spill out her life story to this confident young woman.

Catherine had only one request. "Please, don't call us the Suicide Club."

"Of course not. How awful," Miss Doty replied, as though she did not know that was how a competing paper had described the woman before her. She looked again at Mary Jane, contentedly rolling from side to side on a blanket on the floor. "How old is your youngest?"

Catherine was always all smiles when discussing her children. She followed Miss Doty's gaze to Mary Jane and said, "She is almost a year old. We are so blessed to have her in our lives."

"Of course, you are. A year old, you say. Does she suffer effects of radium poisoning?"

A quick denial was on Catherine's lips, but she managed to squash it. She looked more objectively at Mary Jane. At ten pounds, she was certainly smaller than most one-year-olds, but Catherine tried not to think about it. Instead she said, "Thankfully, Mary Jane is healthy in every way."

"I'm happy to hear it," Miss Doty replied, scribbling notes rather than look Catherine in the eye.

Catherine didn't realize until she read Miss Doty's article that Tom had also spoken to her. His words, stark there in black and white, were so void of hope compared to when he spoke to his wife. Catherine wondered what his true feelings were. Did he believe he would be left to raise their children alone?

Catherine folded up the newspaper and placed it in the violet colored box at the back of her closet. She had not consciously started collecting articles regarding former dial painters, but the box contained a few. Someday, she hoped to look back feeling victorious over the fears and doubts that assailed her today.

As the days went by, newspapers were added to the box at an increasing rate, and people began to wonder if the dial painters hadn't been telling the truth after all. A few neighbors began stopping by again. Others stopped Catherine in the street for a glimpse at baby Mary Jane. She could feel the change. They were beginning to believe her.

†

The women were more determined than ever, but they needed a lawyer. They had little to offer in return for legal expertise. What they really needed was a knight in shining armor.

And legal issues were not even their biggest problem. Catherine had to travel to Chicago, suffering through a series of examinations with different doctors and dentists in an attempt to find a cure for radium poisoning. At times, she was so weak, Tom practically carried her from these appointments and back to the train that returned them to Ottawa.

On one such trip, Catherine morosely watched the Illinois landscape whiz by. Her tongue prodded the abscesses and loose teeth in her mouth, and her memory was flooded with images of Peg Looney. She had been so young, and her life had held so much promise. Now she had been gone six years, and Chuck had married a girl he met at college, though Catherine had heard that he observed the anniversary of Peg's death each year.

Not wanting to feel sorry for herself, Catherine turned from the window to look at Tom. He was so faithful and strong. She wished she wasn't putting him through all this. Feeling her gaze, Tom met her eye.

"What is it, love?" he asked, pulling her close and kissing her forehead.

"Oh, Tom," Catherine sighed. "Can't we just pretend that nothing is wrong? We're so happy together in our little house."

He squeezed her gently. "We take these trips so that we don't have to pretend. Someday, you will look back on this as just a snippet of our lives. We will have many years to watch our children grow and enjoy a peaceful life together."

She smiled and pretended she believed him. So much of her life was make believe now. "It doesn't seem so bad," she said. "As long as we're together, whatever happens."

The sights and sounds of Chicago never ceased to amaze Catherine. The office buildings that reached for the sky and endless crowds of people were such a stark contrast to quiet Ottawa. It made Catherine feel small and vulnerable, and she gripped Tom's arm with all her feeble strength as they made their way through the streets.

Catherine could not remember which physician they were seeing that day, so she trusted Tom to guide her in the right direction. He pulled her along slowly but firmly. She wasn't sure how he so confidently selected one structure out of the forest of office buildings, but when Tom opened a door for her, she entered.

Dr Walter Dalitsch read the plaque on the door.

Tom and Catherine waited without speaking in the

hauntingly quiet waiting room. Catherine tried to steady her breathing and slow the beating of her heart. She used to get nervous about these appointments, wondering what bad news she would receive. Now, there were few ways for her condition to worsen, but she had to prepare for the pain that she knew the examination would bring.

All the poking and prodding had become far worse to endure than the humiliation of removing her clothes and exposing her emaciated body. She would go home, covered with bruises and bandages taped to her arm where blood had been drawn, and she would be sore for days. All in the hope that someone could help her, that eventually it would be worth it.

When Catherine was called back to the examination room, she took a deep breath, struggled to stand, and limped after the nurse who led the way. The nurse went through the routine steps that weren't worth the doctor's time. Height: five feet and four inches. Weight: ninety-one pounds. The blood pressure device squeezed her arm painfully, and Catherine wondered what the bruises would look like. Then, she was given a reprieve while the nurse left to measure another patient's vitals and Catherine waited for the doctor to enter the small, shockingly clean room.

The scent of cologne announced his arrival a second before the door opened. Catherine wondered if he wore it to challenge the scent of antiseptic or because of smelly patients. Then she admonished herself. Maybe he just liked the fragrance and she was growing too cynical.

"Hello, I'm Dr Dalitsch, and you must be Mrs Donohue."

"Very nice to make your acquaintance," Catherine said, shaking his hand. "Thank you for making time for me in your busy schedule."

Dr Dalitsch peered intensely at her, and she knew that her

examination had already quietly begun.

"Your case is . . . unique," he said, still making no further move toward her while his eyes seemed to take in everything from her thinning hair to the watch hanging loose on her wrist. "Your husband sent me a copy of your records. You worked with radium?"

"Yes, until I was dismissed about five years ago." Catherine was grateful that she could make this statement without shame. It had taken her too long to realize how much of a victim she had been.

Dr Dalitsch did not seem to need to refer to the records he mentioned, and Catherine wondered if it was all stored perfectly in his head. She wasn't sure what question she expected him to ask first, but he managed to surprise her.

"How are your children?"

Catherine frowned, although she enjoyed talking about her children as much as any other mother. His question reminded her of the reporter, Miss Doty, and the way she looked at Mary Jane.

"They are well, curious if not precocious. Happy."

Dr Dalitsch smiled. "Very good. And how do you feel. Right now."

Catherine's frown deepened and she sighed. "Tired."

With a low laugh, Dr Dalitsch moved a hair closer. "As are most mothers. Could I look at your jaw?"

Instead of answering, Catherine opened her mouth, not wide because it pained her, but the doctor did not complain.

"You have lost several teeth," he observed without touching her, but Catherine did not respond. Her mouth remained open to his inquisitive gaze. "You have trouble eating?"

He leaned away and Catherine relaxed her jaw and closed her mouth, only nodding in response. The examination continued with Dr Dalitsch making observations and asking questions but touching her as little as possible. Catherine's respect for him grew as his concern for her became clear. Still, she was left exhausted, and by the time Dr Dalitsch was scribbling out prescriptions, she left it to Tom to keep track of what it was all for and when she needed to take it.

As they were leaving, she simply stated, "I like Dr Dalitsch," and Tom smiled in agreement.

The next morning, Catherine gazed down at the large calcium pill in her hand and tried to remember that Dr Dalitsch was kind and trustworthy. The tablet seemed to fill her palm, and she couldn't imagine how she was going to swallow it past the sore tissue of her mouth and throat.

"We need to infuse your body with enough calcium that your bones release the deposits of radium that exist where calcium should be," he had explained. Catherine knew it made sense. She knew that her body faintly glowed in these predawn hours because of the radium stored in her weak, disintegrating skeleton.

She took a deep breath, filled her mouth with water, and popped in the pill. Trying to imagine she was swallowing only water, Catherine willed the life-saving calcium into her system. She choked and sputtered but managed to get it down.

Four times a day, Dr Dalitsch had ordered. She could only pray that it got easier. And that it worked.

By the time Catherine had painfully lowered herself to the toilet and pulled herself up again, using a handle that Tom had nailed to the wall for when she needed support, she was exhausted again. The sun was just peeking over the horizon. Blinking away burning tears, Catherine summoned up her remaining strength to descend the stairs.

She felt like she was at the top of a mountain, but whatever path had led her there had been destroyed by a raging storm. This stairway had been a part of her life long before her marriage, but now it had become an enemy to defeat. Catherine began her slow, painful descent, praying that the calcium pills would begin to take effect. She remembered her uncle spending his dying days upon the bed in the living room and vowed that would not be her, not any time soon.

Pink light of sunrise gave her home a fairytale glow as Catherine's feet left the final step. She stood, grasping the railing and catching her breath, willing away some of the pain that never completely left her. Her eyes longingly searched out the sofa, but she couldn't yet allow herself to rest.

She shuffled to the fireplace and prodded the embers into life. Two small logs were added for the fire to catch, and she left it to Tom to build it up when he arose, which she knew he would be doing soon. He would leave their bed, use the toilet, and come downstairs as though it were no challenge whatsoever.

Catherine sighed and moved toward the kitchen. Once the oven was warming, she could allow herself a rest until Tom joined her. These days, he helped her with morning chores before he left for work. Without his help, she did not have strength for the day.

She laughed, a quiet, humorless sound. She could not get through the day now but didn't know how to tell Tom. They had no money to hire help, and her best friends, those who could be most counted on to lend a helping hand when needed, were also ill and in need. So, she remained silent and carried on the best she could.

Pearl always seemed to appear when Catherine was in deep need of encouragement. This time, she came armed with copies of the *Chicago Daily Times*. It was a grim smile that she offered along with Miss Doty's most recent story. How could she be truly happy with their truth there in black and white? Yet it sorely needed to be told.

Women come cheap in Ottawa, where they have been dying off for more than a decade without any official investigation.

Mary Doty had written with passion and conviction. Catherine was surprised, though she didn't know why she should be, to discover her own words.

I am in constant pain. I cannot walk a block, but somehow I must carry on.

Catherine looked up at Pearl. "Do I really sound so self-pitying?"

Pearl shook her head. "Is that how you believe it sounds? To the contrary, I believe Miss Doty has portrayed you accurately as a strong woman in a hopelessly difficult situation."

"She has written about Mary Jane," Catherine murmured as she continued reading. "I suppose it doesn't matter what she says about me, but she calls Mary Jane a 'wizened little baby.'"

Pearl considered her response. "She means no insult, but she wants the public to take up our cause. We need them to. Mary Jane is a rather small child. Do you think it's because of the radium?"

Catherine lowered the paper. She and Tom never discussed it, as if Mary Jane would grow big and strong if they remained silent. "We just go on as if everything is normal . . . . but it must be true. Mary Jane isn't developing because of the radium or because my body couldn't nourish her properly. It's true, isn't it?"

"You bear many burdens, dear friend, but look at the help you have in your fight. You have Tom, your children, and dear friends." Pearl reached for her.

Catherine felt her hands lovingly held by her dearest friend and did feel a bit stronger. She didn't know if the calcium pills or any of the other medicine was proving effective, but she put her trust in the Great Physician, and He gave her peace.

†

Catherine sat in the kitchen, waiting for Tom to get home from work. The *Chicago Daily Times* was neatly folded and placed in the center of the table where a vase of flowers would have stood when her Aunt Mary was alive. Mary Doty's latest piece was included within the pages, and Catherine had reread it more times than she could count throughout the day.

When Tom did arrive, Catherine almost pushed the newspaper aside. He was so worn and weary. She wondered when the wrinkles had formed that gave him an aura of constant sadness. She greeted him silently by stepping into his arms and took comfort from his consistent strength.

"Was it a hard day, Tom?"

He removed his coat and hat before sighing, "It's always a hard day, but it's better than having no job. The bread line looks longer every day."

"If only I could take in some sewing or washing . . ."

He cut her off with a kiss. "You know I expect you to do no such thing. It is difficult enough for you to see to your own duties without taking on someone else's."

She knew he did not mean for it to, but his comment stung. He was right, of course, but Catherine still hated the fact that she could not help support their family. The nation was in financial crisis, but she couldn't think beyond her four walls.

"What does Miss Doty write today?" Tom asked, spying the paper, as he was meant to, and Catherine felt deceitful for placing it there.

"You do not believe a surgeon will be found for me. She writes that you have no hope that an operation will help."

Tom was quiet for a moment. Miss Doty had taken personal revelations from many of the dial painters and their families and used them to inspire public outrage and sympathy. "I am sorry, Catherine. It is not that I do not have hope. How do you feel since starting the calcium?"

Catherine snorted derisively, not wanting to let him change the subject and not certain the hateful pills were having any impact at all. "They are helping as well as anything else," she flung back at him, then was embarrassed by the spitefulness in her voice. "I'm sorry, Tom. You have sacrificed everything for me."

His arms were around her in an instant. "All that I have done, I have done willingly. You suffer a burden so great, and you have no choice. If you need to rage at me, I can take it."

But his words took all the fury out of her. She slumped against his chest and sobbed.

He stroked her back and murmured into her hair until her thin frame stopped shaking. Then, as if she had not broken down, he continued their conversation.

"I have written to the Secretary of Labor. Did you know she is the first woman to serve on the Presidential cabinet? I thought she might be sympathetic to our case, and she's certainly in a position to do something about it."

Catherine smiled through her tears and wondered how she had thought to accuse Tom of being without hope - of giving up on her. He had written to Washington DC, to someone with the ear of the President of the United States, because he wanted to see her healed.

"I love you, Tom," she whispered and leaned into his embrace.

Chapter 18

*I can't recall a single actual victim of this so-called
'radium poisoning' in our Ottawa plant.*
William Ganley, 1937

Charlotte sat across from Catherine with a pot of weak tea placed between them. Neither met the other's eye nor touched their teacup. Then, Charlotte spoke in little more than a whisper.

"I don't know just what we can do with the men out of work."

Catherine had no words, only a slow, sad shake of her head. Tom and Albert had been working together at the Libbey-Owens glass factory. They had been so thankful for those jobs, even if they had held better positions before the financial downturn had struck Ottawa. Now, each of their families had a pile of medical bills, a stalled lawsuit, and no breadwinner.

"I fed my children mustard sandwiches yesterday," Charlotte continued with an edge of hysteria in her voice.

Her eyes vacant, Catherine pictured the three little ones reluctantly munching on such an unappetizing supper. She had little more to give her own Tommy and Mary Jane, and that was only due to the generosity of Tom's sister, Margaret. Catherine reached for her cup but then let her hand fall to the table. It didn't seem right to sip tea as though everything was alright.

"What will you do?" Charlotte asked.

Catherine shrugged. "What can we do? We depend upon the charity of family we will never be able to pay back, and the grocer occasionally sneaks extra potatoes into my bag. I'm trying to teach Tommy how to manage the garden, because it's simply impossible for me to tend." She slammed her hand on the table in frustration. She was thirty-four years old and less capable of keeping house than her elderly aunt had been. Pain shot up her arm to punish her for her angry outburst.

Charlotte took a deep breath and locked eyes with Catherine.

"What is it?" Catherine asked, an uneasy sensation growing in her gut.

Charlotte's face suddenly changed, and she pointed toward the window. "Is that our little bird? How marvelous!"

Turning to look, Catherine muttered, "It cannot be. Can it?" As silly as it seemed, she didn't want to put misplaced hope in the presence of the canary that they had first seen years ago when they were both happy and healthy.

Fluttering from branch to branch in an apple tree near the house was a bird that certainly appeared much like the one that had made the other visits.

"There's no way to know for sure," Catherine cautioned, but Charlotte's face was alit with joy.

"But it could be," she insisted. "How wonderful to just permit ourselves to believe that it is. What can it hurt after all?"

Catherine allowed herself a small smile. "I suppose you are right."

They contentedly watched the bird's antics for a few moments before Charlotte spoke again, breaking the spell.

"We are moving to Chicago."

The unease that had faded immediately returned and crushed Catherine like a physical blow. She opened her mouth to argue that Charlotte leaving couldn't possibly be the best solution, but she closed it because she realized it probably was.

"Al cannot find work here," Charlotte continued, seeing Catherine's thoughts as clearly on her face as if she had said them aloud. "We have nowhere to turn. He can find something in the city."

There was, of course, no guarantee of a job, even in Chicago, but a big city had much more to offer than a town like Ottawa. Catherine's heart felt like it was in a vise, and she wished she could offer some hope, something that would convince Charlotte to stay.

Then she imagined having to feed her children mustard sandwiches and what she would do if she were forced to do so.

"I understand," she whispered somewhat unwillingly. "I do so hope that Al will find work in Chicago."

"Thank you. That means so much to me," Charlotte said. "You know that I don't want to leave our home and our friends. If we saw any way to stay . . ." She raised her single slender arm as if to encompass the entire town that had nothing to offer them.

Catherine only nodded and reached for her cup of tea.

†

A few days later, Catherine watched as the Purcells left town with their few most treasured possessions. Anything else had been sold for whatever they could get to fund their travel and resettling expenses. Hating that they had to go, Catherine prayed that it would be worth it, most especially that Al would be able to find work in the big city.

When they were gone, Tom wrapped his arm around Catherine and urged her forward.

"We should get home," he murmured.

Sniffing and blinking back tears, Catherine nodded and allowed Tom to lead her. Once home, she asked the question that had been on her mind since Charlotte's announcement.

"Should we go to the city, too?"

Tom shook his head with confidence. "This house is saving us. We've no rent to pay, like others do, and we've got the garden."

"But now there's the mortgage. We don't own it free and clear like we did," Catherine heard the guilt in her voice. Her uncle had entrusted his home to her, and she had mortgaged it to pay for medicines that didn't seem to be working.

"Our situation is still better than many others," Tom insisted.

"How can you say that?" Catherine cried, uncharacteristically raising her voice. "You have no income, a mortgaged house, a sick wife, and two hungry children!"

Tom's voice remained calm. "I have a home, a wife I love, and two healthy children. I will find work."

Catherine squeezed her eyes and mouth shut. He was right. Of course, there were others much worse off, but right now she wanted to feel sorry for herself. Constant pain and the loss of her dear friend put her in a dreary mood. She couldn't even consider attempting the stairs to their bedroom after the walk home, so she shuffled to the sofa and laid down without saying another word.

After a moment, Tom followed and perched on the edge next to her, rubbing her back until she fell into a fitful sleep.

She awoke to the sound of a familiar radio program. The voice of Father Keane was soothing and encouraging as he said the mass and offered prayers for people across the country. Miracles had been worked through the thousands of people who prayed at his church in person or as they listened through the radio as the Donohues did.

As Catherine listened, she wondered how he chose those he would pray for each week. He must get an overwhelming amount of mail.

When the Our Lady of Sorrows choir began a hymn, Catherine tried to join in. Never an excellent singer, her voice had not improved with the damage to her mouth and throat. Tom acted like he didn't notice, happily adding his own pleasant voice to the song and smiling down at his wife.

†

Tom was not able to find work and was forced to register with the government for relief payments. Catherine never attempted to discuss it with him, because she knew how humiliating it must be for a man to confess that he could not support his family. She cursed her body for being the source of so many of their expenses and the reason she could not economize more.

She imagined what she would do in the garden if she had the strength or energy. A couple of chickens and maybe even a goat could have been kept out back if simple tasks hadn't become virtually impossible for her. However, even these blows were not as devastating as having to admit that she could not attend church.

Catherine had grown up at St Columba. Its soaring arches and wooden pews were a part of who she was. But she couldn't climb the steps to the front door, couldn't sit for any length of time on the hard seats, couldn't kneel to pray.

Instead, a priest visited Catherine and gave her communion each week. She was thankful for his thoughtfulness and bitter about what she was missing at the same time. Her life was being stolen from her bit by bit.

Chapter 19

*We just go along as if we were all going to
be together forever. That's the only way.*
Tom Donohue, 1935

Catherine had always loved Easter. She remembered skipping up the steps of St Columba as a little girl, her new Easter dress billowing out around her legs. Inside, the altar was swathed in pure white cloth that seemed to shimmer with a divine light. She felt at home in church, but particularly on Easter. It was a day when Catherine could especially feel God's presence within Ottawa's little congregation.

Easter of 1937 would not be spent at St Columba, at least not for Catherine. Those she had grown up with would still enter that holy place and enjoy the fellowship of joining together for worship. Catherine rested upon the bed that had been set up in the living room for her, waiting for the priest to visit.

It was more than St Columba's steps, hard pews, and kneeling rails. Catherine had been forced to admit that she could not walk the few blocks to get to church or stand for the singing of hymns. There was no part of this everyday event that she was capable of enduring.

So, she laid there, trying not to drown in self-pity. Attempting to feel the grace of God and be thankful for the mercies he had shown her. Oh, how her faith was being tested!

She had kept her smile firmly in place as she kissed the children before Tom scooped them up to get them to Easter service. Catherine would not have the family miss this important event just because she was forced to. However, the moment the door had clicked shut, she allowed herself a few moments of self-pitying tears.

They would be singing.

Christ the Lord is risen today, alleluia!

How Catherine wished to add her voice to the beautiful sound. But the time for feeling sorry for herself had passed, so she closed her eyes, released her tension, and calmed her breathing. Welcoming the peace that came over her, Catherine prayed. She gave thanks for her husband, who stood so loyally by her side even as she was able to perform fewer and fewer of the responsibilities of a wife. She asked God to bless her children. Tommy was strong and active, but Mary Jane was still so very small and not doing the things other children her age could do with ease. Catherine prayed for her friends, Pearl who had little Lotte but would never have the family she desired and Charlotte who had three children but only one arm with which to care for them.

"Let your glory shine through our lives," Catherine whispered before opening her eyes.

The repurposed living room didn't appear as dreary as it had just a few moments earlier. None of her problems were solved, but Catherine felt comforted.

The time must have passed more quickly than she realized, because the sound of her children's voices floated to her from the street. Then her family bustled through the door, and the children ran to her side.

"Mama, look at what Aunt Margaret gave to me!" Tommy insisted, pushing his sister behind him to wait her proper turn. He proudly held up a kit of watercolors for her inspection. A queasy feeling rose in Catherine's stomach when she looked upon the tiny brush included. It was perfect for Tommy's small hands . . . or painting the intricate faces of watch dials.

"You mustn't put the brush in your mouth," she said without thinking.

Tommy furrowed his brow at her. "I know, mama. Why would I put it in my mouth?" Then he stepped aside to give his sister her turn while he further inspected his prize.

Catherine didn't have time to admonish herself before Mary Jane wordlessly presented a tiny rabbit. It was just the size of Mary Jane's hands, though Catherine now noticed that Tom was keeping careful watch, ready to pounce upon the poor thing if Mary Jane allowed it to escape.

"Did Aunt Margaret give that to you?" Catherine asked in a quiet voice reserved for her youngest. Mary Jane only nodded with a sheepish smile on her cherub face. "Well, isn't that thoughtful."

Mary Jane nodded again before placing the rabbit in a box that Tom had at the ready for it. He instructed Tommy to help his sister collect some grass and twigs for the rabbit's home, and they tumbled outside together.

"Was the service lovely?"

Tom nodded and carefully took a seat next to her. "The same as always. Beautiful and comforting in its familiarity."

"Thinking of our resurrected Lord gives me hope," Catherine said, staring ahead as though she were gazing into heaven. "One day, even my broken, weary body will be made perfectly new."

"Amen," Tom said, and they both pretended not to hear the catch in his voice.

Easter supper was a simpler affair than it should have been. The Donohues could not easily entertain guests, and Catherine could no longer cook extravagant dinners, even if they could have afforded the necessary ingredients. Instead, Margaret had provided for this as well, sending a roasted chicken, potatoes, and gravy home with Tom after service.

The aroma was delicious, though Catherine wasn't sure how much she would be able to eat. She remembered how thin Peg had become and knew that she looked worse. When Tom brought her a plate, Catherine was determined to try. The potatoes, at least, would go down quite well, she thought.

The buttery potatoes seemed to melt in her mouth, and Catherine wondered at the number of times she had eaten this simple dish and thought nothing of it. She identified the flavors of garlic, salt, and pepper, as if they were the most exotic of spices.

Then, Catherine felt something hard and rough in her mouth. She moved her tongue to separate the object from the food she had been gently chewing. Carefully fishing it out, she examined the unfamiliar item. It was a similar in color to potatoes, but it was far too firm. The surface was rough and pitted.

A metallic taste flowed over Catherine's tongue, and she touched her napkin to her mouth. It came away red with blood, and she suddenly knew what she held in her hand. How scary it must have been for Peg to have been the first to experience these things. Catherine was terrified enough as she looked down at the piece of her jawbone.

She did not eat any more of her Easter dinner, but she waited until Tom was helping her perform her evening toilet before she told him what had happened.

"Will you get that box that my watch came in?" she asked him once she had taken her pills and washed out her mouth with a salty tasting rinse.

"Here it is. Would you like me to take off your watch?"

"No," Catherine quickly declined. Her ever-loosening

watch was one of the few reminders of normal life she continued to enjoy. "I have something else to keep safe for the time being."

She dropped in the small piece of bone, and Tom peered down in curiosity. Before he could ask, she explained, "It is a piece of my jawbone. It fell out earlier."

"Oh, Catie," Tom whispered. He had never before looked at her with such unadulterated pity, and she hated it.

"The same thing happened to Peg," she said without emotion, as if Tom would not follow through to the part where Peg died. She successfully chased away the pity on his face to replace it with horror. His mouth moved noiselessly. What could he say?

"I'm sorry, Tom."

He blinked and shook himself a little. "Why are you apologizing to me? I stand here, the man who vowed to love and protect you, and all I can do is be a witness to your pain. Do you know how hard it is to be a man and be helpless?"

"I'm sorry," she repeated.

"No, don't," Tom said angrily. He began to pace the floor.

Catherine hung her head as he continued to move about in order to vent his anger. Finally, her illness had taken away the one thing she thought it never could, the closeness of their loving relationship. They were left with their sorrow and anger, suffering from it in quite separate ways.

Chapter 20

*He had no thought of money. He just wants
to help us girls, to help humanity.*
Catherine Donohue, 1937

Marie spent a few minutes greeting the children and listening intently to their latest accomplishments before sitting matter-of-factly at the side of Catherine's sickbed. She gazed openly at her as if making an assessment.

"Your Tom came to see me," Marie announced, seeming to have found whatever she was searching for in Catherine's countenance. When Catherine made no response, Marie continued, "He believes – and I happen to agree with him – that we need to have another go at finding a lawyer, at holding Radium Dial responsible for what is happening to so many of us."

"But we tried . . ."

Marie didn't let her get far. "We didn't try hard enough. We need to try again."

"Alright," Catherine murmured meekly. She didn't do much of anything anymore, and finding a lawyer who would take on their case sounded more daunting than ever.

Marie's face hardened, and she pounced on Catherine's reluctance. "We can't let them get away with it – not Radium Dial, not the lawmakers, not the people of this town who refuse to listen and then avoid us as though we're contagious!"

Catherine felt a glimmer of hope. Marie was so much stronger than she was. Maybe she could make it happen.

"There are some who won't join us," Marie admitted, shaking her head at their weakness, "but there are plenty who will. Pearl, Charlotte, Helen, and Olive . . . we can do this if we do it together."

"But a lawyer . . ." Catherine wanted to believe, but none of them had the money to retain a lawyer.

"We need a lawyer with enough money that he doesn't need to charge us and enough hunger for justice that he wants to be connected with our case," Marie mused, searching the ceiling for answers.

"Clarence Darrow," Catherine whispered. "I will write to Clarence Darrow."

Marie turned her glittering gaze on Catherine. "You might not look like much," she said, patting Catherine's arm with surprising gentleness, "but I'm glad to see you've still got some fight in you."

And so it was agreed. The dial painters of Ottawa were going to pursue justice. Who better than Clarence Darrow to help them, as he had the Pullman workers and others who seemed up against impossible odds.

It took Catherine some time to pen the promised missive to the famous lawyer. She couldn't sit up for long without pain, and writing neatly was a chore. However, she kept at it and finally produced a note outlining the girls' situation. Tom posted it right away, and they all prayed for a response from the octogenarian attorney.

When it came, the event was anti-climactic.

"He is very sympathetic toward our case," Catherine said, staring at the letter, "but he is unable to take it on." She set it down. "He says that he will refer someone else to aid us. Do you think he means it?"

"I hope so," Tom muttered.

"He better," stated Marie.

"Maybe there is something else we can do in the meantime," Catherine said, slowly, as if the thought was still forming in her mind.

"What are you thinking of?" Marie asked, leaning forward in interest.

Catherine gave her what could only be described as a mischievous grin. "Remember Mary Doty?"

Marie laughed aloud. "There's my girl," she said with a wink. "I knew they were making a mistake to count you down and out."

Tom looked back and forth between them. "The *Chicago Daily Times* reporter?"

Marie nodded determinedly. "That's exactly who she is."

✝

Radium Death on Rampage!

In spite of the gruesome headline, Catherine smiled down at the latest edition of the *Chicago Daily Times*. It would certainly get some attention, and, if it didn't, the sympathetic image of Charlotte with her empty sleeve and forlorn expression would.

"Well, done Mary Doty," Catherine whispered to the empty room.

Miss Doty had been exceedingly willing to feature the women's stories. "That's just why it's so important to have female reporters," she had smugly stated. "There are some newsworthy events that men simply never notice."

Tom had taken some offense at that, but Catherine had shushed him imploringly.

Doty's writing invited readers to take up the dial painters' cause without making them sound pathetic. It was the perfect cry for justice.

With their Illinois Industrial Commission hearing just days away, these dial painters are without a lawyer. The women are understandably concerned that legal trickery will win the day. Will justice be served?

Would it? Catherine couldn't help but wonder, but this article gave her more hope than she had felt in quite some time. She was surprised at how confident she seemed where Miss Doty had quoted her.

Radium Dial wants us to feel so hopeless that we all decide to stay away. I suppose the company lawyers would like that.

But it wasn't going to happen. Marie had not been able to rally all of the Ottawa dial painters that were known to suffer from their exposure to radium. There would always be those who were too afraid to stand up for themselves, unwilling to face the wrath of their neighbors, but more than a few were standing together. If only they had a lawyer.

†

Two days before the hearing, Catherine checked her bag and resisted the urge to go over house rules with Margaret. She knew the children would be well cared for, but she still hated leaving them. A few days with Tom's sister would be good for them, while he escorted Catherine to Chicago.

The women had been summoned to a law office on LaSalle Street. If Catherine was still capable of falling to her knees in thanksgiving, she would have. The letter from Leonard Grossman had arrived in the nick of time. He had offered to take the women's case on Clarence Darrow's recommendation, but would he be able to challenge the expensive legal team employed by Radium Dial with so little time to prepare?

Catherine took one last look around the room, zipped up her overnight bag, and said a prayer for Leonard Grossman. The children were in the kitchen with their Aunt Margaret. Tom and Catherine met there to say their good-byes. The children were excited rather than sad, as if they believed their parents were going on a great adventure, and maybe it was better that way. They did not have the weight of the world on their shoulders like their parents did.

"You take good care of her," Margaret ordered her brother.

The command gave Catherine a warm sensation. She was touched that Margaret was now one of her greatest supporters. They had come a long way since Tom's family had expressed their concerns regarding Catherine's poor health before they married. The deed done, Tom's family, especially Margaret, did everything within their power to help.

"Thank you for caring for the children while we're away," Catherine said, forcing Margaret to endure a brief embrace. She was not a physically affectionate woman, and she held Catherine loosely.

"We will all be just fine, won't we, children?"

Tommy and Mary Jane added their enthusiastic assurance as Catherine hugged and kissed them in turn. "Behave well for your auntie."

"We will," they said in unison.

Catherine squeezed them one last time, offered Margaret a grateful look, and took Tom's arm to be on their way.

Catherine had not spent much time in Chicago. During the train ride, she thought about what a very different world the big city was compared to Ottawa. She would have to ask Charlotte and

Helen, who had moved there for greater employment opportunities, how they found it. The tall buildings and crowds of people intimidated Catherine, and she supposed she would always be a small town girl.

The atmosphere on the train changed as they neared their destination. More people got on board who were dressed for business. They hid behind the financial papers and avoided eye contact. Only a few children were in the car, and Catherine wondered what Tommy and Mary Jane would think of a trip to Chicago.

Were she healthy enough to take them swimming in Lake Michigan and shopping on the Magnificent Mile, maybe she would bring them. She doubted they would enjoy a hearing before the state's Industrial Commission.

Arriving at the station, people stood and pushed their way toward the doors before the train had come to a complete stop. Tom and Catherine waited. They had no interest in being part of the bustling to be first, and Catherine could too easily be injured by a casual shove. Once the bulk of the passengers had disembarked, Tom stood, helped Catherine to her feet, and retrieved their bags.

Out on the street, the air was thick and hot. It was amazing how the windy city could be buried under mountains of snow in the winter but hotter than hades in the summer. Hoping she wouldn't be a melted mess before they arrived at the Metropolitan Building, Catherine took the first step forward.

The women had agreed to convene there, where they would meet for the first time the man who had decided to take on their case. Tom hired a taxi, knowing that Catherine could no longer walk the blocks to their destination. She wanted to protest that it was an expense they could not afford. It was, but she also knew that Tom was right. She would never make it on foot. Not anymore.

Riding along in that Chicago taxi, Catherine's mind momentarily travelled only a few years back in time to trips to Starved Rock and dancing at the shack. How she had taken it all for granted. What she wouldn't give to be able to hike through the forest now.

It did not take long to arrive at the impressive façade of the Metropolitan Building. Soaring skyward and decorated with gold, the structure oozed sophistication like nothing Catherine had ever seen. She was relieved to see her friends gathered on the sidewalk. None of them would have to face this alone.

Hugs and greetings were shared all around the instant Catherine stepped from the taxi.

"Isn't this place just fabulous?" Charlotte exclaimed.

"Let's just hope that the lawyer is," Marie interjected.

"Well, he's willing. That makes him the best lawyer in the world in my book," Pearl added.

"Let's go meet him," Catherine said, and she led them inside.

Her polka dotted dress swirled around her skinny legs in the humid Chicago air until they walked through the door. The unfamiliar but welcome sensation of air conditioning replaced the heat of the outdoors. Catherine looked up at Tom in wonder as she imagined what it must cost to constantly cool such a large building.

The women all gawked at the lobby for a few moments – the gold paneling, tiled floor, and artificially cool air were a wonder to the humble visitors. Catherine urged them toward their purpose, and they found the elevator, another marvel that some of them had never experienced before. It carried them smoothly up to the office of Leonard Grossman.

It would have been easy to be intimidated by the office of the successful attorney. The walls were lined with as many books as were held in the Ottawa library. Where the bookshelves left space, impressive certificates hung, giving testament to Grossman's many degrees and accomplishments. His large desk shone as though freshly polished. Were it not for the man himself, Catherine would have been very nervous indeed.

"Welcome, ladies," he said in a warm voice. "I am Leonard Grossman."

Although he wore a suit similar to the unfriendly businessmen that Catherine had observed on the train, Grossman had an open face and broad smile. His hand was outstretched, and the women shook it in turn. His glasses were perched on a somewhat oversized nose, and dark, thinning hair was carefully combed to one side. Catherine felt immediately at ease around him.

The women were surprised to see that Grossman had a stack of files on his desk related to their case. He had already begun tirelessly working on their case, and it was a good thing too, since their hearing was in forty-eight hours. Having been introduced to each new client, Grossman gestured for them to sit in chairs that had been brought in for them.

Once they were all seated, their attorney demonstrated the skills that he would, from that moment on, be using to benefit them. His voice resonated without being too loud or jarring. He would have made a wonderful preacher, Catherine thought.

"I am happy to be in this fight for you," he began. "I have familiarized myself with your case and am passionate about helping you find justice. My heart, like that of many Americans just learning of your story, is with you."

Catherine felt her heart warm within her thin chest. Here was someone on their side, someone who had the power to do something about it. Optimism filled her for the first time in a very long time.

When he had finished, Catherine slowly stood, feeling that it was her duty to represent their little group. "Thank you, Mr Grossman. We were at our wits' end, and you have come to our rescue."

He seemed slightly embarrassed by being painted a hero, but he took her hand and said, "I do this for you and for everyone who is exploited by a greedy employer. You will be heard."

Catherine smiled. She kept her mouth closed to hide the fact that she was missing so many teeth, but she smiled with genuine optimism.

†

The new hope in Catherine's heart invigorated her somewhat. Although it was difficult for her to climb the courthouse steps, she took advantage of the representatives of the newspapers gathered there. Cameras clicked and quotes were scribbled. As much as Catherine hated the limelight and had never imagined it shining on her, she knew that public sympathy was necessary to their case.

Nothing would be decided today. Mr Grossman was planning to request a postponement since he had so recently taken the case. However, he had also coached them in using every opportunity to draw attention to their plight. Laws were not changed without public demand for it. To save others from their fate, the dial painters had to make sure everyone knew about it.

So, Catherine, a quiet Catholic girl from a small town,

became a media darling. It was no longer only Mary Doty featuring the women in stories written to incite public outrage. Just as Catherine had read about the New Jersey dial painters, people across the country were now reading about her.

Inside the courtroom, Radium Dial's legal team was happy to accept the proposed delay in the case. Marie whispered far too loudly, "They're hoping that some of us die before the case is over," and an eerie moment of silence interrupted the hearing before the attorneys awkwardly carried on.

That moment, however, was forgotten when Mr Grossman gave his closing remarks.

"We do not need to have martyrs such as we have sitting around this table, and the many dead who worked with these girls." He paused and made eye contact with each of his clients. "It is a heavy cross to Calvary, but we will bear it, and, with the help of God, we will fight to a finish!"

"Yes," Catherine whispered to no one in particular. "He would make a good preacher indeed."

Chapter 21

*Like the x-ray, radium therapy has been passing
through the shadows of illiterate misconceptions
and unfortunately has been handled at times
by the unscrupulous.*
Dr Everett Lain, 1922

Mr Grossman called them together the next day. He was wasting no time in his preparations. The women all eagerly responded to his summons.

"I would like to introduce you all to my partner in law and in life, my wife, Trudel," he proudly laid claim to a pleasantly plump woman by placing his hand on her arm. "She tolerates my long hours and works many of them with me."

Trudel smiled up at her husband as if it was by his command that the sun shone but said nothing, so he continued.

"As you may have guessed, my Trudel is of German descent and speaks the language fluently, and she will be assisting me with the vital work of translation. In order to learn what Radium Dial should have known about radium, Trudel will be studying the research of European scientists."

He gave his wife a look filled with gratitude before directing his gaze at his clients. "What I need for each of you to do is obtain doctors' statements." His eyes grew harder and intensity emanated from him. "We absolutely must have doctors on our side who will testify that you suffer from radium poisoning, so that is what I task you with."

The women nodded but shared sidelong glances. They had been struggling with the doctors of Ottawa for years. Some still claimed that radium poisoning didn't exist, but how could they not hold up their part of the bargain when Mr Grossman was working so hard for them?

After a few more instructions, he and Trudel left for Chicago. The women gathered at the Donohue home.

"I have written my doctors," Catherine sighed in exasperation. "They don't reply."

"They are worried about protecting themselves," Marie stated.

Charlotte spoke up. "There must be other people willing to stand up with us, doctors who seek justice, as Mr Grossman does."

"Dr Loffler will testify for us," Catherine admitted. "What others?"

Pearl had been quiet and thoughtful. Now she spoke. "We must beg them, convincingly and without ceasing. In person and in writing. We simply must have our records."

The women all nodded in agreement. There wasn't much they could do, but they would succeed in this task.

"There is Dr Dalitsch. We can count on him, but is there anyone local?" Catherine asked, looking to each woman in turn. They had all had the same experience with local doctors, but maybe they would have better luck all working together.

When they next met with Mr Grossman, they had mixed results to share. He didn't seem surprised or disappointed, but he encouraged them to continue in their quest.

"As many doctors' reports as you can obtain. Do not give up." Then he shared one of his own activities. "I have requested documents from Radium Dial."

No one said a word, but shock was evident on their faces.

"They have been ordered to produce records of employee physical examination results. We will discover what they knew and when they knew it. Their negligence will be revealed."

Pearl was the first to speak. "Thank you for the great sacrifices that you are making on our behalf. To be sure, an attorney such as yourself has many clients, yet those you set aside to take on our humble case. God bless you, Mr Grossman."

Murmurings of assent and nodding heads signified the agreement of the entire group, and Mr Grossman accepted the praise with a slight inclination of his head.

"I have decided that Mrs Donohue should be the lead litigant. She is known to the public, and her family situation makes her a sympathetic figure."

Catherine looked down at her hands in her lap. She knew the other, unspoken reason Mr Grossman would put her case front and center. She was likely to be the next Ottawa dial painter to die.

She thought of Inez and how she had died after her day in court but before receiving justice. Would her case be different?

With Mr Grossman gone and the women returned to their daily lives, it seemed almost a dream that they had a champion fighting in their corner. Catherine's routine no longer resembled anything like what it used to be. What it should be.

Instead of sharing their cozy room upstairs, Catherine slept on the sickbed in the living room, while Tom often slept on the nearby sofa. She was usually so sore and stiff in the morning that Tom practically carried her to the toilet and helped her to wash.

The first time Catherine had needed to be carried, she was humiliated. If it weren't for the fact that she was afraid of soiling the bed, she would have never asked it of Tom, but he had done it without a second thought.

He had gently and easily taken her into his arms as if she was his young healthy bride . . . . and carried her to the bathroom.

Catherine had cried after he returned her to the bed, and Tom had gone to the kitchen to prepare breakfast and pretend that he didn't notice.

When he returned with a plate of food on a tray for her, he offered a blessing and waited a few moments before speaking again.

"Catie, we are going to have to hire a housekeeper."

Catherine closed her eyes and bit her tongue on any objection she would make. They couldn't afford it. They couldn't afford anything, but Tom couldn't do it all on his own. The help of his sister was welcome but intermittent. Daily duties were being neglected because Tom was at work and Catherine in bed.

It made a new kind of pain well up in her to admit it, but she said, "You're right, Tom."

The woman selected for the job was Eleanor Taylor. She arrived at the Donohue home dressed smartly but plainly. Her features were pleasantly rounded in a way that Catherine's never had been and never would be, but her respectful habits made it impossible for Catherine to feel any jealousy. Eleanor cared for her and her children like members of her own family, and they grew to love her as one of theirs.

Having Eleanor there made things so much easier when Tom had to take Catherine to her appointments with doctors, dentists, and specialists. None of them seemed to make anything any better, but they couldn't just give up. Once Tom had helped Catherine prepare for the day, the way she should be readying her children each day but could not, he helped her out to a car, borrowed because Catherine could no longer walk.

X-ray treatments were the latest experiment. Catherine didn't entirely understand what was happening when she laid upon the hard, uncomfortable table and a loudly buzzing machine was pointed at the large lump on her hip, but Dr Dalitsch thought it might help, so she endured it.

She endured having to be lifted onto the table like a child by her husband. She endured the pain of remaining still in an awkward position. She endured knowing the treatments were expensive and ineffective. She endured watching hope fade from her husband's eyes and knowing he saw the same thing in her own.

"This was my thirtieth x-ray treatment," Catherine said in little more than a whisper after Tom had carried her back to the car. The day had taken so much out of her that no strength remained to walk to the parking lot on her own.

"Yes," Tom said, placing a gentle hand on her knee. Catherine thought he was not going to say more, but finally he did. "Do you feel any better? Any better at all?"

Holding in a sigh, Catherine considered what she should say. Honesty had always been her policy, especially with Tom, but she did not want to tell him that she didn't feel better. The lump didn't feel smaller. Her hips hurt as badly as they ever did. Then she realized that she had taken so long to answer his question that there was no need to anymore.

"I'm sorry, Tom."

"No, I'm sorry. Sorry that I cannot do for you what you need. Sorry that I cannot even figure out what that is. I would do anything to see you healed."

"Maybe that is not the plan God has for us." Catherine could say it to Tom to assuage his guilt, but she hoped it wasn't true. Surely, God wanted her health to be revitalized so that she could care for her husband and be a mother to her children.

Didn't He?

The car became silent, and Catherine, weary from the stress of her procedure, fell asleep.

†

It took only a few weeks for Catherine to grow fond of Eleanor. She kept the house and cared for the children in a way that Catherine wished she could, but without making Catherine feel guilty that she was doing it for her. Eleanor was careful to ask Catherine's opinion about any decision that needed to be made, giving her a feeling of being needed, even if she could no longer rise from her bed.

"This seems a bit too small for Tommy," Eleanor said, holding up a blue shirt that was in fine condition but was, indeed, too small for the growing little boy. "Would you like me to try repurpose it for Mary Jane or is there someone to whom you'd like to give it?"

Catherine held out a hand for the item, and, taking it, she held it to her face, breathing in the little boy scent and remembering when the shirt had been too large for her son. "If you don't mind making some effort to make it appropriate for a girl...." Catherine said. She didn't need to explain that the family could not afford to replace anything unless absolutely necessary.

"Of course," Eleanor said cheerfully, taking back the shirt and giving it a critical eye. "I think I have just the idea." Before she strode out of the room, she asked, "Would you care for some boiled carrots? I can spare a sprinkle of brown sugar for them."

Catherine was surprised to feel an answering grumble of hunger from her stomach. "Why, that does sound fine. Thank you, Eleanor."

She nodded respectfully and returned to the kitchen.

With so little to do besides think and pray, Catherine gave thanks for Eleanor. Welcoming another woman into one's family was no easy thing, so she was grateful to be sent a helpmate that so well suited her.

It wasn't much later in the day when Eleanor returned to Catherine's little front room with the children in tow. "Go on, then. Show mummy what you've been up to."

Tommy rushed to the bedside. "Look, mama! I painted it myself."

Catherine made appreciative sounds as Tommy held up a page from the newspaper. Over the stories that were of no importance to him, he had created a landscape scene with stick-leg animals and bright colored flowers. "Did you use your Easter present?"

Tommy nodded proudly with a face-splitting grin.

"I used to enjoy painting as well," Catherine said wistfully. "This is quite good. When you go to school, we will have to tell your teachers that you are an artist."

Tommy beamed as Mary Jane toddled up next to him. She held a plate out, but she was a quiet girl and didn't say many words yet.

Eleanor spoke for her. "Mary Jane has helped me bake some soft biscuits for you. We thought you might like them soaked in milk."

"That was very thoughtful of you, my love," Catherine said to Mary Jane, hoping that Eleanor understood the praise was intended for her as well.

Tommy piped up, not wanting to share his mother's attention. "Miss Taylor said that you like foods that are soft and sweet."

Catherine saw a blush cross Eleanor's face as she stepped forward to usher the children out. "Miss Taylor is quite right," Catherine said to let Eleanor know there were no hard feelings. "She is right about most things and takes very good care of us."

Eleanor's blush deepened, but she also smiled prettily. "Thank you, Mrs Donohue."

The children left their gifts and gave their mother gentle kisses before leaving her alone again. Catherine considered tiny Mary Jane. She could not help but think that her lack of development was due to radium, but was the radioactivity trapped within Catherine's body continuing to have an ill effect on her?

A sinking feeling grew in the pit of Catherine's stomach as she realized what needed to be done. The next time Eleanor came in with a routine inquiry, Catherine asked her to stay for a moment.

"I believe that we should limit my time around the children," Catherine stated as firmly as she could. Inside, her heart was breaking, but she blinked away her tears and clamped her lips shut on the objection she wanted to make to her own words.

Eleanor looked at her for a moment as she considered her response. Catherine couldn't meet her eye. She didn't want to see pity. That was one thing she had no shortage of, so she kept her eyes averted.

"If that is what you think is best, Mrs Donohue. Has your doctor suggested it?"

Now Catherine did turn to Eleanor, because it was something she hadn't thought of. "I will ask Dr Dalitsch, Eleanor. Thank you. It's just that . . . ." she couldn't continue. A sob caught in her throat and her eyes burned.

"I understand," Eleanor murmured, sitting carefully on the edge of the bed. "You are concerned about the radioactivity affecting the children."

Catherine released a strangled laugh. "After all this time hating it when people in town acted like I was contagious." She turned large, tear-filled eyes on Eleanor. "What if I am?"

Eleanor stroked Catherine's arm and brushed hair away from her face as a mother would. "Let's see what Dr Dalitsch has to say. Have you mentioned this concern to Mr Donohue?"

It was tempting to foist this responsibility onto Eleanor, as she had all her others, but Catherine shook her head. "I will discuss it with Tom." Eleanor pulled her hands away, and Catherine suddenly didn't want her to leave. "Can you see my bones glow when you check on me in the night?"

She wasn't sure why she asked. Maybe she hoped that the faint glow was a figment of her imagination. Eleanor would laugh and say, "Oh, what an idea," or look at her like she was crazy. Except she didn't.

Eleanor smiled grimly at Catherine and continued to stroke her hair. "You have the light of an angel about you," she admitted, nodding slowly. "It is as though God knows that He has placed a heavy burden upon you, so He surrounds you with heavenly light while you are still on earth."

Catherine could not speak. Eleanor patted her arm a final time before slipping from the room. Only then did Catherine realize that Eleanor had seen this about her all along. Since the first night in her position in the Donohue home, Eleanor had seen the glow that was evidence of the poison that ate away at Catherine's body. Yet, she had never been afraid, had never shied away. What a wonder, that someone who hadn't even known her could show her such love.

Chapter 22

Edgar Allen Poe in all his weird stories never utilized a theme more harrowing than that of death by radium.
Daily Courier, 1928

Entirely bed-ridden, Catherine had not been able to attend St Columba or the make a trip to the grocer in months. Activities that used to be a mundane part of daily life were impossible for her to complete. Tom and Eleanor did it all for her.

The one activity she remained capable of was conversation. In person, in prayer, or by letter, conversing was the greatest consolation left to Catherine.

Tom spent as much time at her side as he could. Sometimes, this was quite a lot when he was between the temporary jobs he was able to scrape up. Eleanor sat with her whenever the children were otherwise occupied. Oftentimes, as Eleanor was leaving the room, Catherine would ask her to help her sit and bring her stationery before she left.

Letters from Pearl were a great joy, just as they had been in their younger, healthier days. Pearl would emphasize the positive things that were going on in her life and ask about Catherine's children. She kept in contact with Mr Grossman and forwarded anything he said to Catherine.

All the women gathered their doctors' statements, medical bills, and anything else they felt might be relevant. In Catherine's case, this included the small jewelry box where pieces of her jawbone were deposited as they fell out.

To Pearl, she wrote about the feeling of isolation that came with her condition. Catherine begged Pearl to visit.

I'm so lonesome and blue. Please, come Sunday if you can.

Catherine looked at the last line of her letter to Pearl. She was afraid that she sounded a bit desperate, but she did not erase the words. Pearl would understand, and hopefully she would come.

Of course, Pearl did come as soon as she could, but she never mentioned Catherine's pitiful plea. When Pearl arrived, she strode in just as she always had, as if both women were not facing matters of life and death. She was like a fresh breeze chasing away the somber cloud that had settled over the Donohue home.

One difference was obvious immediately. Pearl hadn't brought cookies. Once a favorite of Catherine's, she simply couldn't manage to chew them anymore. Therefore, Pearl had brought a jar of sweet tea and warm, spongy cake. Her friend's thoughtfulness made Catherine's heart full.

As Pearl settled into a chair at Catherine's bedside, she sighed and said, "I suppose I could have brought you a bottle of rum now that this experiment with Prohibition is over."

Catherine laughed. "I believe spirits are against doctor's orders."

"Well, what do they know anyway?" Pearl scoffed as she poured them each some tea. It was a rich golden brown in the sun, and Catherine savored the flavor.

"Have they given you any relief? The doctors, I mean."

Pearl snorted again. "What comfort can they give me now. They've already taken everything away."

Catherine knew that she was referring to her hysterectomy, but Catherine couldn't help but feel that Pearl had much left to her. She just murmured, "I'm sorry," between sips of tea and concentrated on not letting it drip down her chin.

"Charlotte's Al has found some work in Chicago. They seem to be doing well." And with that, Pearl launched into a monologue both informative and entertaining, including updates on some people Catherine hadn't even thought about in months.

After a few moments, Catherine laughed aloud, "I've always wondered how you manage to keep track of everyone – and where you even find the time for so much gossip."

Pearl appeared aghast. "Why, it's not gossip! I'm a good Catholic girl." With a harrumph, she insisted somewhat less enthusiastically, "I just like to stay in touch, that's all."

"Oh, dear Pearl," Catherine said soothingly. "I meant no offense. This is good for my soul. You are distracting me from my troubles and reminding me to think of others. I'm so glad you could come."

Mollified, Pearl asked Catherine if she had heard the latest on which nightclubs would be opening up first.

Catherine knew the days were long gone when she might have gone out for cocktails or dancing, but she did smile a little when she added, "We can have Christmas wine this year."

†

On Christmas Eve, the Donohue family gathered around Catherine's wrought iron bed with a little radio on the bedside table.

"We are going to listen to the President!" Tommy told his sister, always happy to impart his greater knowledge for the benefit of little Mary Jane. She simply grinned and nodded in response.

"It's mighty fine to be able to hear Mr Roosevelt all the way from Washington DC," Catherine said, sounding wistful as she imagined how many miles separated them from the event they were about to listen to and how many other Americans joined them.

Blankets hung over the room's windows to keep out the cold, and a fire burned cheerily in the hearth. Tom was careful to ensure that Catherine did not catch a chill. Each holding a cup of hot tea, they waited for the program to begin. When the static of the channel changed to the sound of an adjusting microphone, the family exchanged happy grins.

Their smiles remained in place as the announcer thanked Hobby Lobby, the popular radio show, for forgoing its regularly scheduled broadcast so that listeners could enjoy the lighting of the Christmas tree in Washington DC. Catherine closed her eyes to envision the scene in her head. Tom was prepared to light their little tree at the same time the chimes rang out in the capital city.

First came a prayer, shared by the entire nation, and the children folded their hands and bowed their heads as the pastor read John 3:16. It gave Catherine such comfort to imagine her savior's coming on this holy night.

She couldn't help a small frown when the prayer included a supplication for the end of war. Surely, after the war that had only ended nineteen years ago men were not so eager to take up arms again. Catherine added her fervent prayer to that of the President that the Japanese invasion of China and Spanish Civil War would be swiftly brought to an end. The moment quickly passed, however, as the prayer ended and the family crossed themselves in the name of the Father, and the Son, and the Holy Spirit.

The next speaker talked about the peace of the first Christmas, and Catherine could feel that quiet peace settle over the room and chase away her fears. For just a moment, her great anxiety caused by pain, immobility, and medical bills faded away.

"Let us in America dedicate ourselves to the preservation of the ideal of the first Christmas: peace on earth."

The words reverberated in Catherine's heart as the tinny voice traveled to them through hundreds of miles. New hope swelled in her heart. She felt excitement build as President Roosevelt was addressed by several speakers wishing him a merry Christmas. Enthusiastic applause welcomed President Roosevelt, the bells indicating the lighting of the tree rang out, and Tom switched on their own short string of lights. Then Roosevelt spoke.

When he mentioned "man's inhumanity to man," Catherine knew that he was referring to war, but she thought of Radium Dial. How could they have stood by and watched the dial painters poison themselves? The feeling of peace began to evaporate, and Catherine wished she could physically grasp it and not let go.

"This night is a night of hope, joy, and happiness," the President continued, and Catherine's tranquility was restored. She hoped that he would not mention war again, though she knew that not speaking of it would not make it go away any more than she could wish her illness away.

Were there really "better things to come," as President Roosevelt promised? He shared a story that he had read in the newspaper. Catherine found herself a bit disappointed, because she didn't want to listen to the President read another person's message. She wanted to hear his, but she listened closely, wondering how honored the columnist must feel as the President's voice sent his words across the nation.

"It is the habit of my friend when he is troubled by doubt to reach for The Book," the President read. Catherine nodded her head slowly. It was wisdom applicable to the greatest man in their nation and the poor, bed-ridden woman listening.

"He took the cup and gave it to them all," he continued, noting that not even Judas the Betrayer was left out.

Roosevelt finished his message emphasizing man's duty to show good will to all men, not just those we feel are worthy of it. Catherine couldn't help but hope that Mr Reed and the Radium Dial executives were listening.

As the President recited from the gospels, Catherine's darker thoughts were swept away by the beautiful image of forgiveness and love. She was greatly comforted by hearing the leader of the nation witness his faith in their shared savior.

The President's speech was brief, and when a choir began singing *Oh, Come Let Us Adore Him*, the Donohue family, in their own little living room, added their voices to the mix. As they moved on to *Silent Night*, Mary Jane wriggled in next to her mother with drooping, sleepy eyes. Catherine ignored the flash of fear that it was not safe for her daughter to be so near. On this night, she would set her worries aside and snuggle Mary Jane close.

By the time the benediction was given, Catherine was also drowsy. She did not notice when Tom gently lifted Mary Jane to carry her to her own bed as *Hail to the Chief* played for the President's departure.

†

When Christmas morning dawned, Catherine grasped eagerly at the contented feeling of the evening before. However, waking in her bed, alone in the family room, brought her reality back to her with harsh clarity.

She would have to wait for Tom to wake and carry her to the toilet. Then she would lie abed while he scraped together breakfast from their meager pantry. Tommy could dress himself, but Mary Jane would need tending. With morning chores completed, Tom would take the children to church, while Catherine could do nothing but wait to hear about it.

When they were gone, she delved into her memories of Christmases when she thought she had decades more to worship under St Columba's vaulted ceiling. How she wished she would have counted the number of pews and taken more time to memorize each stained-glass window. She could picture it well enough, but the details were becoming blurred.

She thought of the boys who were proud to be chosen as acolytes, lighting the candles and carrying the cross. Would Tommy someday be chosen? She would never get to watch him serve his church and community as he grew into manhood.

Catherine forced her eyes open, not wanting to linger in her sorrow. They were immediately drawn to the cross that Tom had hung on the wall near the bed. When the visiting priest came to give her communion, this small cross was her substitute for the crucifix at St Columba, and how lovingly it had been provided.

With a deep breath, Catherine cast aside her complaints. Others had struggled in worse places than hers. She was determined to find joy this Christmas Day.

Joy was easier to discover when the children came bounding home from church. With rosy cheeks and a dusting of snow in their hair, Tommy and Mary Jane appeared like little angels. Their cold butterfly kisses brought the scent of the outdoors and faint incense that clung to their clothes. Catherine reveled in the feeling of holding them in her arms.

The paltry offering of gifts under the tree didn't matter as long as they were all together. Tom leaned over the bed and embraced her. It reminded Catherine of when she had leaned over this same bed in this same room to comfort her dying uncle. There was love and devotion in Tom's touch, but no longer passion.

Catherine was grateful when the children's chatter distracted her from that course of thought. She had many other days to contemplate the state of her marriage and the fact that she was entirely at fault for everything they were missing out on. Today, she only wanted to soak in her children's happiness and be grateful for what they did have.

Coats, hats, and mittens had been promptly discarded, and Tommy led Mary Jane to the tree where they sat politely yet eagerly to be allowed to open their gifts. Tom laughed and proposed that they let mother open one first.

Tommy appeared disappointed, but Mary Jane's lit up as she picked up just the right one.

"For me? But, Tom, we agreed that there was only money for a few things for the children." Tears swam in Catherine's eyes as Mary Jane held out the small package to her.

Tom only smiled and nodded for her to open it.

As soon as it was in her hand, Catherine could tell that it was a paperback novel. Her lip quivered as she imagined Tom selecting it for her, knowing there was little else she could do these days besides read. Even writing was a challenge, what with holding the pencil just right and sitting up long enough to complete a letter.

She gently opened the present at the seams, careful not to tear the paper. It didn't matter, since the gift was wrapped in newspaper, but it had become a habit. The book revealed was clearly a used copy, and Catherine was glad that its purchase would not have been too dear.

Gone with the Wind, Catherine read. "Oh, how wonderful!" she cried. "I have been longing to read this. Thank you, Tom!"

Noticing Mary Jane, still standing anxiously at her bedside, Catherine added, "And thank you, Mary Jane. This is a very thoughtful gift."

"I had wanted to get it for you last year," Tom admitted, "but it was still new then." He left it at that, knowing she would understand. He also left unsaid that he no longer searched out penny copies of the newest Agatha Christie novels for her. It just didn't seem likely that Catherine would find as much enjoyment in reading about murder as she once had, as fanciful as the stories were.

"I am certain that I will enjoy it. Now, you must open something, Mary Jane."

That was all it took for the children to dive into their gifts with gusto. Some were handmade, like Mary Jane's doll and Tommy's blocks, but Tom had also been able to find a few inexpensive new items that were purchased with money from Margaret that he knew she would never let him pay back.

As they proudly brought each new item to Catherine, she shared their excitement, asking what Tommy planned to build first and what Mary Jane would name her doll. Feeling the warm glow of affection between them, Catherine reflected that maybe her life wasn't so bad after all.

Chapter 23

*There seemed to be an utter lack of realization
of the dangers inherent in the material
which was being manufactured.*
Dr Cecil Drinker, 1924

January brought a blanket of snow to Ottawa, covering the lawns and cobblestone walkways and drifting around the Superior Street house as if tucking it in for the night. With a fire burning merrily in her dark, little front room, Catherine felt cozy but isolated. Tom and Eleanor left her to rest as often as possible. It was vital that she build up her strength for the upcoming hearing.

The only time they allowed her to be disturbed was when Mr Grossman arrived in a fragile looking four-seater plane to work on court preparations with his clients. Catherine thought that Mr Grossman must believe passionately in their case if he was willing to risk his life flying through winter skies in that thing!

He worked tenaciously with them, going over what questions would be asked and forming concise, effective answers. The sessions wore Catherine out, even though she laid in bed for most of them. What truly challenged her were the mandatory doctor appointments.

Tom had to carry Catherine into the small medical office. The scent of bleach assailed her nostrils, and the lights seemed far too bright. She would rather never leave her house, but Catherine knew how important this evidence was, not only for her own case but for all of the other dial painters, so she persevered. She allowed herself to be examined and measured, trying to ignore the serious expression on the physician's face.

Catherine balanced hesitantly on the scale and took her hand off Tom's arm long enough for the nurse to obtain an accurate measure.

"Seventy-one pounds," she said in a low, awestruck voice.

Catherine blinked as Tom took her back into his arms. She had always been slim, but now Catherine weighed slightly more than half of what she had when she had been healthy. She realized that she must appear to be a child in Tom's arms, rather than his wife. It brought tears to her eyes, but she fought to control them until she could weep and wallow in self-pity in the privacy of her own home.

The potions and powders simply weren't working. Catherine couldn't eat regular food, and pieces of her jawbone continued to fall out, just as Peg's had. But Catherine couldn't let herself think about Peg. She had her children to live for and Mr Grossman on her side. Surely, someone would find a cure before it was too late.

The day before they were scheduled to leave for Chicago, Tom tiptoed up to Catherine's bed with a small cupcake in hand. When he saw that she was awake, he gestured to the children, who had been waiting just outside the room. Together, they sang "Happy Birthday" to Catherine as she smiled at their out-of-tune melody.

"Happy birthday, my love," said Tom, placing the cupcake on the nightstand, where it would remain untouched.

Catherine gazed up at him full of adoration. "You are so good to me, Tom. Better than I deserve."

"Nonsense," he playfully disagreed and kissed her on the forehead.

For a moment, Catherine longed for real kisses, like she and Tom used to share, but that was impossible now. Even if her mouth weren't deteriorating before their eyes, she was far too ill to be a true wife to him now. Their eyes locked on one another, and she felt that he shared her feelings.

The children distracted Catherine from her thoughts of what she was missing. At least she had them. Tommy was growing into a strong little boy, and Mary Jane was sweet and petite.

"Let me hold you a moment longer," Catherine whispered when the children began to pull away from her embrace. To her surprise, they acquiesced and settled into her arms until she indicated to Tom that she could do no more. "Thank you," she whispered and kissed them as they were lifted from the bed.

"How old are you today, mama?" Tommy asked.

"Now, that is not a polite question to ask a lady," Tom reprimanded him, but Tommy was not upset.

He only asked, "Why?"

Catherine laughed and answered her son. "I am thirty-five today."

Tommy looked thoughtful and Mary Jane's eyes grew wide. It seemed so very old to them, so it made sense that their mother was bed-ridden and elderly in her appearance. It did not strike them that their father, who was actually older, did not share their mother's problems.

Tom jumped in before the children could comment further on their mother's advanced age.

"And tomorrow, I'm taking your mother to Chicago."

He tousled their hair and gave Mary Jane a gentle poke in her ticklish ribs.

"Is that a birthday present?" Tommy asked. He had never been to Chicago, but it sounded like a faraway, exotic land.

"In part," Tom lied. "You will have to help Eleanor while we are away for a few days. You will be the man of the house, Tommy."

The little boy puffed out his chest and assured his father that the house was safe in his hands, much to the delight of his proud mother.

"We will be home as soon as possible," Catherine said, giving them each a kiss before they were shepherded from the room so she could rest.

The next day, Tom carried Catherine to Margaret's waiting car. She drove them to the train station and waved from the platform as their train pulled away.

"Margaret cares more than she likes to let on," Catherine observed as she waved to her sister-in-law.

Tom smiled fondly and agreed. "She has always been that way. It is as though love is a sign of weakness, so she would hate for us to point it out, even to express our gratitude."

"I don't know what we would do without her and Eleanor," Catherine sighed as Margaret disappeared and the train carried them toward Chicago.

Tom patted her hand but didn't speak. So much was left unsaid between them now. Their future was so uncertain and the outlook was so bleak, it was better not to mention where it all might end. They lived in the moment. Tom's hands lovingly enveloped Catherine's, and it was enough.

It was difficult to get comfortable on the hard train seats, especially with the tumor on Catherine's hip. It had grown from the early days when her limp had gotten her fired from Radium Dial until it was now the size of a grapefruit. Catherine morbidly wondered how much less she would weigh if the tumor was removed, but doctors agreed that she was not strong enough for surgery.

Catherine shifted and wriggled in the seat for almost thirty minutes before finally settling against Tom and drifting into a restless sleep. She felt as though she had just closed her eyes when Tom gently shook her and said they would depart in a few moments.

She rubbed her eyes and placed a mint leaf in her mouth. Her pain would not allow her to chew it, but it still helped reduce the embarrassing scent of illness and decay that emanated from her own body. Catherine briefly wondered if Tom was ever disgusted with her.

He helped her slowly rise to her feet. Catherine rarely stood or walked anymore, but she wanted to try leave the train on her own. It was one thing to be carried around one's own home. She hoped to avoid the humiliation of being carried in public.

Tom grabbed their bags and held a strong arm out for Catherine to steady herself with. Slowly, they shuffled down the aisle to disembark.

An arctic blast of air struck them as they exited the train. In the winter, when the cold rolled in off Lake Michigan, visitors were left with little doubt why Chicago was referred to as the Windy City. Catherine clasped a hand down on her hat before it could blow away and almost lost her balance. Without Tom, she couldn't have done it, but, somehow, they worked their way to the edge of the street and hailed a taxi.

Tom helped Catherine inside before seeing to their bags and finally taking his own seat. The driver babbled about the city as one who is used to filling silence with their own voice.

"It's a windy one today," he observed unnecessarily. "You know, it's not the lake breeze that gives the city its nickname, but all our blowhard politicians!" He laughed uproariously at his own joke, and Catherine wondered if it were true. Either way, Chicago had more than its fair share of ferocious wind.

Tom only nodded and grunted in response to the cabbie's ongoing commentary, but their driver seemed to desire nothing more than an audience. He wished them a good time in the city as he pulled up to their cheap hotel. It was all Catherine could do to make it to the uncomfortable bed before falling into a deep slumber.

She awoke in the middle of the night to find that Tom had removed her shoes and hat and tucked her in like a weary child. Shifting on the firm mattress, pain shot through Catherine's body and throbbed in her hip. City lights peeked through the hotel curtains, and Catherine wondered what it might have been like if she and Tom had been able to vacation there when she was healthy.

What if instead of visiting doctors and lawyers they could go shopping and dancing? She may as well wonder what might happen if aliens landed on Earth. Catherine might not be able to go out on the town with her husband, but she watched the city lights twinkling merrily and thought of others who strolled beneath them without a care in the world and was happy for them.

She wondered if Tommy would one day court a pretty girl. Or maybe Mary Jane would come to the city on the train with a group of friends. She prayed, not for the first time, that her children would be spared the burdens that had been placed upon her own thin shoulders. She prayed daily for their health, especially Mary Jane who appeared and behaved like a much younger child.

Catherine wished that she could stand and walk to the window, but she had to be content with the sliver of a view offered through the slightly parted curtains. Simple things, like the ability to get out of bed on her own, were what she missed most. Walking down a street through scattered fall leaves, lifting her children into her arms, kissing her husband – how she wished she hadn't taken them for granted.

A slow tear rolled down to Catherine's pillow, and the lights of Chicago blurred into an indistinct glow.

Chapter 24

That was the first time I knew that radium might be dangerous. The company had never told us a thing.
Luminous Processes Employee, 1952

Tom gently assisted Catherine with dressing and preparing herself for court. She watched a wave of grief pass over his face as her dress slid over the bulging tumor on her hip. He quickly controlled his features and offered her a slight smile.

"Feeling alright?" he asked, running fingers through her thinning hair.

"No, but well enough to do what must be done."

His smile turned grim as a reflection of her own, and he nodded.

"You are so strong, Catherine," he murmured and placed a soft kiss on her sunken cheek. "I love you so much."

She pressed her lips harder together and fought with her emotions. When she could respond without her voice cracking, she gazed deep into his eyes, hoping that he would understand everything she didn't say.

"I love you too, Tom. More than you know, but not as well as you deserve."

She saw his Adam's apple shift as Tom gulped down his own emotions. Then he leaned down and lifted his wife into his arms as if she were a small child and carried her to the waiting taxi.

They did not speak as the sights and sounds of Chicago flew by. It was such an alien world of healthy people caught up in routine activities that were beyond Catherine's scope of possibilities. She watched women strolling, laughing, and window shopping and wondered what she would do if she was made whole again.

The view before Catherine's eyes slid away as her imagination replaced it with a vision of herself at home, playing with her children, working in the garden, and making love to her husband. If she could, she wouldn't perform profound tasks or great deeds. She only wanted to do what most other women took for granted every single day.

Catherine forced herself to focus on the skyscrapers and occasional glimpses of Lake Michigan. Today was not a day for daydreams or self-pity. This day in court must be a victory, not just for her family, but for every family devastated by corporate greed and worker exploitation. Though she could barely stand, Catherine would stand up for them all.

The taxi slowed and the door opened. Catherine didn't move. She knew she didn't have the strength, so she didn't try. Tom appeared, dapper in his three-piece suit and slightly tilted hat. Her heart wanted to burst just looking at him, but enough of her was broken so she held her heart together.

Tom asked her to wait as a friend who had arranged to meet them brought a wooden chair from the courthouse to the edge of the street. They had discussed this, but Catherine still hated that it needed to be done. While she was light enough for Tom to carry her as far as necessary, she was easily bruised and even her bones easily broken. Therefore, they had decided to transport her from the street to the courtroom sitting on a chair in a sad mockery of a queen being carried on a throne above her subjects.

Of course, Tom and Clarence did not raise her high above them but kept the chair low and well-protected by their strong bodies on either side. Catherine kept her eyes on her hands folded in her lap. She didn't want to know how many people observed this humiliating scene. She felt, rather than saw, that they made it to the elevator, and the lurch upward put painful pressure on her joints and made her stomach flip.

When the door opened, she risked a glimpse into the hallway and was grateful to see only friendly faces, including Marie, Pearl, and a determined looking Leonard Grossman. Seeing him gave Catherine the encouragement she needed. With the might of Radium Dial standing opposed to her, she felt confident next to Leonard Grossman.

Mr Grossman's suit was distinguished and, Catherine was sure, expensive. Even the air around him seemed slightly scented with what she could only describe as intellectual power. He led the group into a room with little space to spare between the walls and a large conference table, and the men carefully placed Catherine's chair on the floor.

She assumed that this was a room where they would confer as a group before going into the courtroom. Maybe Catherine had read too many novels, for she had envisioned testifying before a judge in white wig and black robes, sitting high above her on a throne-like chair in a large, intimidating room. Therefore, she was surprised when Mr Grossman informed them that this was the room the hearing would be held in.

"The Industrial Commission judge will enter shortly," Mr Grossman said, even pointing to the door he would pass through. "His name is George Marvel, and I have every reason to believe that he will be fair and sympathetic."

Catherine pondered this choice of words. She wasn't sure she would have previously put them together, but she couldn't think of a more suitable way to describe a desirable judge for their case. Mr Grossman was still speaking, so she tried to stop her mind from wandering. He was repeating instructions that he had given the women many times, but instead of being irritating it was calming. They were ready.

A grandfatherly man walked in, and Catherine could tell by the way Mr Grossman respectfully tilted his head toward him that this was the judge. Before she had any time to consider his grey hair and black-frame glasses, more people spilled into the room as if George Marvel had been the dam holding them back.

Catherine wondered which of them were from Radium Dial and was surprised again when many of them took seats set up beyond the table for those who wished to observe. Press, Catherine suddenly realized, spotting a few cameras and notebooks. She swallowed hard and said a silent prayer.

She knew the Radium Dial representatives as soon as she laid eyes on them because they were the only ones dressed in suits more impressive than Mr Grossman's. Idly wondering if they were from Chicago or the even more glamorous New York, Catherine watched them take seats across the table from her. Their lawyer had explained that Radium Dial was sending a legal team with only a single corporate employee. None of the group looked familiar to Catherine, and she wondered if she would rather Mr Reed or some other familiar face was among their ranks.

No, she decided. Better to face an enemy that does not conjure up such a strong sense of betrayal as would one who watched Catherine's deterioration, knew the cause of it, and did nothing.

Each person was introduced as the hearing began, and Catherine learned that Arthur Magid was the sole current Radium Dial employee present. He was comfortably insulated by his expensive legal team and spoke only when required. Not a glimmer of pity shone in his eyes when he dismissively glanced at the ruined bodies of the former dial painters.

The hearing began not with the dramatic banging of a gavel, but with Mr Marvel announcing, "Alright then, let's begin."

As Mr Grossman launched into his opening statement, Catherine discretely touched a handkerchief to the corner of her lips, hoping that none of the sharp-eyed reporters noticed the pus that oozed from her damaged mouth. They might not have noticed, but Mr Grossman did. Catherine saw his face harden in determination to make Radium Dial pay for the condition they had left her in.

He was a born speaker, and Catherine supposed that was what made him such a successful lawyer. Gooseflesh popped up on her arms when he proclaimed, "Under the intrepid Illinois Industrial Commission, larger and larger grows the brightening rainbow of our hopes for the right against the wrong, and the weak against the strong."

Mr Grossman would have made a glorious preacher, but Catherine was grateful that God had made him a lawyer instead. Her lawyer. Seeming to hear her thoughts he gestured toward her.

"Women painted luminous dials on instruments for US forces of the Great War. They have sacrificed their own lives to make others safe. Catherine Donohue is a heroine, and our state owes her a debt."

Catherine blushed and looked down to hide her face. She thought of women who had actually painted the dials for army watches and instrument panels. She hadn't joined Radium Dial until after the war, and she felt unfit to be categorized with those earlier women.

The Radium Dial lawyers seemed unfazed, and none of them less so than the one who stood to make their opening statement. He stood, smoothed his suit as though it didn't already fall in perfect line with his trim frame. Catherine was so mesmerized by his dismissive countenance and gestures that she almost forgot to listen to his words.

As had been the case at the hearing in Ottawa, the legalese was difficult to follow, but Catherine understood perfectly when he stated, "We will demonstrate that radium is not and has never been the source of any of the varied illnesses that these disgruntled former employees bring before the Commission. In addition, while there is a casual relationship between these women's employment and their conditions, radioactive substances may be abrasive, but they are not poisonous, and therefore are not covered by current workmen's compensation legislation. Radium Dial cannot legally be held liable for any disease caused by radium, even if one were proven to exist."

Then it was her turn to testify. Catherine could not hide the damage done to her mouth when she spoke. She had lost count of how many pieces of her jaw had fallen out. Many of her teeth were gone and replaced by unhealing sores. It made it difficult for her to enunciate, a humiliating truth that caused her to hesitate when she needed to be bold.

She saw an image of her younger self marching up the steps of the Radium Dial building as she described the environment with paint dust omnipresent in the air and on their clothes. "I remember wearing my going out dress to work once, so that I would glow like an angel for my Tom that evening." She heard Tom sniff in the seat behind her, but she could not see him.

When the judge asked her to describe dial painting, her reluctance fled. "We dipped the brush into the paint, sharpened the tip with our lips, and traced the numbers on the dials." It seemed so innocuous, so ridiculous that they were dying for it. She cried, "That's how this terrible poison got into our systems. We never even knew it was harmful!"

Mr Grossman laid a calming hand on her arm, and she paused. She breathed in and out. She reached for a glass of water, took a drink, and finished answering the judge's questions in a submissive voice.

Pulling a sheet from the stack of papers in front of him, Mr Grossman requested to introduce a piece of evidence. Arthur Magid was craning his neck to see it and insistently smacked the arm of one of the Radium Dial lawyers once he realized what it was.

"Objection," the lawyer obediently announced.

"This is a full-page advertisement from the *Ottawa Times*, paid for by Radium Dial," Mr Grossman continued, unaffected by the opposition.

Mr Marvel nodded and accepted the page into evidence, overruling the objection with a hard glance.

Catherine's eyes followed the page as it was passed around. Although she could not make out the words, she remembered them. She was glad when the judge asked her if she had seen the advertisement when it was originally published.

"Yes, sir," she stated, feeling foolish that she had not seen it for the propaganda that it was. "After those New Jersey girls died from radium poisoning, we were alarmed, but Mr Reed called our attention to the advertisement." She nodded toward the page in the judge's hand. "He said we didn't have to worry . . . . so we didn't."

Her words had grown quiet, but it didn't reduce the impact of them. The company had lied to them – had known that some of them would die – and lied to them anyway. In the silence that followed her statement, Mr Marvel studied the advertisement, underlining sections and furrowing his brow. What Catherine would have given to read his mind.

Finally, he looked up at her and asked about the examinations that Radium Dial doctors had performed. Catherine dutifully replied, making sure her voice rang clear and true when she testified that the company had declared them all in the best of health.

"When that proved not to be true, what did you do?" he asked.

Catherine took a deep breath. Would things have turned out differently if they had realized the signs when they first appeared? Would she be healthy now if she had quit working at the first sign of a limp? She closed her eyes and willed the questions away, all except the question Mr Marvel had asked.

"We asked for the reports," she slowly stated. "Mr Reed." Now part of her wished he was here to face her. "He told us that if he gave us our medical reports there would be a riot." She pressed her lips together, took another breath, and continued, "We didn't realize what he meant."

She pondered if the judge was wondering how they could have been so stupid. It seemed so obvious in retrospect. Catherine held her head steady because she wanted to shake it in disbelief at her own naivety. Something at that moment caused her to look down the line of her co-litigants, her friends. She was comforted by the feelings she saw reflected in their eyes. They had been fooled, treated like they were less than human, but that was why they were here. Together.

A pile of papers was handed to the judge, and he began to page slowly through them. Catherine was surprised when Mr Grossman introduced them as his next piece of evidence.

"I accept into evidence the medical test results of Radium

Dial employees," Mr Marvel murmured, clearly distracted by his search through the pages. "Where are the years 1925 and 1928?" he asked with a stern gaze toward the Radium Dial legal team.

"We have been unable to locate them," was the nonchalant reply.

Mr Marvel raised an eyebrow but continued his appraisal without further comment. After a moment, he laid them aside with a disappointed snort.

"What were you told about the medical test results?" he asked Catherine.

"Mr Reed said we were perfectly healthy." She remembered when she had stood before him with Charlotte, and he had mocked them even then. "He said he didn't think there was anything wrong with us. He refused to consider our request for compensation."

The judge's round face and friendly eyes made it easy to confide in him. Catherine's voice grew in strength as he eased her story from her with simple questions. She was beginning to shake with fatigue, but she retold every detail of her limp starting and how the pain had slowly spread, slowly enough that the truth didn't dawn until much too late.

A tear rolled down her cheek when she recalled the first time that she had been unable to kneel in church. She referred to notes for the dates that her teeth had fallen out. Then she held out a small box that had been tucked away in her coat pocket.

"What is this?" Mr Marvel asked with an open curious gaze.

Catherine cursed her fumbling fingers as she struggled to open the box. Her joints were stiff, and weariness was weighing her down. Finally, the top sprang free, and she held the box out to Mr Marvel in a quaking hand.

"These are pieces of my jawbone," she stated in a voice

muffled by deformity and mucus.

Silence settled in the room, and Catherine knew they must have been imagining the same thing she was. Dipping the brush into the paint, creating a precise tip with her own lips. The poison had invaded her body and attacked it from the inside, leaving her defenseless and broken.

And they had known.

Catherine was so proud of her testimony that she struggled for a moment to understand what was being discussed afterward. Mr Grossman had introduced another piece of evidence, letters on Radium Dial letterhead, but she had received no such letter. When realization came, she felt as though struck by a bolt of lightning.

"The crux of the matter is that Radium Dial carries no workmen's compensation insurance because they have been denied by ten different companies. Rather than discontinuing the operations that made them uninsurable, they carried the risk themselves and have attempted to hide their assets to minimize their responsibility to my clients."

Catherine deflated visibly when the truth became clear. Only $10,000 in assets had been discovered to pay out to Radium Dial's victims. If they won their case. It wasn't a drop in the bucket compared to the medical expenses they'd already compiled, and each of the women present faced a future filled with continued medical expenses and no cure in sight.

"No," Catherine whispered so quietly that no one heard. All this, and she wouldn't even be able to ease Tom's burden. He would be left with bills long after he ceased to have a wife. How utterly unfair.

Chapter 25

Why go on killing people for more money?
Dr James Davidson, 1924

Certain that she had endured the most difficult portion of the hearing, Catherine relaxed a little. She had said everything she and Mr Grossman had talked about. She had been sympathetic but not pitiful. It was a little disappointing that the hearing carried on when she felt like it should have been over.

But it wasn't finished. Dr Dalitsch was called as an expert medical witness. Catherine did not look forward to hearing herself discussed and analyzed, so she allowed her mind to wander. It snapped back to focus when the judge asked Dr Dalitsch for his opinion on Catherine's diagnosis.

The doctor's dark eyes found Catherine's, and he spoke to her as he answered Mr Marvel's question. "Mrs Donohue suffers from radium poisoning."

Again, Catherine felt like that should be the final word, but Mr Grossman was already asking more questions. Could she work and other observations that were self-evident without a medical degree. Catherine was tempted to drift into daydream when Mr Grossman asked a question that brought everyone to attention.

"Have you an opinion if this condition is fatal?"

Now the doctor did not look at Catherine. He looked at the judge. "Must I answer in the patient's presence?" he asked, sounding a bit like Tommy when trying to wheedle out of something he didn't want to do.

Catherine forgot her handkerchief, and pus began to leak in a thin line toward her chin. She willed the doctor to look at her, but he refused. Is this condition fatal, Mr Grossman had asked. Catherine looked at the doctor, who looked pleadingly at the judge, who looked pityingly at her.

And she screamed.

Any remaining hope she had clung to was washed away by crashing waves of reality. The faces of doctors passed before her eyes. They hadn't told her, but she should have seen it there. Whatever happened today, she was going to die.

Sobs shook her tiny, delicate frame, sending needles of pain into her joints. She covered her face, so that reporters wouldn't get a picture of her mouth, cringingly open and drooling as she lost control. Catherine shrieked and cried and started slipping from her chair.

Hands grabbed her before she could fall to the ground, but she could feel bruises begin to form even as visions of her children passed before her mind's eye. She would not see them grow up. Another scream echoed around the room, drowning out the murmur of reporters, the click of camera shutters, and the quieter weeping of her friends.

She felt Tom's arms around her and realized that he had picked her up out of the hateful chair. His warmth and strength gave her none of the comfort they usually brought. Sobs continued to shake her, and she realized that they were his. Tom cried openly as he carried his wife out of the room, away from her audience, and into a quiet space. But he could not escape the doom that followed them.

Catherine felt a hand on her wrist and wondered which of the doctors was taking her pulse. It did not matter. They knew she was dying. Just like Radium Dial had known. Everyone had known but hadn't told her.

All the potions, treatments, x-rays, and exams. It had all been for nothing. She was dying.

Pearl's voice was trying to break through the mist that was fogging Catherine's mind, but she couldn't make out the words. She was lying down now, but she couldn't imagine where. Wasn't she in the middle of a hearing? She felt Tom's hands slip her glasses off as tears streamed from her eyes. It hurt to cry. Everything hurt. The rest of her life, however short it was to be, would hurt. She bawled harder.

She felt her hopelessly loose watch slide up and down her thin arm in time with her harsh, gasping breath. Pearl and Tom stroked her hair and her arms. Their voices began to reach her in a comforting murmur. Another voice came from within, telling her, "Do not be afraid." Catherine hiccupped and sniffed as a strange office came into focus around her. She was lying on a desk.

With her remaining strength, she clutched at Tom's hand and begged, "Don't leave me, Tom."

He cried something in return, but she did not hear him. She did not hear anything, and the blackness soothed her.

†

She didn't know how long she was there, sprawled across some courthouse employee's desk. Every part of her ached. The traveling and testifying had been bad enough, but Catherine's own emotional breakdown had left her utterly destroyed. And after the doctor's words, she wondered if it was possible to recover from her collapse.

Shifting slightly in an effort to gain some modicum of comfort, Catherine's knees knocked together and sent shockwaves of pain up her legs until it rested in her hips. It brought to mind a familiar hymn. Stricken, smitten, and afflicted – that was how she felt, and she wondered if that was blasphemy.

Is this how Jesus felt when He cried out, when He groaned in pain? Catherine took some strange comfort in knowing that her Savior had also suffered, so He understood her grief. She began to weakly hum the song to herself, attempting to recall the words. Some of them came to her, but many did not. A presence of deep peace came over her when the last lines came clearly into her mind.

None shall ever be confounded who on Him their hope have built.

Catherine rested in that peace, humming disjointedly as her mind wandered around sacred mysteries. When even humming became a chore, she fell silent while images of a possible heaven flashed through her mind, mingled with memories of family and friends. She tried to ponder what it meant, but she was so tired.

"Tom," she whispered, wondering if she was dying, alone in a stranger's office, far away from her children. Or maybe, she contemplated vaguely, this was purgatory.

"I am here," he quickly replied. He squeezed her hand ever so gently, and Catherine realized that he had been holding it the entire time, however long that was.

"Thank God," she mumbled before fading back into oblivion.

When she next woke, Pearl seemed to discern her consciousness before she opened her eyes. A soft hand stroked Catherine's hair, and Pearl whispered soothing words close to her ear. It really was unfair that Pearl had not been able to have more children. Mothering came so naturally to her, but maybe that compassion had been instilled in Pearl for moments such as this.

Catherine wanted to ask what was happening. Had she slept through the night? Had the hearing continued? However, she had only the strength to open her eyes and search out Pearl's kindly face.

Of course, Pearl understood what Catherine needed to know.

"Tom is testifying now, but he will take you home soon."

She did not say that Tom, too, had broken down, that he bravely endured listening to the doctors' continued testimony regarding his wife's inevitable demise. Pearl only murmured and soothed, keeping buried deep in her own heart that grief that had pierced it when Dr Dalitsch admitted that Catherine had not more than months to live.

"She is beyond a doubt in the terminal stages of the disease," Dr Weiner had also stoically testified.

It was Pearl's job to stand between her dear friend and these harsh truths. She didn't need to hear them. There was no way for her not to know as she laid there, scarcely more to her than faintly glowing bones.

†

Catherine felt herself lifted and moved, but one of the doctors must have administered opium or morphine because the world moved around her as if she were not a part of it. The pain was blissfully eased, and Tom's voice assured her of his presence. It was enough.

Catherine was not restored to full consciousness until the next day, when she awoke in her own front room. She breathed in the fragrance of the low fire and simmering soup, feeling an unfamiliar stir of hunger. It made her wonder what time it was and if Eleanor was there.

As of in answer to her thought, Eleanor entered the room

with a bowl of soup in her hands. She beamed when she saw that Catherine was awake.

"How do you feel this morning?"

Catherine wasn't sure. "Hungry."

Eleanor chuckled and drew up a chair close to the bed. "That is good. Let me help you."

After propping Catherine with some pillows, Eleanor began to feed her the rich soup in small spoonfulls. She chattered about the children but said nothing of the hearing until it was clear Catherine had eaten all she could.

"The hearing will continue here today."

"What? Here?" Catherine wasn't sure she had heard correctly. Her brain was still in a medicated fog. "In Ottawa?"

"Here, in your room," Eleanor clarified, gesturing to their surroundings.

"Oh." Catherine didn't know what else to say. She looked around her sickroom and wondered what it would be like to see Mr Marvel and Mr Grossman at her bedside. "But why?"

Eleanor took a few moments making unnecessary adjustments to Catherine's bedding before she responded.

"They just want to make sure you can finish your testimony as comfortably as possible."

"How very kind," Catherine whispered, drifting off into sleep once more.

She didn't think she slept long, because the angle of the sun filtering through the thin curtains seemed the same when she opened her eyes again. Sounds of people moving about in other rooms of the house and preparing for their day surrounded Catherine, but she was helpless to move. The trip had left her weak, weary, and uncertain if she would ever feel better again.

Dr Dalitsch's face appeared before her as he asked if he

must give Catherine's prognosis in her presence as clearly as if he were truly standing there. Past her initial shock, Catherine felt sympathy for the good doctor who had tried to shelter her from the worst, who had concocted what he hoped were cures, and who had done much of it for free since the Donohues could not pay.

She could reflect now upon the news with a stoicism that she had not felt less than twenty-four hours earlier.

The Lord is my shepherd. I shall not want.

"Walk with me through this valley of death," she whispered in prayer. She closed her eyes and asked God for the strength she needed to complete the hearing and see justice done. The sound of shuffling feet brought her out of her divine communication.

"You're awake," Tom observed, somewhat uncertainly.

"I am. I was praying." Catherine added a smile to reassure him that yesterday's scene would not be repeated.

"I feel that I have been doing that all night," he admitted, crossing the room to her and sitting at her side. He smoothed her hair and added, "Pearl is coming early to help you prepare."

Catherine sighed. "I don't know how much preparation I can tolerate." She looked down at her bedclothes, a fine white nightdress that Charlotte had designed and sewed for her. "I would appreciate it if Pearl fixed my hair, but I will remain dressed as I am."

Tom nodded and kissed her forehead. "Can I bring you anything?"

"No. I've had some soup."

"Have you?"

The bright hope on his face broke her heart, but she smiled again.

"I have. Eleanor is a treasure."

Tom returned her smile and left to see everything was

prepared for the judge and lawyers to arrive with a small spring in his step that hadn't been there when he came in.

He deserved a tiny smidgen of false hope. After all, he had been bolstering her up with mountains of it for years.

Catherine breathed in deeply and slowly released it, replaying the words of her remaining testimony in her head over and over again.

Unsurprisingly, Mr Grossman was the first to arrive. He was almost as attentive as Tom, and Catherine enjoyed the warm feeling of having a fatherly figure to look after her. She felt a ripple of strength run through her when she assured him that she could complete her testimony.

"It's too late for me, but maybe it will help some of the others. If I win this fight, my children will be safe and my friends who worked with me and contracted the same disease will win too."

Mr Grossman positively beamed at her. "Good girl," he said, his comforting hand stopping short of touching her fragile flesh. He turned away quickly, but she had caught the glint of tears in his eyes.

Tom greeted him and was faced with the same question.

"Are you up to this, Tom?"

Catherine saw his jaw clench, but when he spoke it was in complete support of her. "Catherine wants to do this, even if the excitement of it . . . ."

Tom did not turn away when tears filled his eyes. He let the lawyer see them, and his passion and grief were like fuel to the older man.

"We will see justice done," Mr Grossman said, firmly grasping Tom's shoulder. "Your wife is an amazing woman."

Tom looked past him at Catherine. "Of course, I know

that," he agreed with a lopsided smile that Catherine realized she had not seen in quite some time. Then it faded. "We've just had so little time together."

A knock on the door ended their moment. It was time to begin again.

Pearl strode in, looking nervous but determined. Catherine was glad to see her tension visibly ease when she saw that Catherine was, at least, awake and alert.

At first, Catherine didn't notice that someone else had arrived with Pearl, but her breath caught in her throat when she did.

"Charlotte!"

"Oh, you poor, dear thing!" Charlotte cried, rushing to Catherine's side and grasping her hand firmly enough to cause pain. "I just had to come." She glanced up at Pearl. "I am just so thankful to Pearl for letting me know what happened. How I wish I'd been there for you."

"This is not the time for guilt or regrets," Catherine insisted. "You are here now and that is what matters."

"You're wearing the nightdress." Charlotte was quick to spot her own handiwork. "How lovely it is on you."

"Little did you know it would be my court day dress."

Charlotte's voice grew quiet and lost its animation. "How I wish that it wasn't."

Pearl interrupted, "Let's get your hair combed and straighten those covers."

Catherine grinned and almost said, "Yes, mother," but caught herself, knowing the words would be hurtful to her barren friend.

As Pearl and Charlotte made the best they could of Catherine's appearance, they chatted and giggled as if they were young girls crowded into Peg Looney's house again. Catherine's mind wandered to those days, remembering Marie pretending to faint in front of the pharmacist and dancing at the shack. They had painted their faces and fingernails with the magical glow-in-the-dark paint....

"They are here." Mr Grossman's voice dragged Catherine back to the present and silenced Pearl and Charlotte's gossiping. The women knelt at Catherine's side, and they prayed together until the lawyers, doctors, and judge were brought into the room.

Pearl and Charlotte stood but remained as close as possible as men squeezed into the small family room. Catherine was so grateful for Charlotte's presence, but she tried not to think about the fact that her friend appeared ill, wrapped in her coat even indoors with an empty sleeve dangling desolately at her side. She recognized the foul odor that Charlotte tried to cover with mint leaves because it was the same that emanated from her own mouth.

Catherine dabbed at the corner of her lips and closed her eyes. She tried to save her strength and waited for the questions to begin.

When she sensed someone kneel at her side, she opened her eyes. She had expected it to be Tom, but he was anxiously standing in the doorway as if he thought he might have to race from the room. Ensuring that the children didn't enter the room, Catherine realized.

Instead, at her side knelt Leonard Grossman, dignified in his three-piece suit but on the floor to more personally and gently question his dying client.

Catherine tried to keep her eyes open, but she was overtaken by weariness. It was too difficult to take in the unfamiliar faces in her home and think about her answers at the same time, so she let her eyelids flutter down and limit the information her brain had to process.

Mr Grossman's biblically deep voice filtered into her head.

"Mrs Donohue, can you show us how you were taught to point your brush?"

Had they discussed this? She wasn't sure, so she forced her eyelids partially open to discover Mr Grossman holding out a small paintbrush. It was Tommy's, from his Easter gift. Her stomach turned at the idea of even pretending that her son's brush was coated in that greenish-white poison, but Mr Grossman met her eye. The understanding and encouragement she found there gave her just enough strength.

As she was reaching out, telling herself to pretend it wasn't Tommy's, just do what she had done hundreds of times before, a harsh voice halted her hand.

"Objection!"

Catherine closed her eyes and dropped her hand.

"We object to the use of this brush, as it is not the type used in the dial painting studio."

It must be one of the Radium Dial lawyers, Catherine thought without opening her eyes to investigate, or that horrible Arthur Magid.

Then Mr Marvel's voice, calm and nonplussed, "Is it possible to obtain a dial painting brush, Mr Grossman?"

Catherine had to smirk slightly at his caustic reply.

"Yes, they are being used now at the Luminous Processes plant, which is using all the equipment of Radium Dial, and employs some of the same women. They even have an official there who is originally from Radium Dial."

She forgave him if he sounded just a bit smug.

"Objection withdrawn," was said much more quietly than it had been raised.

When the quiet lingered, Catherine peeked through slitted eyelids and realized the brush was being proffered once again. So, she raised her hand to take it. Watching her fingers grip the tiny brush, Catherine realized how much her hands had aged in a few short years. Her fingers were bony, and the skin hung loosely from her arm. Her watch slid halfway to her elbow as she raised her hand.

The brush taken, she looked at it for a moment and wondered how such an innocent object could deliver pain and death. She hadn't worked in a munitions factory or any other number of places that one might expect to have accidents or illnesses. Catherine had been one of the lucky few to paint in a studio.

They had thought they were better than other girls their age. She wondered if some of those women laughed at them now. Then she realized that Mr Grossman was nodding at her with eyebrows raised.

Everyone was watching her.

She cleared her throat and said in as strong a voice as she could muster, "Here's how it's done." She mimed dipping the brush in a pot of paint, but decided she should also add, "We dipped it in the radium compound mixture." She saw Mr Grossman smile as she moved the brush from her imaginary paint pot toward her mouth. Her elbow ached with the movement, and her throat threatened to close as if she was truly introducing more poison to her body. "Then we shaped it like this." A sob caught in her throat on the last word as the brush touched her sunken lips.

She twirled the brush, more slowly than she used to do when she did it dozens of times each day. Lord, how had they been so stupid?!

Her hand began to shake and her eyes brimmed with tears,

but she held the brush out toward Mr Grossman. They both stared at its perfectly pointed bristles as if expecting a demon to suddenly appear.

Catherine heard Charlotte sob, and she raised her eyes to Mr Grossman's. He pressed his lips tightly together and took the brush, holding it high for all present to see. Camera shutters clicked and pencils scratched in notebooks.

Into this tense quiet, Catherine spoke again. "I did this thousands and thousands of times. That was the way we were told to do it."

She heard someone else crying and realized it was Tom. Guilt washed over her, and it was worse than any pain she had been forced to endure. Poor, dear Tom. She closed her eyes.

However, Mr Grossman wasn't done making accusations in his best preacher voice.

"Did any official of Radium Dial ever tell you that the use of camel-hair brushes with radium compounds had been officially condemned?"

Catherine's eyes flashed open to see her anger reflected on the faces of her friends.

"No. Nobody ever told us that."

"Objection!"

"Sustained," Catherine was surprised to hear Mr Marvel announce, but Mr Grossman was used to these tactics. He rephrased the question.

"Was there any notice posted regarding the dangers of radium dial-painting with camel-hair brushes?"

"No." Catherine was going to leave it at that, but fury began to build in her. They had done this, and now they were trying to cover it up. They weren't even sorry. "There were no notices of that kind. Mr Reed encouraged us to eat our lunches at our workstations as long as we didn't get food on the dials." She had to stop to catch her breath, but she gasped and went on before anyone could interrupt. "All they were worried about was grease spots on the dials."

Catherine felt Mr Grossman's hand on her shoulder as she wheezed and tried to steady her breathing. He waited before asking his next question. When Catherine gave him an almost imperceptible nod, he continued.

"At any point, did Radium Dial offer you another method of dial painting."

Her answer was a short bark of laughter before she mentioned the glass pens. "We used them for less than a day before asking for our brushes. They gave them back without another word about it. We got more done that way."

Catherine no longer heard the reactions around her. Marie's angry grunts, Charlotte's sobs, and Tom's sniffling faded away as concentrated on the truth that she had to testify to while she still could.

"How did your employment at Radium Dial end?" Mr Grossman asked, and she almost laughed again.

"I had developed a limp," she began. How she hated reliving the humiliation of her demotion and eventual firing. Catherine remembered the disdainful way people had looked at her. Even worse, some townspeople were still defending Radium Dial under the guise of Luminous Processes.

A reporter tried to hide a sob by clearing their throat when Catherine reached the part where Mr Reed told her she would have to leave because her limp wasn't good for company morale.

Catherine took refuge in darkness again while the testimony of her friends carried on around her. Mr Grossman asked Charlotte about losing her arm.

"Thirteen months," she had bitterly stated when asked how long she had been an employee of Radium Dial. Then she sounded even angrier when asked about confronting Mr Reed when they were seeking compensation for their injuries. "He said there wasn't any such thing as radium poisoning."

Murmurs of shock filled the room. How could anyone look at a woman with one arm and tell her there was nothing wrong with her?

Catherine heard a clicking sound while Marie was testifying. It went on so long that she forced her eyes open to determine what it was. She saw Marie's hands furiously clench and release, clench and release. Her rings clicked each time she brought them together.

Each of the women was asked about Catherine's demonstration of pointing her brush. Was it accurate? Had they done it?

Yes and yes, every time.

Then it was Tom's turn, and Catherine didn't know if she could take it. Could she listen to her husband recount the hardship and struggle that he endured because of her? Would she scream, cry, and collapse all over again? She already wanted to.

Mr Grossman asked Tom to briefly reiterate Catherine's condition and how it had devolved since their marriage. "Six years ago," Tom said when asked when they had been married, and Catherine was taken aback to realize it had been that recently. It seemed like a lifetime ago, and she supposed it was.

"How has this impacted your personal finances?"

Catherine almost groaned to hear her husband so thoroughly and publicly humiliated. Tom robotically listed dollar amounts for Ottawa doctors, Dr Loffler, Dr Dalitsch, trips to Chicago, x-ray treatments, medicines, and the list kept going. It was even longer than Catherine realized it would be.

When Tom stopped, Mr Grossman asked him how they had paid for the thousands of dollars in expenses.

Tom took a deep breath. "Well, sir, I have to admit that I have been forced to mortgage our home. Twice actually. My parents and my sister have also given us generous gifts, and we have exhausted the inheritance that Catherine received from her uncle."

"The uncle from whom she inherited this house?" Mr Grossman urged him to continue.

"Yes, that's right."

"Therefore, Mrs Donohue is at risk of losing her entire inheritance, is that correct?"

Tom's head drooped, and the answer was a mumbled, "Yes."

Mr Marvel was closing the hearing and giving the legal teams their instructions for submitting their written arguments when Catherine realized she had dozed off. She tried to look around and see if anyone had noticed her sleeping, but her eyelids were so heavy. The sun seemed far too bright streaming in the window. Could it really only be midday?

As Catherine was considering this, Mr Marvel shuffled his way around through the crowd. He wanted to be back in Chicago tonight, Catherine thought as she imagined this sympathetic man around a dinner table with a happy family.

Before she realized what she was doing, she reached out to him. If Mr Marvel was shocked, he didn't let it show. He simply took the thin, delicate hand in his own and said, "God bless you, Mrs Donohue," before he left.

As the men filed out, sounds of giggling and stomping feet came from the stairway. Tommy and Mary Jane rushed into the room with Eleanor hot on their heels.

"I'm sorry, Mr Donohue. They somehow knew the hearing was over. Shall I take them back upstairs?"

"That's quite alright," Tom reassured her. "I'm sure they saw people leaving from the window seat." He raised an eyebrow at his son, who grinned mischievously. "Their mother would like to see them for a moment before she gets some rest."

Mary Jane needed no more invitation. She scooted up close to Catherine and began babbling about the games she and Tommy had played while they waited upstairs.

"You were very well behaved," Catherine agreed, smiling but still fighting to stay awake.

"A picture please, ma'am?" a lingering reporter asked politely but eagerly. Catherine heard Tom begin to object, but she raised her own voice.

"Yes, please," she said, remembering the power of the *Times* articles. Let the world see what Radium Dial had done to her and her children.

Tom reluctantly helped her sit up and the children scrambled up next to her. Catherine was still struggling to keep her eyes open when she heard the camera shutter click.

"Thank you, ma'am."

Finally, everyone was gone, and Catherine slept.

Chapter 26

I belong to a class of woman of which the medical profession does not know the reason for their illness.
Pearl Payne, 1937

"I have an idea," Pearl gushed, unable to contain her excitement.

Catherine had not been able to leave her bed since the hearing and had stopped wondering if she ever would. If the thought occurred to her, she fixed her eyes on the crucifix that Tom had hung on the wall near the head of her bed. If it was God's will, she could accept it.

"I have an idea, Catherine," Pearl repeated in an attempt to get Catherine to focus on her words.

"I'm sorry, dear Pearl. What is it?"

"I've written to Mr Grossman." When Pearl could see that this did not seem important to her friend, she carried on. "I've suggested that we begin a humanitarian organization that will help people like us, people who have been harmed by their employers and need help."

"That's a brilliant idea," Catherine said without much enthusiasm. "I'm not sure what I can do."

"You are already doing it," Pearl said. "Winning this case. Being the media darling. Raising awareness that people like us exist."

Catherine smirked. Media darling was a bit of a stretch, but it was nice to see Pearl excited about something.

"He has agreed to meet with some of us." Seeing Catherine's wrinkled brow, Pearl made a show of rolling her eyes. "Mr Grossman!"

"Oh, of course," Catherine murmured. It was such a struggle even to think anymore.

Pearl left in a flurry of excitement, so Catherine only heard later what her friend had decided to name the new organization: The Society of the Living Dead.

Not sure how to feel about this, Catherine looked down at her emaciated body. It was barely perceptible beneath the blankets required to keep her warm and comfortable. She concluded that the name was appropriate.

Tom brought her a thick green file, and he smiled when Catherine asked what it was.

"Mr Grossman has submitted his legal brief to Judge Marvel." He held up the stack of paper and made a show of leafing through it. "This is your copy."

Catherine's eyes, so often heavy-lidded with sleepiness, opened wide. "Oh my!" she gasped. "It is longer than an Agatha Christie novel."

His boyish grin in place, Tom admitted that she might be right. "I don't rightly know just how it compares, but the secretary said this brief – though that's a funny word for it – is eighty-thousand words if it's a page."

"Eighty-thousand," Catherine murmured in amazement. And it was all about her. Written by Mr Grossman, who was receiving no fees. "God bless him."

"Indeed," Tom agreed, still thumbing through the hundreds of typed pages. "He may not be using a sling-shot, but he's the closest thing to David I've ever seen."

Tom also read bits of news articles to her regarding the

progress of her case, and Catherine was astounded by the sight of her own picture on the front page. He stopped when he saw her eyes closing and her mind wandering.

"Tom," she whispered sleepily. "I am hoping for a miracle. I pray that my children will not grow up without a mother like I did."

He was silent for a moment, so Catherine opened her eyes so that he would know she was awake and waiting for him to respond. After a heavy breath, he did.

"I have been uncertain whether I should tell you this, but Dr Dalitsch has mentioned trying a more aggressive calcium treatment. It might help."

Suddenly feeling more awake than she had in days, Catherine begged Tom to tell her more.

"I don't know if I'm explaining all of this right, but he said that since the radium is depositing in your bones like calcium should that high doses of calcium might be able to replace it."

"That makes sense," Catherine said. She remembered that he had said something similar before and allowed in a tiny sliver of hope. "I am willing to try anything." Even as she said it, she remembered the huge calcium pills and how hard it had been to swallow them. However, Tom appeared unconvinced, so she added, "Can we afford it?"

His laugh was sharp and without humor. "We can't afford anything. If only I could find work, but everyone is in the same place. There's just no work to be found."

"Mr Roosevelt will find a solution." Catherine wasn't sure why she said this except that something had to get better soon, didn't it?

Tom just shrugged. "I don't know if he will or not, but if the doctors suggest calcium, I will find a way to pay for it."

Catherine pressed her lips together but did not reply. She thought she was doing the right thing, giving every possible cure a chance and testing every treatment. It was for the sake of the children, she had often told herself. However, in this moment, she wondered if she was right.

The family was going bankrupt trying to keep her alive when there was nothing proven to help in any way. Would she be doing more for her children by protecting whatever assets that remained to them?

Tom halted her doubts. "We will do whatever the doctors recommend."

And that was that.

A few days later, Tom rushed to the front room that Catherine never left.

"What is it, Catie?" he asked in a poorly controlled panic.

Catherine's brow furrowed in confusion. "What do you mean?" she asked, but she wasn't really listening because pain seemed to flow through her veins. There was no escape, no relief. If only she could go to sleep.

"Catherine." Tom was at her side, his lips close to her ear. "I am here."

"What? Why?"

"Sweetheart, you're groaning. Are you in pain?"

She could only laugh as tears streamed down her face and her body pulsed with agony. Tom's hands were on her, attempting to soothe and comfort, but she all she felt was white-hot pain until everything went mercifully black.

For days, Catherine only was vaguely aware of her friends and family gathered around her. Their voices filtered into her brain without any comprehension of their words, but she was comforted by their presence. Their murmured prayers and conversation steadied the beating of her struggling heart as she drifted in and out of sleep.

When Catherine regained consciousness, Father Griffin was praying over her. The Latin words seemed to chase the pain from her body until only a dull throb remained. A wafer of communion bread was placed on her tongue where it slowly dissolved as her own silent prayers joined those of the priest.

Catherine slowly came to the realization that he was administering her last rites, and she wondered without emotion if it were as bad as all that.

Noticing that she was awake, Father Griffin reverted to English and inquired about her well-being. She didn't have the strength to speak but managed to say, "Better with your prayers."

"And through the strength of the cross," he added with a meaningful look toward the relic kept close to Catherine's bed.

"Yes," Catherine whispered, but she wished she could say more about how precious was that fragment of the True Cross that the nuns had brought to comfort her. "It is like having God in the house with me," she weakly added, uncertain if Father Griffin heard her.

He was a man used to ministering to the dying and understood how wearying any interaction could be. Therefore, Father Griffin shared only a few more soothing words and a final prayer before blessing Catherine with the sign of the cross upon her forehead and leaving, promising to visit again in a few days.

A peace surrounded her even after he had gone. The fire crackled, and a train rattled through town. She realized that she didn't hear the children, but that concern faded away as she fell into a dreamless sleep.

Margaret came and forced Catherine to eat some soup. She brought the children into the room to see their mother and discussed family issues with Tom at the kitchen table the way Catherine wished she could. When Catherine wasn't sure if Margaret was visiting, she could squint toward the window. If a car was parked out at the curb, she knew Margaret was there. She was the only one in their family who owned a car.

Tom's twin sister was bossy to a fault and struggled to hide her anger when Catherine refused to eat, but she was just what the little family needed to keep them going as Catherine's condition worsened.

In her lucid moments, Catherine knew that Margaret must be giving them money and groceries, but most of the time practical matters were far from her mind. She lived in a fog of pain interspersed with moments she tried to make the most of with her family and friends. She was aware that any one of them could be her last.

In her bed-ridden world, one of Catherine's favorite pastimes was listening to Tom read her letters. Sometimes, she read them herself, but it was so much nicer and less tiring to hear her friends' words in Tom's soothing tenor.

Pearl wrote long pages about the news coverage of their case. Catherine was embarrassed to see herself the subject of so many news stories, but Tom reminded her how important her fate was to countless women.

"You are their beacon, Catherine. They look to you for hope."

When Tom said things like this, Catherine would be humbled and bemused. Looking at her body, wasting away under her handmade quilt, she did not feel like a beacon of hope.

What most astounded Catherine were how many letters she received from complete strangers. When the first one arrived, she had thought it sweet and thoughtful, but a bit odd. As time went on, they arrived by the hundreds, and Catherine received a boost to her spirit from each letter. She was so encouraged to know that people were cheering for her from as far away as California. A few even contained small donations that helped keep the Donohue family afloat.

Sometimes, Catherine would sit up in bed for a few minutes in order to respond to her letters, especially those from Pearl. As Tom helped her reposition herself, she smiled gratefully at him.

"It feels good after so long lying flat," she said, but soon the position would become painful and Tom or Eleanor was summoned back to remove the extra pillows propping her up.

"I did mange a short letter to Pearl, though," Catherine sighed wearily, holding out the note to be posted. She hoped that he would not read it. Would he be hurt that she admitted how lonesome she was, begging Pearl to visit? Tom was her rock, but she missed the cheerful chatter of girlfriends.

Tom also shared excerpts from Mr Grossman's legal brief with Catherine. He had thoughtfully read through the pages and highlighted sections that he thought might interest her. As they prayed for a just outcome of her case, they reviewed some of Mr Grossman's work.

"*My clients were lulled into a false sense of security by dastardly and diabolical false and fraudulent misrepresentations,*" Tom read. He looked up from the file to nod at his wife. "We are truly blessed that this man has taken on our case." Then he continued reading. "*Radium Dial Company knew the legal duties owed to its employees and murderously refused them.*"

Catherine gulped at the word 'murderously.' Sometimes, she felt that people forgot that she was not dead yet. Tom continued reading, but she could bear no more, however good his intentions. She closed her eyes and let his voice lull her to sleep as she refused to listen to the words he said.

She must not have dozed for long, because Tom was still speaking when Catherine opened her eyes. "The judge will render his verdict on April 10." It was March 28.

"Two weeks," Catherine murmured. "I can't decide if it sounds like forever to wait or if I'm worried that he is making his decision too quickly."

Tom brushed hair away from her face and smiled in understanding. "We will trust this to God as we have all things."

She nodded. "If Mr Grossman hasn't made a winning case for us, I don't know who could have."

"He is impressive," Tom declared, picking up the brief file once more. "*This case is an offense against Morals and Humanity, and, just incidentally, against the law.*" His smile broadened. "You have been through so much, but I think your victory is at hand."

Catherine forced herself to smile in return. She shared Tom's confidence but found little comfort in it. Victory she might have, but a life she would not.

"Just one more line," Tom insisted, shaking his head in wonder at Mr Grossman's words. "*I cannot imagine a fiend fresh from the profoundest depths of perdition committing such an unnatural crime as the Radium Dial Company did. My God! Is the radium industry utterly destitute of shame?*"

Catherine only nodded and said, "He could have been a preacher."

Chapter 27

*Our citizenship is in heaven, and from it we await a
Savior, the Lord Jesus Christ, who will transform our
lowly body to be like his glorious body, by the power
that enables him even to subject all things to himself.*
Philippians 3:20-21

Catherine ran through the woods, the lithe muscles of her legs taking her down a leaf strewn path to the base of a steep hill. She climbed Starved Rock, savoring the sensation of bones, ligaments, and muscles working together in perfect harmony until she reached the top. The scent of the river came to her on the breeze and made her more eager to gain the summit.

When she did, she threw her arms wide, taking in the panoramic view of trees, valleys, and water rushing by. The wind was strong on this high plateau, blowing her hair back and chapping her cheeks, but the sun felt warm and inviting. She closed her eyes to luxuriate in the vivid sensations of nature.

The sound of crashing waves changed, and Catherine opened her eyes to investigate. The river was gone and had been replaced with a cheering crowd. A football game was being played before them and Chuck was on the field leading the team. Joy lit up Catherine's face even before she realized that Peg Looney was standing next to her, shouting herself hoarse in admiration of her man. The girls grinned at each other and screamed as Chuck threw a touchdown.

In a blink, the screaming crowd became children screeching

and giggling at the playground, where Catherine sat on a bench watching Tommy and Mary Jane at play. When Tommy ran over and asked her to play catch, she happily stood and caught the ball he tossed her way. Mary Jane skinned her knee, and Catherine squatted down to kiss her tears away. The little girl embraced her mother with the unconditional love that only a child can give.

Closing her eyes to relish the embrace, Catherine opened them to discover herself in Tom's arms. He smiled and kissed her, gently at first but with rising passion. His hands explored her strong, healthy body, and she responded eagerly to his affection. He was so handsome and loving.

But she made the mistake of closing her eyes, and he was gone. The dream was replaced by her new reality. The front room with shades drawn, the faint scent of illness and decay, low embers in the morning chill, and a body that could no longer do any of the things Catherine dreamed of. In the dim, pink light of dawn, Catherine wept.

Chapter 28

There is no hope. My clients will all die.
Leonard Grossman, 1938

"The verdict is in."

Tom stood in the doorway of Catherine's sickroom as he made this announcement. Catherine's heart broke when she looked upon the dark moons of shadow under his eyes that stood out in stark contrast against his pale face. Then his words sank in.

"It is five days early . . . . isn't it?" She had some trouble tracking the days, but the countdown until the tenth, when the verdict was anticipated, had been carefully kept.

Tom nodded, eyes wide and wondering. Her own question was mirrored on his face. Was this good news or bad?

He left to prepare for the trip to Chicago without another word. There was no discussion of Catherine going. She no longer left the bed or the room where her uncle had also spent his last days.

She listened to the sound of Tom moving around in the bedroom above her. What would she have to live for with her case decided? She could no longer do anything for her husband and children, was only a burden to them. Would the Lord end her suffering once this race had been run?

Why was the verdict five days early?

†

The beads of Catherine's rosary slowly slipped through her fingers. She lost count of how many prayers she had said since Tom had left. If she had failed to uphold some of Christ's teachings, the admonishment to 'pray without ceasing' had been followed almost without exception, at least since she was restricted to her bed. She found that it was true what the preachers said. In times of weaknesses, when left with no earthly solutions, God's children desperately turn to Him.

She hoped the Lord did not hold it against her that she had not been quite so attentive when a greater range of physical activities had been available to her. How humbling it was.

The sound of her children at play comforted her. Catherine was no longer bitter that she could not join them, only thankful that they were healthy. If there was any evidence that her illness had impacted Tommy and Mary Jane, it was found in the little girl's tiny size and slow development. Catherine prayed that she would eventually grow to overcome it as she thanked God for Tommy's robust health.

And what about Tom, Catherine wondered as her rosary beads stilled. She thought about the evenings that she had come home coated in the dust of radium paint or the earlier date nights when she had playfully painted her fingernails a glowing green. Tom seemed perfectly healthy, but had he been exposed in a way that would more slowly affect his health?

Catherine returned to the comfort of prayer as the beads moved through her thin hands once more. Only God knew the answers to her questions, and she would likely not know until she met Him. She had to release her anxieties and receive His peace.

A sharp knock at the door broke into Catherine's reverie, and she dropped her rosary with a gasp. Most of the visitors to the Superior Street house, of whom there were few recently, knocked lightly on the door and entered whispering as if Catherine were already dead and they were attending a somber wake. She struggled to shift in the bed enough to see who it was.

Eleanor was at the door in an instant. She must have left the children in the back yard, because their shouts and laughter remained unchanged. Somewhat short of breath, Eleanor greeted a familiar, if not friendly, face.

"Hello, ma'am. I'm from the *Ottawa Daily News*. If I could have just a moment with Mrs Donohue. We'd like to know her reaction to the verdict in her case."

Catherine's breath caught in her throat. She would hear the news, not from Tom but from a reporter. Her heart galloped too hard and too fast, and she willed it to calm as she considered what she should say depending upon what news the reporter brought.

Without waiting for Eleanor to welcome him in, the young man slipped into the house and took several steps toward Catherine while remaining far enough away that she knew he, too, was afraid of what might happen if he drew too close to nearly-dead, radioactive woman. Holding in a sigh, she waited for his announcement.

Pencil and notebook in hand, trying to keep his nose from wrinkling at the faint scent of urine that permeated the room, he looked eagerly at Catherine and asked, "How do you feel about winning your lawsuit against Radium Dial?"

Catherine closed her eyes as they welled up with tears. She thought her heart might stop beating for good, but it carried on at its unsteady, weak staccato. She had to swallow hard before she could answer him, and when she did the sound of her voice struck her as if she was hearing it for the first time.

It was thick with mucus and mushy in enunciation. So much of her teeth and jaw were gone that she had trouble accurately creating the sounds that had once come so naturally, but she tried to speak as clearly as she was able.

"I am glad for the sake of my children and my husband." Her attention was stolen by the sunlight reflecting off the band of her watch. It had been the perfect fit when Tom had first given it to her. Now it hung loosely, not to mention uselessly. She had nowhere to go, no appointments to keep.

"I never dreamed of the decision so soon."

"Your happiness is understandably tempered," he observed, glancing around the sickroom.

Catherine wished Tom was there, that he was the one giving her this news instead of a heartless stranger. She moved her mouth as if it needed to be warmed up in preparation for speech.

"The money will help Tom. He has been out of work for many months, though he does start a new position at the glass factory next week."

The reporter talked about the case for so long that Catherine began to drift off. Her mind couldn't remain attentive for so long anymore, but she caught Judge Marvel's name.

"He is just grand," she whispered. "He is very fair. This should have happened a long time ago, but it means a lot that he is so just."

The man asked about Catherine's suffering, as if it weren't obvious. She almost snorted.

"I'll have to suffer more. I may not live to enjoy any of the money myself, but I hope the other girls get theirs before their conditions get as bad as mine."

She was half asleep and didn't know what the reporter had said or if he had said anything, but before her world became black she murmured, "Radium Dial will finally be forced to do the right thing."

The joy that had not rose within her when the reporter broke the news flooded into her when Tom got home. He looked so happy that she couldn't help rejoicing with him. Justice delayed was better than justice denied, after all.

"Oh, Catie! You won! For us and for all the other girls – you won!"

Finally, she smiled as she had not been able to when he was away.

"Mr Grossman did a fine job, didn't he?"

Tom was exuberant. "He's a gift from God. There's just no other explanation. After all those other doctors and lawyers refusing to help . . . ." He paused darkly for a moment, but then his face lit up again. "But now, justice will be served, and Radium Dial will have to pay all the girls."

"That's just wonderful, Tom."

His face changed when he heard the fatigue in her voice. He sat close to her, gently taking her hand in his. "I'm sorry, my love. I know none of this changes anything, not really."

"It does though," Catherine wearily disagreed. "It will mean all the difference to you and the children. You can pay off the debt that we've been forced to incur. You won't be burdened with it after I . . . ." she couldn't bring herself to say it as she watched Tom's face fall.

They both knew. There was no need to speak of it.

"I love you today as much as the day I married you," Tom said with husky insistency. "I need you to know that."

Catherine wanted to laugh. How could it be true? Tom could be married to someone healthy, living a normal life. He must be disgusted with what she had become.

Seeing her doubt, Tom squeezed her hand as firmly as he dared. "You are God's gift to me."

She couldn't speak, but grateful tears streamed from her eyes as he held her close and whispered, "Don't you dare ever doubt it."

Chapter 29

Well done, good and faithful servant.
You have been faithful over a little;
I will set you over much.
Enter into the joy of your master.
Matthew 25:23

A welcome calmness settled over the Donohue home in wake of the verdict. Although nothing had yet changed, there was a peace found in knowing that they had fought the good fight and Catherine could rest easily for the remainder of her days.

She stopped trying to force herself to eat. It wasn't as though she had given up, but she was also done trying so hard. Catherine had pushed herself through treatments and potions, most of which hadn't helped, in her quest to see justice done. Now that it had been, she wanted to live – or die – on her own terms.

Tom seemed to understand and did not press her, even if he was less ready for the inevitable end than his wife. To most others, Catherine was already a corpse that had lived longer than made people comfortable.

It was an ideal two weeks, or as idyllic as two weeks could be when one was undeniably dying. Then news arrived that hit the Donohue family like a freight train.

"Radium Dial has filed an appeal."

Tom had said it in little more than a whisper, but the words echoed through the room as though he had screamed.

Catherine hadn't even realized they could do that. What

did it mean? She wanted to ask, but a feeling of heavy depression kept her from speaking.

Holding a letter from Mr Grossman, Tom read that the lawyer, at least, had anticipated this move and already had a plan of his own.

Charlotte and Pearl were at Catherine's bedside within days, taking photographs of the Society of the Living Dead for immediate media release. In return for the photographs, newspapers were asked to include a plea for funds. Catherine was likely to die before receiving anything from Radium Dial. Could the public help?

Catherine's thoughts were only for Tom. While she appreciated the help of her friends and knew that the failure of her case would also impact theirs, Tom's welfare consumed her. What would he do when she was gone with no settlement money to cover the mountainous medical bills they had built up?

It was only this concern that gave Catherine the strength to speak to reporters and stay awake for pictures to be taken. She forced herself to eat again, as painful as it could be.

One day, Charlotte was sitting with Catherine as they awaited the arrival of yet another reporter. Pearl was in the kitchen, preparing tea and cookies. Catherine was barely awake and talking grew increasingly difficult, so Charlotte chattered away almost to herself

"Oh look, it's just like that bird we saw at Starved Rock!" she cried, pointing toward the window.

Catherine forced her eyes open and then almost smiled. A cheerful yellow and black canary was indeed bouncing about the bushes outside her room. "Wouldn't it be a wonder if it were the same one?" she murmured.

Charlotte grinned broadly. "I am going to choose to believe

that it is. He is our little friend, here to cheer us when we need him most."

Amused, Catherine almost laughed, but it came out as one heavy breath.

"Don't you laugh at me, Catherine Donohue," Charlotte insisted. She refused to treat Catherine as if she was made of glass, and Catherine appreciated the normalcy of their conversations. "I do think he's the same bird. Why, look at his tailfeathers. I swear, they are just the same."

"You must be right then," Catherine agreed with a sunken smile. "How nice of him to visit." She had almost said, "one last time," but was glad to have stopped herself.

"He should have a name, don't you think?" When Catherine did not reply, Charlotte agreed with herself. "Yes, he should. What should it be?"

Before Charlotte could continue to answer for her, Catherine spoke. "Hope."

Charlotte smiled sadly. "That's a lovely name for him." She walked over to the window. Her face was away from Catherine, but she heard the tears in her voice. "Hello, Hope. How nice of you to visit us."

Catherine watched the bird and Charlotte's back shaking with sobs until she drifted into a restless sleep.

Charlotte gently woke her when a reporter named Frederick Griffen from the *Toronto Star* arrived. Pearl welcomed him in, and Catherine left the introductory small talk to them because she wanted to save her strength for saying important things. He wrote frantically as Charlotte and Pearl talked about their odd society.

"We chose to call ourselves the Society of the Living Dead, admittedly, to get attention, but also because it's true." Charlotte's voice lowered. "Each of us is dying, and it is a difficult truth to live with day by day. Every little ache or pain gives us a scare because we don't know if it is a portend that death is near."

Turning to Catherine, he asked what she would like to add to Charlotte's testimony.

"Please, mention Leonard Grossman. No one would know our story if it weren't for him, and our families would have no hope of compensation and relief from debt if it weren't for him. He is a courageous, faithful man, who is doing this for no more compensation than knowing that he is doing the right thing."

Charlotte nodded enthusiastically. "That's right. We are so thankful for Mr Grossman. He is even paying all of the court costs himself, when he's the one who should be getting paid!" Charlotte sat up straighter, as if strengthened by the thought of Mr Grossman's integrity. "He knows that we need better laws, and that's why we formed the Society of the Living Dead – not for us, but for those who will benefit from those new laws."

"Do you live in fear?" Mr Griffen asked Catherine.

The question startled her, for out of the many emotions that she experienced daily fear was not one of them. She narrowed her eyes at him. "I sometimes lie here wondering if I am living my last day. I know that it is possible that I might not see tomorrow, but I do not live in fear. I am comforted by my faith and the love of my friends and family. We know that this is not the end."

Mr Griffen focused intensely on his notebook, his face hidden as he sniffed and scribbled.

Less stoically, Pearl added, "I am missing so much. I can never be a mother again, never be the wife that my husband deserves."

The women nodded together. Their inability to serve their families as well as they wished was difficult to bear.

The women's heartfelt testimonies and photographs in

hand, Mr Griffen left. Gathered around Catherine's bed, the women prayed that his article would be honest and captivating, and that it would help their case be resolved on the side of justice.

†

This time, when her friends left, Catherine did not attempt to write. She could not sit up and did not bother putting her glasses on each day. Her days became a routine of fighting off pain with carefully timed and dosed narcotics. Dr Loffler had warned Tom about the strength of the drugs compared to Catherine's shrinking, weak frame.

Although pieces of her jawbone continued to break and disintegrate, Catherine sipped soup as often as she could bear it. She was determined to live long enough to see her case end in victory.

On one of these occasions, Catherine felt liquid trickling down her chin. It was a common enough sensation given the condition of her mouth. She regularly and humiliatingly drooled and dribbled, so she didn't give it a second thought until she saw Tom's face go pale.

He tried to remain calm, slowly stating, "Catherine, you are bleeding. Let me get some rags."

The way he ran from the room revealed his panic. Before she could blink, he was back with kitchen rags, holding them to her mouth with his eyes full of fear. She was surprised when he removed one blood soaked rag to replace it with another, almost fearful when he replaced it again.

Their eyes locked on each other's. If this was the end, she wanted him to find only love there, so Catherine forced herself to remain calm. There was nothing more she could have done to prepare for this day. She was ready to meet her Lord.

Of course, she could say nothing with her mouth full of blood and rags, so she could only hope Tom understood. Her world turned suddenly to darkness.

When Catherine next opened her eyes, part of her was disappointed to see the sickroom and her thin body scarcely making a hill under the covers. She wondered if it was selfish to long for heaven and renewed strength and health, knowing she would be leaving Tom with so many burdens. She was still here, so she supposed it didn't matter.

She heard Tom's voice and realized that he was speaking to another man in the kitchen. It didn't take her long to identify Dr Loffler since he was one of her most frequent visitors. That's when she realized that her mouth was free of rags and the taste of blood. Her tongue explored her broken jaw, few teeth, and sore gums, but she was unable to determine the source of the hemorrhage amid all the damage that had become her new normal.

The men moved from the kitchen to the front door, neither glancing to see if Catherine was awake.

"The next time it happens, you will need to take her to the hospital. She can't afford to lose that much blood."

Catherine's heart sank at the thought of going through that again, of putting Tom through that again. But Dr Loffler spoke as if it were a foregone conclusion. Tom murmured his acceptance of directions and bid the doctor farewell before turning toward his wife.

"How do you feel?" he asked, shuffling to her side. His hair was disheveled and turning grey at the temples. Had she noticed before?

"Poor Tom."

His grin was half-hearted and lopsided. One eyebrow lifted.

"Poor me?"

"I'm such a burden to you."

He was suddenly stern. "Don't ever say that. I treasure every moment I have you with me. You are never a burden. Do you hear me?"

Catherine could only nod as tears spilled from her eyes and drool ran from the corner of her ruined mouth.

†

Only a few days passed before Catherine's mouth hemorrhaged again. This time, Tom was quick to wrap blankets around her and bundle her off to the hospital, holding a rag to her mouth as he held her emaciated body in one arm and her head drooped onto his chest.

The hospital staff worked quickly but uncertainly. No one quite knew what to do with a woman in Catherine's condition until Dr Loffler could be consulted. Even once he had been, there was not much to be done. Catherine seemed to be holding on to life by sheer will alone.

On only one thing did the doctors agree. Catherine should remain hospitalized. She begged Tom to make them see that she was content at home, that she didn't want to stay there all alone, but doctor's orders won the day. When visiting hours ended, Tom went home and Catherine sobbed until her mouth began to bleed again, bringing another crew of nurses and doctors to her bedside.

The next day, she was bruised from their treatment and aching in every inch of what remained of her body. She felt heavily drugged and couldn't focus her eyes. But she heard Tom's voice, and it was all she needed to relax and be at peace.

Catherine was uncertain how many days passed as she slid

in and out of sleep and drug induced haziness. She had picked up enough whispered conversations to know that the hospital had no intention of releasing her, but she was determined not to die in this sanitized prison surrounded by strangers.

"Tom?" she mumbled, hoping he was there. "Tom?"

Voices and the sounds of other lives carrying on surrounded her, but she was alone. She swallowed as saliva threatened to spill over her chin again. Her eyes squeezed tightly shut to keep tears from escaping.

"Tom?"

"I am here," he said, sounding as though he was approaching as he spoke. "Are you alright?"

Catherine shook her head. "I'm so lonesome. I want to go home."

"I know Catie, but . . ."

She didn't let him finish. "They can do nothing to help me except let me go home," she insisted. "Please, Tom."

He rubbed her hand softly. "Alright. I will see to it." He sounded dejected, like some small part of him had thought she might find healing here that was not possible in their front room.

"I'm sorry, Tom," Catherine whispered.

He squeezed her hand in response and patted it as he stood. She prayed that the doctors would see reason and listen to him.

Catherine must have dozed off, because she was awakened by a slightly heated discussion taking place near her bed.

"It is my opinion that any activity, including moving her anywhere, could prove fatal," came the voice of one of the doctors, not Dr Loffler. He had his own practice and had to leave Catherine in the care of local physicians.

"We understand the risks," Tom quietly countered. "My wife would still like to go home."

"I cannot support this decision." There was the sound of papers and a clipboard. Catherine's thick medical record.

"All the same," Tom insisted. "Catherine would like to go home. There is nothing that can be done for her here. At home we can give her the love and comfort she needs."

A snorting harrumph was the doctor's only response to what he must have considered sentimental nonsense. The sound of footsteps, then his voice from farther away. "Very well. Take her, but it is on your conscience, not mine."

"Thank you," Tom muttered far too quietly for the retreating physician to hear. Then to her, "Catie, are you awake?"

Catherine mumbled a response and smiled when she felt his hand brushing back her hair.

"I'm going to take you home just as soon as I can have it arranged."

Her eyelids felt so heavy, but she forced them up long enough to thank him. "I love you, Tom," she sighed before drifting off again.

Catherine knew she was home before opening her eyes. The scent of simmering soup, the sound of children's laughter, and the warm sunlight on her face were enough to let her know where she was. A deep peace washed over her. This was where she was meant to be.

She caught only snippets of what happened around her.

Mary Jane: "Mama, are you awake? Papa, is she going to wake up again?"

Tommy: "Mama, Aunt Margaret said that I'm going to start school soon!"

Dr Loffler: "Tom, you need to be ever mindful of these doses. According to the hospital records, she weighs only sixty pounds now."

Even Eleanor spent time at Catherine's side, singing as she did for the children at bedtime.

And Tom. Dear Tom. Sometimes he cried when he was certain she was in a deep sleep. Other times, he would reminisce about happier days. But mostly he just reassured her of his great love for her and prayed at her bedside.

During one of her lucid moments, Tom updated her on the status of her case. "Mr Grossman is striving to win this for you. When Radium Dial requested a postponement, you would have thought he was Moses demanding of Pharoah, 'Let my people go!' He was having none of it, and the judge agreed."

A smile brightened Catherine's countenance as she imagined the scene. "I am glad he is on my side," she whispered. Her speech was slurred and quiet, but Tom understood.

"He is indeed. And it's a good thing, too, because that old Mr Reed is trying a new tactic now. He's trying to claim that he never told anyone that radium was good for them. That all you 'gals' are lying."

Catherine's mind cleared as anger chased the clouds from her consciousness. "He said what?!"

Tom nodded. "You heard me right. He gave sworn testimony."

Catherine was bewildered. How could he tell such a lie? Would anyone believe him? To think she had once believed that he had cared for her something like a father.

"But the ad in the paper," she remembered. "It said that nothing about our job was harmful."

"Right you are, my love, and Mr Grossman reminded them of that too. Don't you worry."

"How could I?" she asked, "When I have Leonard Grossman on my side."

Tom laughed, and Catherine treasured the sound. When had he last laughed? Yet there was still much heartache ahead of him.

"Tom, I would like to do something. We need to beg for prayers and ask God for a miracle. I simply cannot die now. I want to write to Father Keane."

Pearl came to help her, and together they wrote a heartfelt message to the radio preacher asking for help. They wondered if he would mention her on his program with tens of thousands listening. Would it be enough prayers to make a difference? Was any amount enough?

Pearl wiped at her eyes and held a tissue to her nose as Catherine dictated the last line.

They say there is nothing that can save me – nothing but a miracle. And that's what I want – a miracle. But if that is not God's will, perhaps your prayers will obtain for me the blessing of a happy death.

A week later, Tom brought her the newspaper. Her letter was on the front page. "It's everywhere," he said. "In all the papers. On the radio. Everyone is praying for you, Catie."

"Oh, Tom," she gasped. "God hears the prayers of the faithful, but how will he answer?"

"I don't know, sweetheart," he murmured shaking his head in wonder of it all. "I just don't know."

That evening they listened to the radio as Father Keane himself instructed the nation to pray for Catherine Donohue, and the next day she saw proof that they were obeying. A few letters wishing Catherine well and offering words of advice had been arriving ever since her first newspaper story, but now they came by the hundreds. It was if she was a celebrity receiving fan mail, and Catherine didn't know what to do with it all.

"They are all so thoughtful, Tom, but I cannot hope to

answer them."

"Of course not," he soothed her. "And they wouldn't expect you to. All these good people just want you to know that you are loved."

"It's just so wonderful," Catherine sighed, admiring the stack of envelopes at her bedside. "I do think I'm feeling a little bit better."

Tom had laughed then, but by the end of the week, Catherine was insistent. "I want to sit up. I don't want to lie down anymore. Could you bring me some soup?"

His eyes had widened, but he quickly fulfilled her requests. He and the children sat chatting with her, and she even wrote a letter to Pearl. She hadn't felt so good in weeks. When they prayed together as a family, they sent up abundant gratitude for her good turn, none of them daring give voice to the truth that it could not last.

Nervously waiting for something bad to happen, the Donohues were shocked when good news came. Radium Dial's appeal was thrown out of court.

Catherine had won.

Tom would receive money to cover her medical expenses, although it would not be enough to pay off the mortgages that he had been forced to take out.

The girls all came to see Catherine to celebrate. She sat up in bed with Charlotte, Pearl, and Marie gathered around her, and was truly happy for a brief, shining moment. Their chatter was such a balm to her soul.

"Can you believe the Reeds? Lying under oath!"

"Mr Grossman was more than a match for them."

"Yet he took his victory like a gentleman. There is no arrogance in him."

"Well, maybe just a little. He does like the sound of his voice."

They giggled like schoolgirls, and Catherine smiled contentedly.

Pearl was the next to speak. "I have been feeling hope for the future. It is such a strange sensation after all that we have been through."

"My heart feels lighter with the case settled. It is a great burden relieved," Charlotte agreed.

But Marie was watching Catherine. The case may be over, and the rest of them may enjoy enough health to live for years yet, but Catherine was still dying.

"How are you, dear?" Catherine could tell Marie was worried when she spoke so sweetly.

"I am at peace."

It was enough. It was more than she had anticipated during her weeks in the hospital. She enjoyed days of summer sun streaming in the front room window and joyful visits from her children, breathless with their latest accomplishments. Tom read to her from the kind letters of strangers in the evenings, and he always kissed her goodnight. It was not only enough, it was more than she could have hoped for. It was her miracle.

Then came the day that Tom entered her room looking as though he had been mobbed in the street. His face pale, hair mussed, and shoulders stooped, he clearly did not want to tell her what had happened.

"It is not one of the children?" she cried. She could take anything, as long as it wasn't that.

"No," Tom whispered, running a hand through his hair. "The children are fine."

When he gazed out the window without speaking,

Catherine urged him on.

"What is it, Tom?"

He sighed hopelessly and turned to her. "Radium Dial has filed an appeal with the circuit court."

Catherine stared at him wide-eyed, and what was left of her jaw dropped open. Tom would receive nothing. It had all been in vain. Her hope had been false.

Her world went dark.

†

The sun dawned brighter than it ever had before, but Catherine realized that she had no need to shield her eyes. She swung her legs over the edge of the bed and strode toward the light. Expecting to see the morning scene on Superior Street, she gasped at the pink light covering trees and wildflowers. Spinning around, Catherine realized that her bed wasn't there. She wasn't in her front room.

The omnipresent scent of broth was replaced by citrus and exotic blooms and spices. She reached down to touch a species of flower that she had never seen before and saw her watch firmly fastened on her wrist. Her fingers were long and elegant. She brought her hands in front of her face. They looked so strong!

Catherine gasped and looked down at her legs. She was standing! Filled with joy and energy, she began to run across the meadow. Her hair flew behind her while her lungs drank deeply of the sweet air. She didn't know how long she ran, but she was not out of breath when she decided to stop.

A cacophony of voices and music filled her ears, and she realized that she was not alone. Catherine was surrounded by smiling faces. Seeing her mother, she squealed and threw herself into her arms. Soft kisses covered her face, and she felt as if she could linger there forever.

"Mama," she whispered.

"And your father," came the gentle, peaceful voice.

Catherine pulled slightly away in disbelief, but it was true.

"Oh, papa!" And she was in his arms. His laugh rumbled so deep Catherine could feel it in her chest, and it made her laugh along with him.

"We are so happy to see you, but there is one who loves you even more," her mother whispered, putting a hand on Catherine's back to guide her.

Those gathered stepped back as one, creating a path for Catherine to follow. She could not see the end, but a familiar voice beckoned.

Catherine stepped forward.

Epilogue

Charlotte Purcell sat on the porch swing of the Superior Street home that held so many memories for her. How many more times was she likely to enter, now that her dear friend was gone?

She had no more tears left to cry, and even her anger had dissipated in her great grief. She felt nothing as she sat, wondering if she would ever again feel passion, or happiness, or even hunger.

The sound of a bird's merry song stirred something like anger in her. Joy had no place in this world, or at least not this home where so much suffering had occurred. Charlotte scarcely had the energy to move her eyes in search of the source of the dissonant sound, but when she did her heart swelled and her breath caught in her throat.

When she could speak, it was only in a whisper, "Well, hello, Hope. Where did you come from?"

Afterword

Catherine Donohue died on July 27, 1938, the day after Radium Dial filed for an appeal in circuit court. She was thirty-five years old. Her body had been ravaged by the effects of radium poisoning, but she had bravely held on for so very long.

An inquest was held, and a jury officially ruled that Catherine had been the victim of radium poisoning.

Leonard Grossman continued to work the case, which was appealed all the way to the Supreme Court. Catherine's victory was upheld when the Supreme Court denied to hear the case.

Pearl, Charlotte, and Marie lived surprisingly long lives, although they experienced a myriad of health problems due to the radium that would never leave their bones. Tom died in 1957, having never remarried.

Catherine had been afraid that her children were affected by the radium in her body when she was pregnant, and those fears were not misplaced. Tommy died of Hodgkin's disease at age thirty, and Mary Jane faced a lifetime of health problems before dying of heart failure at age fifty-five.

In 1984, Catherine's body was exhumed for research purposes. Her body remained luminous.

Additional Reading

For those interested in reading more about the historical figures featured in this novel, I recommend the following sources:

Radium Girls: The Dark Story of America's Shining Women by Kate Moore

Radium Girls: Women and Industrial Health Reform, 1910-1935 by Claudia Clark

The Pearl Payne Collection at LaSalle County Historical Society

Deadly Glow: The Radium Dial Worker Tragedy by Ross Mullner

http://www.lgrossman.com/pics/radium/ by Len Grossman

Author's Note

I had not considered writing 20th century historical fiction until I listened to Kate Moore's *The Radium Girls* on audiobook. I knew immediately that I had to write about Catherine Donohue. It was a unique experience to write about women who lived so recently and in a place I could easily visit.

My trip to Ottawa, Illinois helped me feel so close to Catherine as I worshiped at St Columba, went hiking at Starved Rock, and slowly cruised down Superior Street. The Environmental Protection Agency has spent millions of dollars cleaning up hazardous waste in and around Ottawa, but there are still areas off limits due to high levels of radioactivity.

Using letters and newspaper reports, I have tried to stay as close to the truth as possible and used direct quotes where suitable, but this is a work of fiction and should be treated as such.

Catherine Donohue died not knowing that she had won a landmark victory for dial painters. However, Tom only received about $5,700 in compensation, and the other litigants received even less.

Because of their perseverance though, laws did change, and future workers had greater protection. Unfortunately, worker exploitation continues in various forms to this day. As Mark Twain allegedly said, "History doesn't repeat itself, but it often rhymes."

Connect with Samantha
at SamanthaWilcoxson.blogspot.com
or on Twitter @Carpe_Librum.

Printed in Great Britain
by Amazon